A silent warning went off in his head, reminding Cody of who he was, but, more important, who *Savannah* was.

She was patience and permanence; he was wild and wandering. She was day; he was night and all the darkness that came with it. She wore her emotions on her sleeve for the world to see; those who knew him would swear he'd never had a real emotion. She loved openly, honestly, wholeheartedly; he couldn't—wouldn't—love anything or anyone.

But he hadn't realized his life had been dull and boring until she came along and added a spark of something good. Being with her and her son made him happier than he'd been in years.

But it was only temporary. It couldn't be anything more. He had nothing to offer her, nothing of permanence, anyway.

He was a loner, and he intended to stay that way.

Dear Reader,

Happy New Year! I hope this year brings you all your heart desires...and I hope you enjoy the many books coming your way this year from Silhouette Special Edition!

January features an extraspecial THAT SPECIAL WOMAN!—Myrna Temte's *A Lawman for Kelly*. Deputy U.S. Marshal Steve Anderson is back (remember him in Myrna's *Room for Annie?*), and he's looking for love in Montana. Don't miss this warm, wonderful story!

Then travel to England this month with *Mistaken Bride*, by Brittany Young—a compelling Gothic story featuring two identical twins with very different personalities.... Or stay at home with *Live-In Mom* by Laurie Paige, a tender story about a little matchmaker determined to bring his stubborn dad to the altar with the right woman! And don't miss *Mr. Fix-It* by Jo Ann Algermissen. A man who is good around the house is great to find anytime during the year!

This month also brings you *The Lone Ranger*, the initial story in Sharon De Vita's winsome new series, SILVER CREEK COUNTY. Falling in love is all in a day's work in this charming Texas town. And watch for the first book by a wonderful writer who is new to Silhouette Special Edition—Neesa Hart. Her book, *Almost to the Altar*, is sure to win many new fans.

I hope this New Year shapes up to be the best year ever! Enjoy this book, and all the books to come!

Sincerely

Tara Gavin
Senior Editor

Please address questions and book requests to:
Silhouette Reader Service
U.S.: 3010 Walden Ave., P.O. Box 1325, Buffalo, NY 14269
Canadian: P.O. Box 609, Fort Erie, Ont. L2A 5X3

SHARON DE VITA

THE LONE RANGER

Published by Silhouette Books

America's Publisher of Contemporary Romance

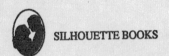

SILHOUETTE BOOKS

ISBN 0-373-24078-3

THE LONE RANGER

Books by Sharon De Vita

Silhouette Special Edition

Child of Midnight #1013
*The Lone Ranger #1078

Silhouette Romance

Heavenly Match #475
Lady and the Legend #498
Kane and Mabel #545
Baby Makes Three #573
Sherlock's Home #593
Italian Knights #610
Sweet Adeline #693

*Silver Creek County

SHARON DE VITA

is an award-winning author of numerous works of fiction and nonfiction. Her first novel won a national writing competition for Best Unpublished Romance Novel of 1985. This award-winning book, *Heavenly Match*, was subsequently published by Silhouette in 1986.

A frequent guest speaker and lecturer at conferences and seminars across the country, Sharon is currently an Adjunct Professor of Literature and Communications at a private college in the Midwest. With over one million copies of her novels in print, Sharon's professional credentials have earned her a place in *Who's Who in American Authors, Editors and Poets* as well as in the *International Who's Who of Authors*. In 1987, Sharon was the proud recipient of the *Romantic Times* Lifetime Achievement Award for Excellence in Writing.

She currently makes her home in a small suburb of Chicago, with her two college-age daughters and her teenage son.

HOW TO FIND A MAN FOR YOUR MOM
(and the perfect dad for you)

1) Ask your best friend, Louie, to come up with a real good plan.

2) Make sure your ma doesn't find out what you're up to 'cause she says she doesn't need a man.

3) Make sure the guy you pick doesn't eat your ma's cookies, 'cause they taste like dirt and you want him to like her.

4) Tell him all the good stuff 'bout your ma, like she smells good most of the time, 'cept when she's been mucking around the barn with Miss Sophie, the bull.

5) Ask him to move in with you—that way he can help with the chores!

6) Ask real nice for him to marry your ma—after all, who could resist such a cool ma?

Prologue

All *important* fourth-grade problems, plots, deceptions or decisions were planned and muddled over in excruciating detail while hanging upside down from the monkey bars of the Silver Creek County Day School.

How high you hung on the bars immediately told your comrades-in-arms how critical the current problem or situation.

On this blistering-hot day in May, when ten-year-old Joey Duncan raced from the sturdy red school building, heading full tilt into recess, and saw his best friend, Louie, hanging upside down on the *top* rung of the monkey bars, he knew something was up.

Something big.

In the five years Joey had lived in Silver Creek, only once before had Louie opted for the all-important *top* rung, and that was when Louie's grandma had broken her hip. Full of mischief and imagination, Louie had taken one look at the sleek, black-haired, red-lipped nurse his daddy had hired to tend to his grandma and decided the woman was a . . . vampire. Louie was convinced the nurse's real mission was to steal his grandma's soul.

Determined to save his grandma, Louie had wailed and worried, plotted and planned, skulking around his daddy's ranch for a good two months trying to get the goods on "the evil vampire nurse," all to no avail. Consumed by the problem, Louie had finally decided that like all good heroes, he'd have to solve this particular problem on his own.

But by the time Louie had finally figured out a herolike plan, Grandma Louisa's hip had healed nicely, and one evening the evil vampire had disappeared into the night like no more than a puff of smoke. But Louie wasn't fooled. He knew how vampires worked; he knew she'd be back for those she'd left behind. Ever vigilant, he kept a constant eye out for any sign of her return.

Yet it wasn't evil vampire nurses on Louie's mind this hot Thursday morning, but something far more important, something he couldn't wait to share with his best friend, Joey.

Joey raced toward the monkey bars, nearly knocking over a playground monitor in his haste. He was breathing hard, and the sun tattooed a heated pattern across the top of his golden head as he skidded to a halt to avoid a collision. After mumbling a swift apology, Joey sidestepped the invader and raced toward the monkey bars.

"What's up?" Joey called, tilting his head back and squinting against the sun.

"Something big." Swinging upside down, Louie rolled his eyes expressively. "*Real big.* Come on up."

Nervousness pumped through Joey, weakening his slender legs and dampening his hands. He hated heights, hated the thought of having to slowly climb, inch by inch, higher and higher up the hot metal bars. But he'd never admit such a thing to Louie, who was the bravest person he'd ever met. Hadn't he single-handedly driven off a vampire?

Not wanting his very best friend to think he was a baby, Joey kept his fears to himself, relieved that disasters of the top rung were few and far between.

Grateful it was only he and Louie this morning, Joey took a deep, shaky breath for courage, wiped his sweaty hands down his jeans, then began his ascent. His palms were slippery with nerves and each new bar brought him closer to the top—and farther and farther away from the security of the solid ground.

He refused to glance down, knowing if he did he'd fall. *Don't look down.* He forced his gaze to stay fixed on the bar just one rung up until his moist hands were wrapped securely around it, then he swung his long, gangly legs up, hooking them securely over the rung. And then he'd reach up and grab the next rung and begin the process all over again.

"Hurry up," Louie admonished, watching impatiently as Joey took his time climbing to the top.

"I'm coming. Hold your horses." Pausing to take another deep, shaky breath, Joey began the final ascent. His heart was pumping like a steam engine, and his hands were so damp and shaky he feared they'd slip right off the metal rung.

The sun had scorched the metal to a blistering heat, and he couldn't keep his hands on the rung for too long without risking skin burns, but skin burns seemed minor compared to the terror of falling.

Blowing his hair out of his eyes, Joey once more wiped his hands on his faded jeans, then slowly made his way up to the final rung, wrapping his arms tightly around the bar and hugging it close. Relief flooded through him. His stomach felt like the gelatin his mother sometimes made for dessert. And his legs felt like spaghetti, all limp and wobbly. But he was up and safe—as long as he didn't look down.

"We've got trouble." Still swinging upside down, Louie blew a big pink bubble from the ever-present wad of gum he kept in his mouth. It popped all over his face. "*Big* trouble."

"More vampires?" Joey asked with a frown.

"Nah." Plucking remnants of sticky gum off his mouth and nose, Louie shook his head. "Bigger."

"What's bigger than vampires?" Joey asked, wide-eyed.

Louie glanced around quickly, then lowered his voice to a level reserved for triple-threat secrets, indicating the importance of the discussion. "You gotta move," he whispered.

"Move?" Scowling, Joey rubbed his itchy nose. "Whatcha talking about? Whatcha mean I gotta move? Move where? Louie!" Impatient, Joey grabbed Louie by the shirt and swung him upright. He couldn't talk to Louie when he was swinging upside down. It made his stomach feel all funny.

Louie clung to the metal rung in front of him, then leaned closer and lowered his voice again. "Heard my pa talking on the phone this morning." Louie's pa was the sheriff of Silver Creek and always knew things firsthand. As did Louie, who was *real* fond of eavesdropping. "You know Mr. Kincaid, the man who owned the ranch you live in?"

Cautiously Joey nodded.

"Mr. Kincaid died."

"I know that," Joey wailed in exasperation, rolling his eyes. "*Everybody* knows Mr. Kincaid died. My ma's even going to his services this afternoon." Scrubbing at his itchy nose again, Joey shook his head. He climbed all the way up here for *this?* If Louie wasn't his best friend, he would've smacked him.

Everybody in the county knew that Mr. Kincaid had died in the big fire at his ranch last week. Joey felt sad inside when he thought about it because he liked Mr. Kincaid. A lot. But his ma had assured him that they wouldn't have to move, that Mr. Kincaid had arranged for them to stay in the little ranch house as long as they'd like.

The Kincaid land spread across almost five thousand acres. His ma had told him that their ranch, which sat way back from the road and even farther from the main ranch house, used to be a foreman's house. It wasn't nearly as big as Mr. Kincaid's, but they had their own chickens and gardens and stuff, and even a bull named Miss Sophie. Joey had his own room with a television, and in the living room there was a big old fireplace. On cool nights, he and his ma would light a fire and roast marshmallows. Even though the house wasn't as big and fancy as Mr. Kincaid's, Joey loved it. He never wanted to leave. Ever.

A frown puckered his brow, and he pursed his lips. But maybe Louie knew something his ma didn't.

Grinning like a cat who'd swallowed a canary, Louie began swinging his legs back and forth again. "So everybody knows Mr. Kincaid's dead." His eyes took on a mischievous look. "But I'll bet nobody knows his son's come back."

"Mr. Kincaid had kids?" Joey's frown deepened as he tried to assess what this bit of news had to do with anything—*him* specifically.

Louie giggled. "Cody's not a kid. He's a...a..." Louie frowned, trying to remember what he'd heard his father call Cody this morning. He brightened suddenly. "Oh, yeah, my dad said Cody Kincaid was a renegade."

Joey's eyes widened. "Holy cow!" he whispered reverently, then a frown slowly puckered his brows again as his eyes clouded suspiciously. "Uh, Louie? What's a... renegade?" He sure hoped it wasn't anything as bad as .vampires.

Louie shrugged. "Don't know." Still swinging his legs, he blew another bubble. "Probably nothing good, though."

Joey made a mental note to look in the dictionary when he got home. Scrubbing at his itchy nose again, he tightened his grip on the bars. "So what does this Cody guy have to do with me having to move?"

Louie leaned closer and lowered his voice again. "Heard my pa tell Cody if he was planning on staying in town, he'd better plan on staying outta trouble." Louie shook his head slowly. "You know my pa hates trouble. And I guess Cody caused a lot of trouble back in the old days when he was young."

"So?" Really impatient now, Joey squinted against the glare of the sun, waiting, wondering what all of this had to do with him moving. Louie sometimes exaggerated stuff. He hoped this was one of those times.

"So." Supremely confident, Louie blew another bubble. "If Cody's planning on staying in Silver Creek, he'll need somewhere to live, right?" Louie shrugged. "So you'll have to move." Louie poked him in the chest. "His father's house burned to the ground, remember?"

"I remember," Joey said glumly, chewing his lower lip in a nervous gesture he'd had since he was a baby. Now he understood. Mr. Kincaid's son was going to want his house back.

Oh, boy.

A flash of fear skittered over Joey, chilling him in spite of the heat of the day. What was going to happen to him and his ma?

Where were they going to go? Where were they going to live? What if they couldn't find another place to live in Silver Creek?

Joey's heart began to pound as if someone had dropped a jumpy frog down his chest. If they had to move, that meant a new school and new kids and *no* friends. Joey almost groaned aloud, unable to even bear thinking about it.

He loved Silver Creek. They even had the actual Silver Creek running right along the back of the property. On real hot days like today, he and Louie and the rest of the gang would race back to his house and go wading in the cool water. Because none of them could swim except for Petey and little Katie, his ma only let them go in the water up to their knees, but still it was fun.

And lots of times at night, he and his ma would make a snack and take it down by the creek and just sit and look at the moon and stars and stuff.

This was the only home he could remember, and since they'd lived here, real good things had happened. He'd met Louie and the gang, got Miss Lynch for English and sat behind Susie Barker in homeroom. Where else would such good things happen?

Nowhere. He was certain of it.

Did his ma know they were going to have to move? Joey wondered suddenly. He had a feeling she would be pretty mad and sad when she found out. She loved Silver Creek as much as he did. She always said it gave her peace.

Since Joey didn't have a pa like everyone else, he tried to help his ma out as much as possible. They shared chores and took care of their part of the ranch together even if there were some things that not even the two of them could do, like control Miss Sophie. But his ma always said Miss Sophie had a mind of her own. He liked tending to the chickens and hens, gathering eggs every morning before school and feeding the stock.

But, oh boy, if they'd have to move... Joey glanced at Louie, knowing he'd never, ever be able to find such an awesome best friend. Unable to bear even the thought of moving and leaving Louie or the gang behind, Joey dejectedly propped his chin on the top of his hand and closed his eyes against the terrors that leaving his friends, the ranch and Silver Creek would bring.

"Hey, Joey?" Louie poked him.

"What?" he asked gloomily, not even bothering to open his eyes. At least with his eyes closed, he didn't have to see how far away the ground was and Louie wouldn't be able to see how miserable he was.

"I got a plan." Louie grinned, a mischievous grin that had given more than a few grown-ups reason to worry.

Joey's eyes popped open, and he felt a huge wave of relief. He should have known! Louie was a "plan man"; he always had an idea or solution to *everything*. It was because of one of Louie's plans that they'd met. Because Louie was smaller than almost everyone else in their class, he was an easy target for the bigger kids. Like any school, Silver Creek had its share of bullies. Because Joey was the *biggest* kid in class, he made sure he looked out for the smaller ones. He didn't like bullies, and he didn't like to see anyone getting pushed around just 'cause they were little. His ma always told him he had a...responsibility to do right and good, and he tried to—mostly.

One day one of Louie's grand plans had backfired, and a few of the bigger boys had him cornered behind the school building. Louie was sweating and talking real fast, until he spotted Joey, who hadn't even opened his mouth. Louie had darted around the boys holding him hostage and skidded behind Joey, using him as a shield. The three boys took one look at Joey and decided to come up with a different plan of their own, one that hopefully didn't involve Joey. From that day on, he and Louie had been inseparable.

Joey grinned suddenly, brightening his eyes and revealing a small dimple on the left side of his mouth. He should have known Louie would come through for him. "So what's the plan?"

Louie scooted closer. "You and your ma take care of the ranch alone, right?"

"Right," Joey said slowly, wrinkling his nose and wondering just what kind of plan Louie had. He hoped it didn't involve vampires.

Louie's grin flashed. "So maybe your ma could hire Cody to do some of the chores, and in exchange maybe he could live at the ranch with you." Louie shrugged again. "You won't have to move, and he'll have some place to live." Louie's grin was back. "And as a bonus, you won't have to do no more chores." As he crossed his arms over his chest, Louie's grin widened into pure male satisfaction. "Problem solved."

"I don't know, Louie," Joey said with a worried shake of his head. "My ma doesn't like having strangers around." Especially *men* strangers, Joey thought, but didn't say.

"Cody's not a stranger, he *owns* the ranch." It was Louie's turn to frown. "So that means he's not a stranger, right?"

With his brows drawn tightly together, Joey tried to process the thought. "I...guess so."

Louie let loose a long-suffering sigh. Joey was his best friend in the whole wide world, but Joey was always worrying about *something*. Even stupid stuff like math tests and vocabulary quizzes. "What are you worrying about now?" Louie asked in exasperation.

"What if...if this Cody guy doesn't want to do chores?"

"Nah." Louie shook his dark head. His legs were swinging back and forth again as he scanned the playground below. "Not a chance. My pa says if you own a ranch, you gotta do chores. Think it's a stupid law or something."

Concentrating, Joey scrunched his brows together as he picked at an itchy mosquito bite on his arm. "Yeah, but what if this Cody guy doesn't want to live with me and my ma?"

Louie looked stunned. "What?" He whacked Joey on the shoulder to get his attention. "Why wouldn't he want to live in his own house?" Shaking his head, Louie concluded, "Nope. That's just stupid."

"But what if—"

"Jooooeeey!" Louie wailed, grabbing him by the shoulder and giving him a little shake.

Joey's heart leapt into his throat, and he almost lost his balance. Righting himself, he shook off Louie's hand and tried to hide the sudden surge of fear that caused a trickle of sweat to roll down his back.

Louie clapped a hand on his best friend's back. "Joey, Joey, Joey! Stop your worrying. You're always worrying. What have you got to lose? Nothing, I say. Absolutely nothing. I came up with a perfect plan. If you don't do *something*, you're gonna have to move. Is that what you want?"

"No," Joey muttered morosely.

"Then it's settled." Louie blew another bubble. "You gotta go talk to Cody."

Joey's head snapped up, and his eyes widened into saucers.

"Me?" he asked in sudden alarm. "Why do I have to do it?" He wasn't sure he liked this part of Louie's plan. Somehow all of Louie's plans involved him having to do something, usually something he didn't want to do. Like talk to a renegade, especially when he didn't even know what it was—yet. Oh, boy. His throat was suddenly dry, and Joey swallowed hard.

"'Cause you're the man of the house, right?"

Joey nodded slowly. "Yeah ... so?"

"So then it's your job." Louie spotted Susie Barker in the playground below and blew out his cheeks and sent his gum sailing toward the top of Susie's head. "Bull's-eye!" he declared loudly, earning a scowl from Susie and a quick grin from Joey.

In the distance, the school bell rang, signaling the end of recess. They began to clamber down the bars. Going down was much easier and faster than going up.

"Want to go with me after school?" Joey asked hopefully. He took a deep breath and swiped his damp hands down his jeans as his feet landed on the ground.

"Can't." Louie popped another wad of gum in his mouth, then grinned. "Got to go to the stupid dentist."

"We'd better hurry up," Joey cautioned, glancing at the school building, where the rest of the gang was waiting. He tried not to be alarmed at the fact that the doors had started to close.

"You're worrying again, Joey," Louie said with a soulful shake of his head. "You gotta stop doing that." He nudged Joey. "Come on, have any of my plans failed?"

Joey considered for a moment. There was the time that Louie figured out if they stole the vocabulary quiz they wouldn't *have* a quiz that week. It didn't dawn on him until later that the teacher might have another copy, or that when she realized the original quiz was missing, would substitute another one—which was exactly what happened. They both flunked the quiz and spent another week in detention when it was discovered who was responsible for the missing quiz. That didn't even take into account the trouble they'd gotten into at home when his mother and Louie's father had found out what they'd done.

Oh, boy. That had been *some* week.

There were plenty of glitches in some of Louie's other plans, but Joey didn't want to hurt Louie's feelings, especially when he was trying so hard to be so helpful.

"No, I guess not," he finally responded, coming to a halt in the playground and crossing his fingers behind his back so the lie wouldn't *really* count.

"So what ya got to worry about?" Smug, Louie whacked him on the back. "Another problem solved by Louie the Magnificent." Grinning, he glanced at Joey. "Race you to the doors."

Without waiting for an answer, Louie took off, kicking up a cloud of playground dust, with Joey fast on his heels, his mind churning as fast as his feet.

Maybe Louie was right. What did he have to worry about? If he did nothing, they'd have to move. He had to do *something,* not just for himself, but for his ma. Now that his pa was gone, he had to look after her, take care of her 'cause he didn't want her worrying. Joey's pace slowed for a moment. Now he just had to figure out what you said to a . . . renegade?

But first, he thought with another frown, he'd better find out just what a renegade was.

Chapter One

Cody Kincaid had some unfinished business to settle. Tense and keyed up, he had driven out to the ranch hoping for a little time alone before his father's burial. He needed some peace, and maybe just a little time to bury the demons he'd been carrying around with him. So he'd saddled one of his father's prize stallions and headed out. He planned to ride long and hard, long enough to ease some of the tension coiled inside him like a snake and hard enough to help clear his head.

Cody's eyes scanned the familiar horizon, and he felt an uncommon ache. He shook his head, trying to banish the unfamiliar feelings. He still couldn't believe his father was gone. In the past seven years since Cody had left, he'd returned briefly a few times, hoping the strain of his relationship with his father would have eased—but it hadn't.

Seven years ago, he'd stormed out the door after an angry, bitter argument with his father. He'd never realized that those angry words they'd shouted at each other would still be ringing in his ears seven years later.

Seven long, lonely years later.

He'd loved his father deeply. Their relationship had never been easy, but that had not affected the way Cody had felt about him. Now his father was gone, and there was no way in the world to take back the painful words that had built a wall between them.

Regret and remorse ran deep, and Cody swallowed the painful lump of memories. No matter how he tried to deny it, reality couldn't be denied. His father was dead, and the only home he'd ever known had been burned to the ground, leaving him all alone with nothing but regrets and memories.

Cody's eyes scanned the barren landscape again.

Everything he'd ever loved was gone.

With his eyes stinging, Cody shook his head again. Something about his father's death still puzzled him. It was so odd, his father perishing in a fire. His father had always been a careful, cautious man, and a man didn't change his ways, at least not *his* father. There were a lot of perils in ranching life, and because of the desert and drought conditions, not to mention the distance between the ranches and town, fire was always treated with the respect reserved for something that could put an end to a life, or a way of life. So he couldn't understand how or why his father had been so careless. Something just didn't add up.

One of the reasons he'd come out here this morning was to have a look around. Last night it had been too dark to do little more than stand and stare helplessly at the pile of gray ashes where the Kincaid ranch house had once stood.

The news of his father's death had churned up a lot of old memories and feelings. But to his surprise, he'd found the anger he'd carried around for so many years had finally faded, and now there was just an empty feeling in his gut.

He'd loved his father, but couldn't get along with him, didn't understand him. His father had been rigid and very set in his ways with strong opinions and strong beliefs that he'd expected his only son to subscribe to. Unfortunately, for as long as Cody could remember, he'd been his own man with his own ideas and his own beliefs. Something his father couldn't—or wouldn't—understand.

About the only thing they'd had in common was the love of this land.

Cody found himself smiling. When he was a boy, he'd spend days and days in the open air, riding from one end of Kincaid land to the other. Camping out down by the creek, he'd take only his camping gear, his fishing pole and a hunting knife. He'd sleep on the ground with only the stars and the night for company, and eat only what he could catch in the creek, snare on the land or pluck from the trees and bushes. He loved this land, every square inch of it, loved the peace and serenity that nothing else in his life had ever given him. He'd ridden and climbed over every hill and valley until he'd intimately come to know every square inch of it.

When he was fourteen, his father had given him his first stallion and his first rifle. Glancing around, Cody smiled in a bit of possessive pride. It was out here, in the open, that he'd learned how to shoot and ride.

By the time he was sixteen, horses and rifles no longer satisfied him, at least not in the way he discovered a woman could—one certain woman: Lucy Miller. His jaw clenched in remembrance. At the time, he'd been too inexperienced and too bewildered by the emotions and hormones raging through him to realize that the only woman he'd had eyes for was interested in him because of *who* he was and what she thought he could give her.

It was because of Lucy that he and his father had had their first—and last—fight. In a fit of anger, his father had called him a renegade. The label had stuck, much to his chagrin. Maybe he'd earned the label by being so defiant and disobedient, but he'd been young and hopelessly in love, fighting a torrent of hormones so strong he couldn't see straight, but that didn't mean he had to like the nickname. Even now, after all these years, the term still grated on him simply because it reminded him how different he and his father had really been.

A small smile claimed Cody's lips. As different as they were, he had to hand it to his old man, who'd been shrewd and wise—about everything, *especially* women.

Gold digging women.

His father had seen right through Lucy, but Cody had been too blinded by lust to see anything *but* her. It had taken him six long years, not to mention being jilted at the altar, to realize his father had been right all along. Lucy had played him for a fool, pulling his strings just as if he were a damn puppet.

Once he'd seen the truth for himself, he'd vowed never to let it happen again. He'd never let a woman—*any* woman get that close to him or his wary, battle-scarred heart again. He'd share his body willingly—and there was always a willing woman available—but not his heart. He'd learned the hard way women weren't to be trusted, and he was a man who never forgot a lesson.

Now his father was gone, and it was too late. Too late for him to apologize for his words and his behavior. Too late to tell his father he *finally* understood why the elder Kincaid had been so adamant about Lucy.

It was a shame wisdom came with age and not with hormones. The other way around would make life a whole hell of a lot simpler.

Reluctantly Cody banished his bittersweet memories, pushing them to the back of his mind as he inhaled deeply of the clean, fresh, air and felt the warm rays of the sun. He just needed some time to be free in the open country.

Urging his horse on, he rode hard and fast, eating up the ground. The hot, dry wind had shifted, bringing with it the scent of wildflowers from the north pasture. For the first time in days, he began to relax. He'd been cooped up in the city of Austin for so long he'd forgotten how peaceful the open land could be. Or how much he'd missed it. There was a solitude out here that he knew he'd never be able to find anywhere else on earth.

He was in the back quarter of the ranch, riding hell-bent across land that had been in his family since before the Civil

War, inhaling the sweet smell of sunshine and freedom, when he first spotted the stranger.

The *female* stranger.

The moment he caught sight of her, he quickly reined his stallion in, not wanting to frighten her.

Or the angry, thousand-powerful-pound Angus bull facing her.

Shaking his head, Cody ground his teeth as he quietly watched her, unable to believe his ears. It sounded as though she was trying to *sweet-talk* the contrary animal back behind the fence he'd just broken through!

Cody's eyes moved over the broken fence to the pasture beyond. The Hooper ranch ran along the western perimeter of the Kincaid ranch, and Hooper had a pasture full of prime cows. From the determined look in the Angus's eyes, Cody had a feeling the lusty bull was eyeing the beautiful bovines with a lot more than courting on his mind.

But apparently the woman was oblivious to the danger she was in.

He couldn't tell if she was drunk, or just plain stupid. He almost ruled out the drunk part, since it was only ten o'clock in the morning. But then again, he'd learned the hard way never to rule out *anything* when it came to women.

Tipping the brim of his Stetson back in order to get a better look at her, he hoped like hell she was drunk, because *no one* could possibly be that stupid. Antagonizing an Angus, an animal not known for its cheery disposition, was tantamount to suicide. The angry beast probably outweighed her by nine hundred pounds. Nine hundred romping, stomping pounds. One wrong move, and the woman would be squashed like a watermelon under a semi.

Scowling, Cody let his gaze travel over her. Her back was to him, so he couldn't see her face, but what he could see made his scowl deepen. The woman was small and slender...*delicate* was a word that came to mind. If she weighed a hundred and twenty pounds soaking wet, he'd be surprised. Her hair was the color of wheat and tumbled recklessly down her back in a mass of silky curls. Jeans, worn white in spots, clung lovingly to her feminine shape. In spite of her petite stature, her legs were long and shapely and seemed to go on forever.

For an instant, Cody felt a primitive tightening in his gut, recognized it, then dismissed it for what it was as he continued his visual appraisal. A blindingly white blouse with the sleeves rolled up gave just the barest hint of the curves that lay beneath the pristine material. Her boots were leather, probably hand tooled, and could qualify as ancient. And likely added several inches of height to her frame, so she was smaller than he'd originally believed.

Curious, he studied her for a moment. He knew his dad had rented out the old foreman's ranch house a few years back. He'd noticed the chicken shed and the gardens when he rode in last night, but none of it had really registered until he spotted her. Now he realized she was probably his tenant.

But that certainly didn't excuse her incredible stupidity.

Watching her, Cody shook his head, wondering if she knew that dealing with an Angus was always a delicate proposition. And when that bull had loving on his mind, it could get downright dangerous.

Normally he was a man who minded his own business—especially when it came to women—but *this* woman was on his land, and as such, he figured she was his responsibility. Especially since she was apparently too damn stupid to look out for herself.

"Looks like you could use a hand."

Absorbed in what she was doing, Savannah was totally unaware she was being observed. The deep, gravelly masculine voice had the same effect as a cannon going off in her ear. She screeched, and the sugar treats she held in her hand in order to coax the contrary bull back home went airborne.

Swearing under his breath, Cody ducked the sweet, flying weapons and kept a tight rein on his horse and an eye on the Angus.

"Easy, boy," he murmured, patting his spooked horse's mane in comfort as his hooves started dancing, itching to run.

Clutching a hand to her racing heart, Savannah whirled in the direction of the voice, determined to give the trespasser a proper dressing-down for sneaking up on her, never mind scaring her.

The moment her gaze collided with his, her jaw flapped open as if it had come unhinged and her breath crawled back down her throat. Instinctively she took a step away from him—and closer to the bull, some female instinct warning her which beast was the more dangerous one.

Staring openmouthed at the stranger, Savannah held back the angry words that formed in her mouth. *Dangerous* and *disreputable* were the first words that popped into her mind. Patting a hand to her still-galloping heart, Savannah swallowed, surprised to find her throat suddenly dry. Perhaps it would be wise not to voice her angry thoughts. She wasn't certain it would be prudent or healthy to anger a man of his size—not unless she had her late daddy's Colt handy.

And loaded.

Savannah attempted to gather her composure as she tried to take him all in. Sitting atop a horse that was as black as midnight only made him appear larger than life. He was so tall, so broad, he shadowed the sun from her view as if an eclipse had suddenly fallen from the heavens. He wore faded jeans that molded tightly to the contours of his long, powerful legs, and a black T-shirt stretched wide across his muscular frame. His arms were long and tanned, the hands holding the reins huge. The black Stetson he wore was pushed back far enough on his head give her a glimpse of blue-black hair. His face was slightly etched and weathered and achingly masculine. His jaw, which hadn't seen a razor in more than a few days, was a series of fierce slashes and blunt angles.

But it was his eyes that caught and held her attention; they were as blue and brilliant as the creek that bubbled along the back of the property. Yet they were unreadable; there was no hint of emotion visible, not in his eyes or his face. His expression told her nothing, not even if he was friend or foe. But something about his eyes made her feel as if he was seeing right through her—all the way to the secrets hidden in her soul.

In spite of the heat, Savannah shivered, averting her gaze from his. Lord, he was big. Her late mama would have described him to the good ladies in her sewing circle as the kind of man a woman wouldn't know whether to run to—or from.

And at the moment, Savannah wasn't entirely certain which to do, either.

Cody met the woman's frightened gaze, feeling as if his horse had just kicked him in the gut. The golden mass of curls framed a face that was as beautiful and feminine as the rest of her. Her skin was as pale and translucent as the finest porcelain, touched by a hint of rose. Her nose was delicate, with a smattering of freckles just across the tip; her lips were full and lush, glistening with a hint of something soft and shiny, making him ache to know what she'd taste like. Sweet, he'd bet. Very sweet.

Her eyes were huge and blue, but there was something in their depths. Wariness, definitely, but something more, some hint of hidden vulnerability that went far deeper than fear, and it instantly tugged at something deep inside of him.

Muttering an oath, Cody sighed wearily. He didn't need any grief in his life now, especially *female* grief. And experience had taught him that any woman who looked like her could only mean one thing—trouble. And plenty of it. Cody sighed again.

She looked like the kind of woman who should be draped in silk and swathed in diamonds, sipping some delicate aperitif in a glittering suite on the French Riviera as she exchanged pleasantries with some intellectually and economically superior male whose idea of comfortable clothes was a penguin suit. There was something about her, an elemental elegance that shrieked she didn't belong. *Not here.* Definitely not here.

What the hell was she doing in the middle of the dusty, drought-ridden Texas plains? he wondered in disgust.

Standing perfectly still under his visual onslaught, Savannah struggled deep to find her voice. She'd lost it the moment her eyes had landed on the interloper. Even though she was scared witless by the sudden appearance of this lethal-looking stranger, she knew better than to show fear. She'd learned a long time ago to fend for herself.

Determined to get rid of him as quickly as possible, Savannah bravely lifted her chin, planted delicate hands on her hips and looked him square in the eye, even if it did make her heart begin a series of world-class gymnastic moves.

"You're trespassing." When angered, her deep, Georgia accent became thicker, gently curling around her words.

The soft, sexy drawl slid over Cody like warm honey, awakening his nerve endings.

He cocked his head, trying to hide his sudden amusement. "Excuse me?"

"You're trespassing," Savannah repeated, as if he were a blockhead. She forced herself to take a step closer. He shifted his frame in the saddle, and she resisted the urge to turn tail and bolt. No doubt a man of his size was capable of sending her flying into the next county with one powerful sweep of his arms. But she held her ground, determined. A woman alone couldn't be a chickenheart. She couldn't let a little thing like one huge, cantankerous man frighten her. Savannah's gaze found his, and she swallowed. Hard. Well, she could *try* not to let a huge, cantankerous man frighten her. But she'd die before she ever let him—or anyone else—know he'd startled her. Pride alone prevented it.

"What are you doing on my land?" she demanded, tilting her head back to look up at him. His blue eyes collided with hers, and Savannah felt her pulse kick up. Balling her hands into tight little fists, she tried to ignore the increased beat of her heart.

Her land? Cody glanced around, trying to hide his amusement. "You own this spread, do you?" he asked casually.

Savannah stiffened, suddenly suspicious. After the mysterious fire last week that had cost John Kincaid his life, everyone was suspect. Especially a stranger. Why, the sheriff had even questioned her and Joey! It was an outrage! An absolute outrage! As if she'd ever do anything to hurt John Kincaid. The man had been nothing but kind to them. He was the only friend she had—by choice.

An extremely private person, she chose not to make casual friends. She preferred her solitude to friendships she couldn't return. As in all small towns, people in Silver Creek loved to gossip, and a woman alone with a small son to raise couldn't afford to be gossiped about. So she kept to herself. Not that the people in Silver Creek hadn't tried to be kind and helpful. But it wasn't in her nature to need anyone. She was used to being a one-woman entity. Doing things for herself, by herself. She'd never had the luxury of any kind of support, and had learned the hard way never to lean or depend on anyone—especially a man.

She knew what people said about her because of the looks and the whispers she heard when she went into town. They thought her odd; strange, because she was polite but decidedly distant, making it clear she wasn't interested in casual friends or idle chitchat. She didn't particular care what anyone thought or said about her. She had to protect herself and Joey, which took precedence over anything and everything, and she knew the only way she could do that was to keep to herself.

That was why this large, dangerous, disreputable-looking man had startled her so. Other than the Kincaid ranch hands, rarely did anyone come this far onto the ranch. Generally she could wander about in relative ease, not to mention solitude, knowing she'd never be bothered by anyone. And she hadn't been until *he* showed up.

Savannah studied him for a moment, wondering why something about him seemed so familiar. He definitely wasn't one of the Kincaid ranch hands. And she knew if she'd ever seen this man before, she certainly would have remembered him. He was not the kind of man a woman forgot.

So who was he and what on earth was he doing here?

Still frowning, Savannah didn't know if she should try to detain him and attempt to subtly question him about his motives, then perhaps report her information back to the sheriff. Or should she just try to get rid of him as quickly as possible?

Lost in her own thoughts, Savannah forgot about the cantankerous bull, and was still looking at the stranger blankly, trying to decide what to do.

Amused, Cody shifted his weight. "Question too hard for you, ma'am?" he inquired.

Savannah blinked up at him. "Excuse me?"

"I asked if the question was too hard for you."

Savannah scowled at him. The man was an arrogant, insolent, insufferable boor. And those were probably his good points.

"What question?" she forced herself to ask.

Cody sighed. "I asked if you owned this spread."

For a moment, she contemplated how to answer him. She didn't want to lie, but nor did she want to divulge too much information until she knew exactly who he was and what his intentions were.

"My house is right over there." Lifting her arm, she vaguely waved in the general direction of her house, not wanting to let him know specifically where she lived. "Not that it's any of your business," she found it necessary to add. Her chin went up a notch. "And unless you leave immediately or tell me what you're doing here, I'll be forced to take drastic measures." She had no idea *what* drastic measures she would take, but surely she'd think of something.

Rubbing a hand across his stubbled chin, Cody bit back a smile, never taking his eyes off of her, not certain if he should be amused or annoyed. As she stood with her hands on hips, blue eyes blazing, there was no mistaking the challenge or the implied threat in her words. She wasn't big enough to make spit in a well, but she was standing here, bold as brass, facing him down. She might be stupid, but she sure as hell had spunk, and he had to admire her for it.

Obviously she didn't have a clue who he was, which suited him fine—for the moment. He glanced at the bull before bringing his gaze back to hers.

"What I'm doing here, lady, is trying to save you from getting your little butt kicked." Cody nodded toward the bull, who was now mournfully staring at the contented cows in the next pasture. "That's an Angus, lady, and obviously you have no idea how dangerous that animal can be when riled."

At his words, her mouth fell open in shock, and she could feel the heat rising in her cheeks. Dragging her gaze from his, Savannah looked at the bull. She knew perfectly well just how dangerous this particular bull could be. She was the one who had to deal with the blasted animal on a daily basis. But no matter how dangerous or disruptive, the bull was an investment, a very expensive investment that she hoped would pay off in a big way. She planned to use the bull for stud service to the surrounding ranchers. The income she received would go a long way toward easing some of the enormous financial burdens she faced and hopefully allow her to provide some future financial security for her and her son.

But it was one thing to put up with a cantankerous bull who would bring about some financial security, and quite another to put up with a rude, cantankerous man who had the unmitigated gall to treat her as if she were some kind of an idiot.

Her chin lifted another inch, and her blue eyes grew icy. "I'm well aware of just how dangerous Miss Sophie can be," she assured him with an intimidating gaze that would have felled any reasonable man on the spot. He didn't appear to be phased. "And besides," she added, her tone growing even icier, "I don't recall anyone appointing you as protector of my—"

"*Miss* Sophie?" Cody interrupted with a confused frown. "Lady," he growled, "that's a bull."

A faint flush crept slowly up her porcelain cheeks; a dastardly childhood trait she'd never overcome. She was angered by his arrogance and embarrassed that she had been caught doing something that appeared so foolhardy, when she knew perfectly well what she was doing and just how dangerous it was. Still, someone had to handle Miss Sophie, and like it or not, that someone was *her*.

However, it certainly wasn't necessary to speak to her as if she were some kind of dim-witted fool! This man wasn't just dangerous and disreputable; he was unbelievably rude, as well.

Grinding her teeth together in an effort to hang on to her temper, Savannah blatantly met his bold, engaging gaze. "Yes, I'm well aware that's a bull," she said with maddening patience, nodding her head slowly, as if speaking to a young child. She was using her best mother's voice, deliberately soft and elementally feminine. It was a tone her son, Joey, always said let him know he was in trouble. *Big* trouble. But apparently *this* man didn't have the sense of a ten-year-old, because her deliberately deceptive tone certainly didn't seem to phase him, judging from the calm, cold look on his face.

Watching her through narrowed eyes, Cody shifted uncomfortably. The honeyed thickness of her voice licked a path over every nerve ending, making his blood heat and thicken. Annoyed at himself, he wondered if she was laughing at *him* since anyone with a dollop of common sense could see she was riled but determined to be a lady about it. He would have found it amusing if he wasn't so damn annoyed. And he wasn't certain if he was more annoyed at her. Or at himself.

It had been a long, long time since he'd reacted to any woman—beautiful or not—with the elemental, gut-level, male-responding-to-female reaction he'd had the moment

she'd turned around and seared him with those beautiful
blue eyes.

Watching him carefully, she rocked back on her heels as
she tucked her hands in the back pockets of her jeans, not
realizing the movement stretched the thin cotton fabric
tightly across her breasts, emphasizing her curves—which
immediately drew Cody's attention. He shifted his weight
again as his annoyance—and his interest—grew.

Ignoring his fierce scowl, Savannah smiled benevolently
at him. "But thank you so much for pointing out that Miss
Sophie is a bull." Her smile brightened in proportion to his
scowl. "Why, if you hadn't pointed it out, I might never
have realized it."

The deliberate sweetness of her voice made him scowl.
Damn! She was making fun of him, and it galled him to no
end. Cody's eyes darkened dangerously, and his hands
tightened on the reins. Leaning down off his horse until he
was almost eyeball-to-eyeball with her, he was sorely
tempted to shake some sense into her. She wasn't just stupid, but dangerous, as well.

"Are you telling me you named a thousand-pound Angus bull *Miss* Sophie?"

Savannah blinked in surprise. He was so close, every
breath she took was filled with his scent. It wasn't the typical flowery cologne, but something pure, raw and male. It
made her head spin and her knees nearly buckle. There was
nothing soft about him; he was power, strength and incredible virility.

He was so close she could see the smudge of long, inky
black lashes shadowing his cheeks; could see the shards of
black and navy that composed his eyes, eyes that seemed to
see through her, to read her, to see her secrets and her soul.
No man had ever been able to do that before, and it made
her unaccountably nervous because something about this
man seemed familiar, far too familiar. It was as if he somehow *knew* her. Perhaps it was the unreadable look in his eyes
or the cold, implacable, *knowing* expression on his face.
Whatever it was, it was making her incredibly nervous.

In spite of the heat of the day, her palms grew damp, and she drew her hands out of her pockets to wipe them down her jeans, drawing attention to her long legs.

Cody's eyes dutifully followed the movement of her hands, lingering on her long legs until she almost blushed again. But he didn't back down or glance away.

And neither would she.

She refused to step back, to give an inch. Holding her ground, she tried to ignore his closeness even though having him so near made her want to run in the opposite direction as fast as her legs would carry her. But she'd vowed never again to show any kind of weakness to a man, and she wasn't about to start with *this* man.

But Lord have mercy, if he didn't back up and give her some space, she wasn't going to be able to tell him *anything*. The last time a man had been this close to her she'd had a tooth extracted, and she didn't recall that situation too fondly, either.

Savannah tried to take a deep breath, but it felt as if something had constricted her lungs. She couldn't get a breath, let alone form an intelligible word.

She had absolutely no idea why she was having such a ridiculous reaction to him. He was just a man. And she'd been forced to deal with hundreds of men over the years, but not one had ever made her react this way. It was…odd. And perhaps just a bit disconcerting, leaving her slightly off balance. She didn't like it. At all.

"I…I—"

She never had a chance to finish. Out of the corner of his eye, Cody saw the bull lower his head. His powerful hooves started pawing the dry, drought-ridden ground. Instinctively Cody knew the animal was getting ready to charge, and he knew, too, that the little Georgia peach had just overplayed her hand. Left to her own devices, she'd probably end up as peach juice. Cursing under his breath, Cody clamped an arm around her slender waist and hauled her off her feet and out of the bull's range.

Stunned by being suddenly airborne, Savannah screeched like a hyena. "Put me down!" Too furious to be frightened, Savannah pummeled him with her fists. The blows glanced off his broad shoulders like flies sliding off ice cream. "Damn it, take your hands off of me!"

Ignoring her protests, Cody scooted back in the saddle, then unceremoniously dumped her in front of him, twisting her around so she faced him. Her chest collided with his, nearly knocking the breath from her. His chest was like a wall of steel.

Glancing down at her, Cody tried not to smile. Her hair was a tangled mess, and she was sitting half in, half out of the saddle, her long legs dangling over one side of the horse. She looked mad enough to spit nails.

"How dare you...*manhandle* me," she fumed, walloping him again. "How dare you touch me. Who the hell do you think you—?"

"Shut up," Cody said calmly, spurring the horse in the opposite direction and out of the bull's way, "before you spook that bull any further. And stop hitting me," he ordered in a voice that made her do just that. Grabbing her flailing wrists, he looped her arms around his neck. Her wrists were so slender, he could wrap his fingers around them and still have room to spare. The thought of what could have happened to her had the bull charged her both frightened and infuriated him. "And hold on to me," he ordered none too politely when she started to pull her arms down. "Before you fall flat on your face."

Pushing the tangled hair out of her eyes with one hand, Savannah glared at him for a long, silent moment, letting the angry stream of words accumulate in her mouth, ready to spout, until reality took over and forced her to face her situation. She was alone, all alone, with this...this... She couldn't think of a word bad enough to call this... this...person.

For an instant, she thought of screaming, then realized it would do no good. No one would hear her. Most of the

Kincaid ranch hands had been given the day off for the funeral.

She forced herself to meet his gaze, and her pulse began to thud at his nearness. She began to tremble when she realized her arms were wrapped around his neck. His full, lush mouth was only inches from hers, and they were pressed together in a way that was far too intimate for her peace of mind. She mentally struggled to put some distance between them.

Averting her gaze from his, she lifted her chin haughtily. "If you're thinking of robbing me, you're out of luck. I don't have much money."

He darted a hard glance at her that told her exactly, without a word, that it wasn't her money he was interested in. Savannah swallowed nervously.

"What . . . what *are* you planning on doing with me?" Chewing her lower lip, she waited, worried.

"Drowning has real possibilities," he said mildly.

Savannah's eyes widened in shock and it took a few heartbeats to realize he had no intention of doing any such thing. Furious that he could joke when she was feeling so confused and unsettled, Savannah narrowed her gaze.

"If you lay a hand on me, the sheriff will be on your tail before you even get out of the county."

Her words almost caused Cody to laugh. He wondered how the Georgia peach would feel if she knew *he* was the law. As a Texas Ranger, he had jurisdiction over all of Texas, over and above the sheriff of this or any other town. But he didn't feel inclined to let that information slip, not until he had some answers to his father's mysterious death. People would talk more freely to him if they thought he was merely a grieving son, and not the long arm of the law.

So he held his tongue and let his gaze lazily drift, then linger on her mouth for a long moment before gliding back up to meet her furious gaze.

Damnation, if she wasn't a sight to behold when she was riled. Would she be as volatile in passion? he wondered. Would she be slow to heat, or would she ignite like dry timber on a Texas plain? He didn't know, but damn, his hard, aching body was suddenly dying to find out.

"Lady," he growled softly, trying to gain some perspective, "I don't intend to lay a hand on you." At least not now. Not yet. But soon. *Very soon.* His gaze slowly, deliberately swept the length of her again, lingering on every single feminine curve and hollow as if measuring her.

"Would you like to see my teeth?" she snapped, sorely tempted to wallop him again for appraising her as if she were a side of beef!

"No, thanks," he said grimly. "I've seen enough. To tell you the truth, you're not my type."

It was a bold, blatant lie. He needed to protect himself and keep her at a distance. He'd never let another woman know what he was thinking or feeling; he'd never allow himself to be that vulnerable again. Cody's smile turned to a grimace as his gaze, now cold and emotionless, swept intimately over her again. "You're much too skinny for my tastes."

Pain chased the last edges of anger away. His words slipped past the cobweb of scars that covered Savannah's tender heart, and she felt the sting of tears. He was blatantly *rejecting* her, and not even bothering to be subtle about it.

Rejection.

The word echoed hollowly through her mind, like a haunting, painful memory. It didn't matter *what* the reason; what mattered was the fact.

Swallowing the sudden lump that clogged her throat, Savannah furiously blinked back the sudden rush of hot, salty tears, unwilling to give him the satisfaction of knowing he'd hurt her. She'd never reveal that much of herself to another man, never let another one know that he had the power to hurt her.

She'd thought the years had cushioned her from the pain of such a blow. But it hadn't. The jagged claws of rejection still burned deep, renewing a whole host of feelings of inadequacy she wasn't certain how to deal with. Not now. Not with *him*.

Hiding her pain behind a mask of fury, Savannah glared at him.

"I am *not* skinny," she declared fiercely, sorely tempted to wallop him again. In spite of the fact that he was dangerous and disreputable looking, some female instinct assured her he wouldn't physically hurt her. But that didn't mean she had to put up with his high-handed, arrogant manner! Or his insults about her femininity.

Furious, Savannah considered her options, then gauged the distance to the ground, wondering how badly she'd get hurt if she jumped. And then, of course, there was the little matter of trying to outrun his horse. Her legs were long but not *that* long.

"Don't even think about it," Cody said calmly, as if reading her thoughts. Her gaze flew to his, and she wondered how he knew what she'd been thinking. Their gazes held for a moment, and she could feel her heart dance a wicked beat. Her gaze drifted to his mouth again, so soft, so close. So *dangerous*.

Mortified by her reaction to him, Savannah tried to gather her dignity. Taking a deep breath, she avoided his gaze, looking at everything but him. Maintaining any dignity in this situation was impossible, she realized glumly. She was practically sitting on top of him; the curve of her hip was intimately pressed against a very delicate part of his anatomy. Embarrassed, Savannah squirmed in the saddle, trying to put some distance between them.

"Sit still," Cody ordered, looking directly at her. She swallowed, vividly aware of his closeness and helpless to do anything about it. With every movement of the horse, she was jostled closer and closer to him until she was practically in his lap. Every time she was thrust against him, she collided with the hard wall of his chest. With her arms looped around his neck, she could feel the heat of his skin, warmed even further by the sun. Feeling slightly breathless, and more than a bit uncomfortable at her reaction to him, Savannah squirmed again.

"Damn it, woman," he growled, his eyes narrowed, "sit . . . *still*." Eyes closed, Cody took a slow, deep breath. The woman *was* trying to kill him. He was absolutely sure of it. Her sweet, delicate scent was nearly making him drunk with desire, reminding his hard, aching body just how long it had been since he'd been with a woman. Her scent wasn't sweet as he thought it would be, but something a little dark, and erotic, reminding him of sultry nights and wonderfully sinful sex. He almost groaned aloud.

This beautiful, cantankerous, *stupid* woman with the delicate curves and legs that went on forever was practically on top of him. Every slender curve teased his starved senses. Having her pressed so intimately against him was making him ache in a way he hadn't ached in a long, long time.

Usually the ache could be assuaged by *any* woman; it didn't really matter. There were always plenty of women willing and anxious to spend an hour or a night with him, ready to accept what little he had to offer them—a few pleasant moments and perhaps a fond, lingering memory. But that was *all* he ever offered, could offer; he had nothing else to give. Certainly not his heart, or his soul—they'd been ripped from him years ago.

Opening his eyes, Cody slowly released the pent-up breath he'd been holding. He silently cursed stupid, beautiful women and his own weaknesses and desires.

"If you move or squirm one more time," he said quietly, forcing the words through gritted teeth, "you won't have to worry about jumping. I'll dump you off this horse so fast you won't know what hit you. *Now sit still!*"

Savannah opened her mouth, determined to give back as good as she got, but one look at his face and she decided to try something else.

"Where are you taking me?" she demanded, trying without success to stay perfectly still. It was impossible. Every time the horse moved, she was jostled against him.

"Back where you belong." He looked at her. In spite of his aggravation, she was a damn beautiful sight with her hair all tangled and falling in her face and her eyes as wide as a deer's. Once again he saw that wariness shimmering deep in her eyes, and he cursed under his breath. How could she be afraid of him when he'd just saved her butt? He was almost insulted. Fear sure wasn't the usual reaction he got from women. So what was with her? He didn't know, and he wasn't certain he wanted to find out. What he wanted at the moment was to be rid of her as quickly as possible so his poor, aching body could have some peace.

"I'm taking you home, lady, and I expect you to stay there and stay put, at least until I get that bull calmed down and back where he belongs and that fence fixed."

Thoroughly confused now, Savannah simply stared at him, unable to look away. His statement didn't make any sense. Why would he be concerned about Miss Sophie or the broken fence?

"Do you work for the Kincaid ranch?" she asked with a genuine frown, suddenly more curious than cautious. Unconsciously her eyes drifted to his mouth again.

"Nope." Cody reined in the horse as soon as he reached the outskirts of her part of the ranch, knowing that if he didn't get her off his lap, he was going to be in big trouble. The kind of trouble he didn't need, especially now, especially with a woman like *her*.

Seeing her house, Savannah sighed in relief, then turned her attention back to him with another frown, clearly and utterly confused. "Then why on earth would you be worried about Miss Sophie or the fence?"

Cody glanced away from her, annoyed that he was beginning to like looking at her. And her scent. Damnation, it was a scent that could make a man go mad with wanting, teasing him through the night, making him ache with longing. For an instant, the idea of burying himself deep inside of her until he was drenched in her scent was nearly overwhelming.

Restraining his thoughts, Cody tried to get some perspective.

"Were you drunk when you named that bull?" he finally asked, attempting to put some distance between them. He brought his gaze back to hers.

The question startled Savannah for a moment, and she pursed her lips, almost making Cody groan. Her mouth was close, too close. Soft and shiny, it made him ache to taste her.

"Certainly not," Savannah said primly, wondering why he was staring at her mouth as if she'd just uttered a string of vulgarities. It made her nervous, and she self-consciously licked her lips as his eyes followed the movement of her tongue. It made a ball of warmth curl tightly low in her belly. "I've . . . I've never been drunk in my life."

Cody nodded grimly. "Figures."

Her chin went up in a way he recognized now. Every time he got her dander up, that chin went skyward. It amused him.

"And I didn't name that bull. My son did," she said defensively, pushing another tangle of hair off her face and daring him to make some comment about her son.

Cody shifted his body in the saddle. So she had a son, he thought, wondering about a husband. He'd already checked out her hands, and she wore no rings of any kind. He'd seen no sign of a male anywhere, so he figured she probably wasn't married. No man in his right mind would let his woman behave so irresponsibly, especially around a bull. For some reason, the thought pleased him.

"How old's your son?"

"Joey's almost ten," she said with unabashed pride. Realizing she was telling him more than she ever intended, she snapped her mouth shut.

Cody took one long, last look at her, then sighed as he circled her waist with his hands and gently lowered her to the ground, so gently it surprised her. She wondered how a man so huge could be so gentle. Unbearably, unbelievably gentle. His hands lingered at her waist for a moment, and her skin warmed from his touch, a warmth that crept over her like a silky shawl.

When he finally released her, when her feet were safely planted on land, Savannah suddenly felt off balance. Pushing her hair out of her face with shaky hands, she looked up at him, shading her eyes against the blistering sun.

"Who are you?" she finally whispered, growing more curious and confused by the moment.

Cody finally smiled, a beautiful, glorious smile that made her feel as if someone had suddenly turned up the sun a notch.

"Name's Kincaid." He touched the brim of his hat. "Cody Kincaid." He glanced at the surrounding landscape before bringing his amused gaze back to hers. "And the last time I checked, lady, *I* owned this spread."

Chapter Two

If there was an open hole in the ground, Savannah would have gladly jumped in it. Lord have mercy, she couldn't have been more stunned if the man had just announced he was the Lone Ranger!

As she stared after him in utter shock, Savannah's mouth hung open as if someone had sprung a trapdoor. She shook her head in utter disbelief.

Cody Kincaid.

The name reverberated over and over in her mind. Still shading her eyes against the blazing sun, Savannah blindly stared after him even though he had long faded from her view, leaving little more than a trail of dust behind him.

The impact of *his* identity and *her* actions engulfed her, and she almost moaned in distress.

What on earth must the man think of her? In the space of just a few moments, she had insulted him, assaulted him and threatened him.

Lord, why hadn't she held her tongue? she wondered dismally, turning on her heel and trudging into the blissful coolness of the house. She dropped down into the nearest kitchen chair and inhaled deeply of the cool air. He'd frightened her. She wasn't accustomed to disreputable-looking strangers prowling around the ranch, and the sudden appearance of such a lethal-looking man had thrown her for a loop, especially in light of the mysterious fire and John's death. It was only natural that she react the way she had, she assured herself. Any woman would have done the same thing.

Savannah scowled, shoving a wad of hair off her face. Then again, not every woman would have been quite so tart or outspoken, not to mention downright rude.

Remorse engulfed Savannah. The poor man had enough troubling him with his daddy's death and all; a crazy lady running around loose on his land was the last thing he needed to worry about.

Propping her chin on her hand, Savannah sighed deeply. Her late mama always told her that one day her smart, sassy mouth would get her into trouble. And Savannah had a feeling she'd just run into trouble, *big* trouble. But holding her tongue had never been in her nature. She'd never learned to...filter, as her late mama politely used to say. Everything she thought came out of her mouth, and she had to admit there were times she deeply regretted it. And this was definitely one of those times.

Well, it wasn't entirely her fault, she thought reasonably as embarrassment quickly turned to indignation. *He* was just as much to blame. He could have simply told her who he was instead of skulking around mysteriously, scaring her half to death. Realization had Savannah scowling again. He'd *deliberately* given her vague answers, and Savannah had a feeling he'd thoroughly enjoyed letting her make a complete and utter fool out of herself.

He knew damn well she didn't own this spread— Oh, another thought quickly raced through her mind, and Savannah felt a slow, sick feeling uncoil in her stomach.

Cody Kincaid knew she didn't own this spread, because he *owned* it.

And everything on it, including her house.

Her house.

Oh, Lord! The thought brought her head up. After five years, she thought of the house as hers, but it wasn't; it belonged to John Kincaid. Or rather, it *had* belonged to John Kincaid. But John was gone and now the entire Kincaid property belonged to... Cody Kincaid. Swallowing hard, Savannah vaguely wondered if she was going to be sick.

After what had just transpired between them, she wouldn't blame the man if he tossed her out on her ear. Which was probably exactly what he planned to do.

Oh, Lord, she *was* going to be sick!

Savannah shivered as she glanced around the familiar kitchen she'd lovingly decorated. She couldn't help but smile. She loved this house, loved every nook and cranny, loved the way the house seemed to be a comfort and a buffer from the harsh world outside. She'd worked hard to make this a real home for her and her son.

When they'd first moved in, the place could have best been called a disaster. The paint was peeling, the ceiling leaking, the tile curling up off the floor. John had had the ceiling repaired and the floor replaced, but she had scraped and patched and papered the big kitchen, buying matching fabric to make curtains, a tablecloth and even padded seat covers for the chairs. It had been a labor of love, because the moment she'd walked into this place, it had felt like...home. A real home. A warm, comfortable cocoon, a welcoming haven to protect them from life's harsh realities.

She'd always been a homebody, had always loved making and keeping a home, decorating it, cleaning it, enjoying it, snuggling up on cool nights in front of a roaring fire. Here in Silver Creek, she'd found everything she'd been searching for, and this house had given her a sense of peace and stability she longed for. Maybe because she felt as if she finally belonged somewhere. She belonged here.

This *was* home.

Five years ago, when she and Joey had had to pull up stakes and move, Savannah had carefully looked around and specifically chosen Silver Creek because of its small-town atmosphere. She wanted her son to grow up in a safe environment, with lots of open air for him to play in and explore. Big-city life had never been for her. The thought of putting up with traffic, harried crowds and a fast-track job while leaving Joey in day care or with a sitter while she moved up the corporate ladder did not appeal to her in the least.

She wanted her son to grow up with the benefit of having his mother nearby, specifically *because* she was a single parent. Supporting them was much easier living on a ranch. She had put her teaching degree to good use by starting a small tutoring business, which she ran out of her home so she would always be available if and when her son needed her. She had very few needs and supplemented her income by growing her own fruits and vegetables, raising chickens and selling the eggs, and now there was Miss Sophie, whom she hoped would pay big dividends. She'd saved for two long years to buy that blasted bull, knowing that stud fees would go a long way toward providing some future financial stability for her and Joey.

They weren't rich, and there were times money was extremely tight, but whatever hardships lack of money caused were worth it to be able to be a full-time parent to her son, which was the most important thing in the world to her.

Savannah had never envisioned that she would end up being a single parent. Engaged, she'd been thrilled at the prospect of motherhood. Unfortunately her fiancé hadn't been quite so thrilled. In fact, the idea had appalled him. Fearing it would interfere with his life-style, he'd announced that the "timing" was all wrong and it would be better if she didn't continue the pregnancy. Stunned, Savannah had finally seen Gary for what he really was: a spoiled, immature child pretending to be an adult. When she'd refused to even consider the idea of ending her pregnancy, he'd broken off their engagement and disappeared from her life without a backward glance. At the time, his rejection of her and their unborn child had devastated her. Pregnant, alone and with no one to turn to, she'd had no choice but to assume full and total responsibility for herself and her baby.

Only later could she look back and realize that Gary walking out of her life was probably the best thing that could have happened to her because she certainly didn't need *two* children to take care of.

She'd realized then that she could *never* need, lean or depend on anyone else ever again—*especially* a man. She'd learned the hard way that just like stockings, men had a tendency to run when you really needed them. She had trusted Gary completely, and he'd abused that trust. She'd vowed never again to blindly give her trust away to any man.

And she hadn't.

It was a harsh lesson to learn at a young age, but it had helped to make her a stronger, better person, not to mention a better mother.

Savannah sighed heavily. But as much as she loved and adored her son—and he *was* her life—to no one would she admit that at times, like now, the enormous responsibility she carried weighed heavily on her slender shoulders. Once in a while, when a particularly prickly problem crept up, she felt totally alone, not to mention lonely. At times like this, she longed to have someone to share her burdens with. It wasn't the big things she missed so much, but the little things. A shoulder to cry on, a hand to hold, someone to make her laugh, someone to make her feel *alive*. But in order to have all those things she would have to *trust*, something she wasn't certain she could ever do again. It was too much of a risk. So she'd accepted her fate in life, accepted what she could and couldn't have. And she had long ago realized that she could never have the life of a *normal* woman, a woman allowed to have feelings, emotions or a relationship, because this time it wouldn't be just her heart at risk, but her son's, as well. And she'd never, ever do anything to jeopardize Joey's security. So she'd buried her natural feelings and desires, buried them under the cloak of motherhood, and she'd never regretted her decision until . . . this morning when she ran full tilt into Cody Kincaid, a man who made her *feel* things she knew better than to feel.

Savannah's brows drew into a frown. Perhaps that's why she'd been so surly with him, so mistrusting of him. The moment her eyes had collided with Cody's, she'd felt . . . something. What, she wasn't entirely certain she could or wanted to name at the moment. But the fact that she felt *anything* was more than enough cause for her to worry. It had been so long since she'd felt anything, she'd just assumed she was emotionally dead inside, at least when it came to men. Knowing she wasn't came as a supreme shock.

Until this morning, she'd honestly thought her tender heart had been buried under an avalanche of pain. She couldn't remember the last time she had been quite so acutely aware of a man. Or the last time she'd been so vividly aware that she was a woman—a young, healthy woman.

A woman who *wanted* a man's touch.

Savannah's throat thickened with unshed tears, and her eyes slid closed in an effort to stall them. No matter what she felt, it didn't change the facts of her life, and she might as well accept it. Cody Kincaid was far too dangerous to her bruised and battered heart, not to mention her tenuous emotions, so she had to stay away from him. It was as simple as that.

She could never put her heart at risk, nor her son's security or happiness. The man she'd loved had rejected her and their child, something her son still did not know to this day. She had simply told Joey his father had been killed in an automobile accident before he was born. Joey had accepted her story as the truth, as all children accepted what their mothers told them, and if she had her way, Joey would never know the truth. It would hurt him too much, especially now that he was old enough to understand and perhaps be hurt by the circumstances of his birth. And the day Gary had abandoned and rejected her, she'd vowed that nothing—nothing!—would ever hurt her child. Not as long as there was a breath left in her body. Nor would she ever allow another man into their lives who could have the power to reject them, either of them. The risk was far too great to both of them.

The thought of Joey brought on another well of despair.

As soon as Joey had learned of John Kincaid's death, he had asked her about their house, worried that they'd have to move. She'd assured him they would have to do no such thing. In reality, she'd had no basis to make any assurances, but at the time, she'd thought it a fair and reasonable assumption, and sought only to relieve the worry from her young son's shoulders. Chewing her lower lip, Savannah closed her eyes in disgust for a moment. So much for a mother's assurances.

John had given her an open-end lease, telling her that she was welcome to stay in her little house as long as she liked. She'd always assumed her future was secure—until now. Now John was gone.

As well as all of her security.

If she'd had any doubts, Cody Kincaid's appearance this morning had wiped them out. Once again she was dependent on a man for something: her security rested in Cody's hands, and she didn't like it. At all.

An unexpected shiver raced over her, and she rubbed her arms with her hands, hoping to brush away the bout of cowardice and fear that seized her.

It had taken a long time to build the security and happiness she and Joey now enjoyed, but she'd done it. All by herself, with no one's help, she thought proudly. After all these years of hard work, with the specter of Miss Sophie and the monetary rewards he would bring, she was finally satisfied their future would be secure. And now, just as she was finally beginning to think they had some real security, Cody Kincaid showed up, throwing a wrench into the idea of any kind of security at all.

With another weary sigh, Savannah pushed her hair off her face, wondering why Cody had returned home after all these years. To bury his daddy, certainly, but she had a feeling there was more to it than that.

Even though she loathed gossip, it would have been impossible to live in Silver Creek all these years and not hear the hushed whispers about the infamous Cody Kincaid. His reputation had preceded him.

Savannah scowled. Now that she'd met Cody, she understood some of the whispers. No wonder men generally shifted uncomfortably when his name was mentioned, while the women in town fairly swooned. And she was no exception, she realized furiously, embarrassment flaring anew at her behavior.

She hated to admit Cody Kincaid was everything he was rumored to be, and more. Much more.

A *renegade*.

A rebel, he was the kind of man who followed no one's rules, but made up his own. A man who needed nothing and no one.

A loner.

With the big ranch house gone, there was nowhere for Cody to live. Savannah glanced around her little kitchen, unable to picture a man as big as Cody Kincaid feeling comfortable here. But comfortable or not, she realized if Cody had a mind to stay in Silver Creek and move in here, she had to face the fact that she and Joey would have to move. Like it or not.

Pushing back the sorrow and worry that thought brought on, Savannah, always practical, took a deep breath and tried to concentrate on what had to be done. Proud or not, this time she had to swallow her pride and apologize for her inexcusable behavior this morning. Then she'd have to find out exactly what Cody Kincaid's intentions were, because if they were going to have to move, she wanted it done as quickly as possible so as to produce minimal disruptions in Joey's life. Luckily it was nearly the end of the school year, so if they did have to pack up and move, hopefully they'd be settled in somewhere else before school started again.

Feeling more unsettled than she had in years, Savannah was unable to even bear thinking about leaving her little house. Sighing, she stood up, pushing her chair in and taking one last, loving look around the kitchen.

She couldn't sit here mooning all morning. She had some fences to mend and an apology to make, and it was best to get it over with as soon as possible. Perhaps today wasn't the proper time, what with John's burial and all, but the sooner this situation was resolved the better. She didn't like her future hanging in limbo.

She'd apologize, then throw herself on Cody's mercy, praying he had a sense of humor. Because if he didn't, she and Joey were sunk!

The afternoon sun was hot enough to raise blisters on a turtle's back. Grateful the services were almost over, Cody fingered the brim of his Stetson with damp, nervous fingers as the black horse-drawn hearse carried his father to his final resting place. He was to be buried next to his late wife, high in a meadow of wildflowers in the south quadrant of the ranch. Cody had stood here once before burying a loved one—his mother—and he didn't like it any better now than he had then.

Once again the whole town had turned out to pay their respects, but this time respect was mingled with curiosity. Everyone was angling for a better look at the wayward, prodigal son who'd finally returned home.

But Cody couldn't deal with their curious stares. Not now. His throat was dry, clogged with grief and regret, forming a solid lump that seemed to spread all the way to his chest. He had no way to vent it. He was not a man accustomed to releasing his emotions, but controlling them. He'd learned a long, long time ago to hide his feelings; allowing people to see your vulnerabilities gave them the power to hurt or destroy you. A lesson he'd learned the hard way. But a lesson he'd never forgotten.

As the Reverend Michaels said a final prayer, Cody watched the mourners turn, almost en masse. It was like a

battery of heat-seeking missiles searching him out. Not able
to deal with them right now, he wanted to turn, to walk
away, but he couldn't. Not even he could be that rude. The
people of Silver Creek were good people, and he wouldn't
dishonor his father's memory because of his own discomfort. Besides, after what he'd learned this morning, before
long he would need the help of some of these good people,
and it wouldn't do to alienate them.

With a sigh, Cody gave in to the heat and his own discomfort and yanked his tie off, stuffing it into his pocket
before loosening his collar. Wearily, he rubbed the back of
his neck. It had been a long, exhausting day, and what he'd
learned had left him tired, unsettled and angry—very angry.

After corralling Miss Sophie and fixing the fence, he'd
ridden back over to what remained of his father's house.
He'd spent hours going through the ash and timber, until he
found something that confirmed his suspicions.

Someone had murdered his father.

The thought burned through him. Cody shifted his weight
and lifted something out of his left pants pocket. The
smooth metal was cool against his fingers. His eyes narrowed as he fingered the thin gold chain. The medallion had
belonged to his father. His mother had given it to his father
on their wedding day. And his father had worn it every day
of his life.

Under his white dress shirt, Cody wore one exactly like it.
He'd received it on his fourteenth birthday, as his mother
had planned, but she'd never lived to give the gift to him.
Instead, his father had given it to him, explaining how much
the medallions had meant to his mother. They were a sym-
bol of their connecting lives and loves. Something his
mother wanted to share with the two most important men
in her life—something to link them together forever.

Except now his father was dead.

And the chain of the medallion his father had never taken
off, was broken, as if it had been ripped from his neck.

Cody knew his father would never have willingly taken the medallion off. So someone else had taken it off for him—ripped it off him, most likely, judging from the evidence.

Fisting the medallion in one hand, Cody let the cool metal bite into his palm, allowing his emotions to cool. He couldn't think with the heat of his temper; he had to let it cool, get ice-cold, then it would fuel him and help him do what he had to do, which was find out who wanted his father dead, but more important, why?

He had a few ideas of his own, but nothing concrete. This area of Texas had been suffering from severe drought conditions for the past two years; water was at a premium, and for ranchers, water wasn't a luxury but an absolute necessity. The Kincaid ranch was the only ranch that encompassed Silver Creek, a source of water for livestock and animals. Even though he hadn't lived on a ranch in seven years, he knew that to a cattle rancher, who had his entire livelihood and fortune tied up in livestock, water was a valuable commodity, and more than enough of a motive for murder.

Cody had thought about going to the sheriff with his suspicions, but he'd decided to wait, at least until after he'd had some time to think and do a little investigating on his own. Seven years was a long time to be gone, but some things never changed, like life in a small town. He knew he could pick up some information by just hanging around.

He hadn't planned on staying in Silver Creek after the funeral. There wasn't anything here for him anymore. Cody allowed his gaze to drift over the familiar land he'd once called home. But now that he was here, he realized how much he'd missed it—home. His home.

No, he wasn't heading back to Austin, not for a while anyway. He'd already phoned his boss and been granted a leave of absence. He was going to stick around and poke around until he found some answers that satisfied him. Otherwise, he would never be able to live with himself. And he knew his father would never be able to rest in peace. He owed it to his father and his memory to do this. And he didn't intend to rest until he found the person responsible for his father's death.

The only thing left to figure out was where he was going to live. The image of a spitfire little blonde floated through his mind, and he cursed under his breath. She was here, at the services. He'd noticed her the minute she arrived. Like him, she too had stood away from the crowd, and he wondered why.

Absently, he glanced at her now. There was just something about her that got under his skin. He'd been thinking about her a lot since their encounter this morning. He didn't want or need any distractions right now. He needed to concentrate on what had to be done. Still, his eyes skimmed over her slowly. He almost smiled. She cleaned up pretty good, he thought, taking in the cool, sleeveless black dress she had on. Probably silk, he realized, wondering which was softer, the silk or her skin? He had a feeling it might be interesting to find out. Interesting, but not likely. He was old enough and smart enough now to recognize danger when he saw it, and this woman had Danger stamped all over her. She was the kind of woman who burrowed under a man's skin and infiltrated his mind, tying him up in knots of want and need. Just the kind of woman he needed to stay away from—far, far away.

"Kincaid?"

The voice had him turning, the woman forgotten for a moment as he stuck out his hand with a smile.

"Judd. How've you been?"

The sheriff of Silver Creek, Judd Powers, stood before him. Almost the same size, they were eye level with each other. Judd had been a few years ahead of him in school, and although they knew of each other, they'd never actually been friends, but they did respect each other. Judd was a good sheriff. A damn good sheriff.

"Fine," Judd said with a smile. "How about you?"

Cody nodded. "Doing all right."

"How's Austin?"

Judd was one of the few people in town who knew he was a Texas Ranger. About two years back, Judd had called him for some background information on a case he was working on.

"Fine."

The sheriff shifted his weight, wiping his forehead with the back of his hand, then glanced up at the sun before bringing his gaze back to Cody's. "I'm sorry about your dad."

Cody's eyes darkened. "Thank you."

"He was a good man." Judd studied him for a moment. "You still planning on sticking around?"

"Yep." Cody nodded. Something caught his eye. The little blond spitfire was making her way toward him. He tried not to stare, finally dragging his gaze back to the sheriff's. "There's some things I've got to do." He had little doubt that Judd had anything to do with what had happened to his father, but still he'd learned over the years it was prudent to be cautious rather than careless.

"I understand." Judd fingered the buff-colored Stetson in his hands. "If you need any help, Cody, just let me know. Our preliminary investigation wielded no evidence of foul play." He paused for a moment. "But could be we missed something."

"Thanks." Cody managed a smile. He knew the man was sincere, but at the moment, he preferred to work alone. "I may stop by tomorrow morning to talk to you." Cody frowned suddenly. "Anything unusual been going on? Anything suspicious?"

Judd shook his dark head. "Nothing out of the ordinary, at least not that I know of. The drought's been bad, though. Ranchers are all nervous about losing their livestock. It's been a hard two years for them."

Cody nodded. "I know."

Aware there were others waiting to pay their respects, Judd stuck out his hand once more. "I'd appreciate it if you didn't stir up any trouble, Cody." Judd looked at him carefully as Cody took his hand with a smile. "Things have been mighty peaceful up until now, and I'd kinda like to keep it that way." Judd shook his hand. "Take care, Cody. If there's anything I can do, let me know."

Aware that Savannah was standing behind and a little away from Judd, waiting to see him, Cody let his gaze follow the sheriff's for a moment before bringing it back to hers.

"Ma'am."

Savannah hesitantly stepped forward when Cody extended his hand toward her. A little unnerved, she stared at his large hand for a moment, remembering the feel of his touch as if it had been burned into her. Admonishing herself for being silly, Savannah took his hand, surprised to find it callused and warm. Very warm. It burned all the way through her, making her realize she hadn't imagined her reaction to him this morning.

Lifting her gaze to his, she swallowed hard, praying she could control the nerves this man seemed to bring out in her. If she thought this morning was a fluke, she realized now she was sadly mistaken.

"Mr. Kincaid, I'm truly sorry about your daddy," she said quietly, unable to stop looking at him. Those eyes, she thought with a sigh, ought to be outlawed. She felt as if he were seeing right through her. "John was a good and kind man."

"Thank you, Ms.... ?" He realized he didn't even know her name.

"Duncan," she replied. "Savannah Duncan."

"Well, Savannah, I appreciate you coming, but please, after what happened between us this morning, I think you should call me Cody, don't you?" The lazy way he said it made it seem as if a lot more were between them this morning than a broken fence and a cantankerous bull. Infuriated, Savannah realized he'd done it deliberately. Just what she needed, the whole damn town talking about her!

Rocking back on his heels, Cody almost smiled when Savannah flushed beet red. The way her chin angled, he had a feeling she was itching to use that powerful right of hers. On him. Again. It amused him now as much as it had this morning.

"Yes... well..." Caught off guard, Savannah hesitated, loathe to discuss her personal business, but it couldn't be helped. She glanced back at Cody, then averted her gaze because she couldn't seem to speak or think coherently when she was looking at the man. In spite of her discomfort, she wanted to get this done and over with so she could escape his penetrating gaze.

"I... I'm truly regretful about this morning," she began, taking a deep breath.

He noticed her accent seemed to be a bit thicker.

"And I wanted to let you know how much I appreciate you taking care of Miss Sophie and that fence." She forced a smile she didn't feel, certain her lips were going to melt and slide right off her face. He was still holding her hand, and it was making her insides quake like a sapling in a storm. Gathering her courage, she pressed on. "I know this might not be the proper time or place, but I was wondering... what, uh, you intended to do about the old foreman's house, the one I've been renting." With her gaze locked on his, she held her breath, feeling her heart beating like a drum.

"Well, Savannah," Cody began slowly. He found himself mesmerized by the vulnerability and wariness he found in her eyes. "I have to admit it's a bit of a problem, seeing's how the big ranch house is gone and I don't have anywhere to stay."

His words caused her heart almost to still. He smiled suddenly, that heart-stopping smile that made her knees feel weak.

"How about if I stop by tonight so we can discuss the matter further?" Tilting his head, he looked at her carefully. Living right on the ranch, she might know something about what had happened to his father. Even though her house was miles from the sight of his father's, it was worth a shot. She might know something and not even be aware of it. "That is, if it's all right with you?"

Stunned, and a little taken aback, Savannah merely stared at him for a moment, her mind whirling like a dervish. Trying to bank down the sudden fear that had crawled along her nerve endings at his words, she nodded dully.

"Of course," she said, deliberately withdrawing her hand from his. Obviously he was going to drag this out. It annoyed her to no end. She didn't like hanging in limbo. "I'll see you this evening, then."

With that, Savannah gathered her shaken dignity and walked away, leaving Cody staring after her.

Tonight, she thought to herself. She'd have to wait until tonight to find out their fate. Pausing to kick off her high-heel shoes, Savannah scooped them up, cursing heels and heat all in one breath. She decided to walk in her stockinged feet back to the house.

What on earth was she going to tell Joey? she wondered, stepping over a small, prickly cactus?

Joey tended to worry much too much for a child his age, but then again, she thought with a sigh, wiping her forehead with the back of her free hand, he'd come by his worrying naturally. She was the worrying champion. She supposed it came from being totally responsible for everything, knowing she had no one or nowhere to turn, and she was always playing without a safety net.

Until this moment, she'd never realized how precarious the missing safety net was. Now, she realized, their whole lives might be tossed and turned upside down. Again.

Lifting her chin, Savannah shifted her shoes to her other arm and trudged toward home. No matter what happened, she and Joey had each other, and that was all they needed, she assured herself. She'd handle this just as she'd handled everything else. And then they'd go on.

If they were forced to move, so be it. Surely there would be something else available in Silver Creek. She frowned slightly, opening the gate to her yard and glancing around. A veil of sadness seemed to fall over her, and she sighed heavily, closing the gate behind her. But this was and always would be home.

Still gazing at her little ranch house, Savannah released a long, weary sigh. She certainly didn't want to uproot Joey, take him out of school and away from his friends, but she'd do whatever she had to, whatever was necessary to make sure her son's life was safe and secure.

But until she knew for certain what the future—and Cody Kincaid—had planned for them, she'd keep this new worry to herself. Joey had enough things that he worried about, and she didn't want to add to the list. Resolutely Savannah trudged into the house with a mournful sigh. She had a feeling that until tonight, and her next run-in with Cody Kincaid, she'd be doing enough worrying for both of them.

Chapter Three

The Silver Creek Bar and Grill didn't have a bar, and they didn't know much about grilling. They specialized in home-cooked meals, the kind your mother used to make, and they served coffee—hot and strong—as well as an occasional cup of tepid Earl Grey tea for the finicky Miss Tulip. At ninety, she was the oldest living resident of Silver Creek, and thus accorded special privileges.

Tucked on the ground floor of the Silver Creek Hotel—the only hotel within a thirty mile radius—the B and G, as it was known to the locals, was a gathering place for gossip. All the latest news that was fit to talk about was generally heard floating from booth to booth.

On the afternoon of John Kincaid's burial, the B and G was jumping. Rumors were flying, not only about the mysterious death of John Kincaid, but also about the mysterious reappearance of his renegade son, Cody.

Even though he'd checked into the Silver Creek Hotel, no one had actually expected Cody to show his face in the B and G. Not after the way he'd taken off seven years ago.

Jilted by his fiancée and locking horns with his daddy, Cody had up and taken off, leaving his daddy high and dry to run the Kincaid spread all alone. As he was the only Kincaid heir, his actions were unthinkable, never mind unforgivable.

Running a ranch the size of the Kincaid spread was a heavy responsibility; fully expecting his son to run the ranch one day, John had been grooming his son to take over ever since he was knee-high. But Cody had always been a wild one, and when he'd up and run off, the rumor mill had worked overtime speculating about his behavior and his whereabouts.

So when Cody sauntered into the B and G only hours after burying his daddy, a hushed, wary silence fell over the room.

But Cody always prided himself on never doing things people expected of him. He figured that's what made life so interesting.

After exchanging rather loud pleasantries with a now-rather-deaf Miss Tulip, he accepted her apology for not attending his daddy's burial, and then accepted her sympathies as well, before taking a booth in the back of the room.

Aware that every eye was upon him, Cody looked each man and woman in the eye until they grew uncomfortable and turned away, leaving him to his peace.

He ordered coffee and a cheeseburger and fries, grateful to have a few moments to himself.

The waitress bustled over, chomping on her gum, refilling his coffee and sliding his food in front of him. The aroma made his stomach growl, reminding him just how hungry he was and how long it had been since he'd had a decent meal—not that you could call a greasy hamburger from the B and G decent. But he was grateful for it anyhow.

Digging in, Cody let his thoughts wander, allowing his ears to pick up the sounds surrounding him. He figured it would take about a week of being home before people got used to seeing him and he'd stop being a novelty. Then folks would relax and just act natural around him. He was still one of their own, and one thing about the people of Silver Creek, they looked after their own. That's what he was counting on. Then he'd be able to start checking things out.

Cody's head suddenly came up, and the hair on the back of his neck stood on end. He'd been on surveillance long enough to know when he was the object of someone's intense scrutiny. Not wanting to alert whoever it was, Cody casually continued eating, but his eyes did a slow, roving inventory, pausing on a boy who was standing just at the corner of his booth, staring at him wide-eyed as if he were checking out a circus sideshow.

Cody kept chewing, watching him, banking down a smile. Setting down his burger, Cody took a sip of his coffee, then wiped his hands on his napkin. Slowly he raised his eyes to the boy again. The kid was shifting his weight from foot to foot as if itching to run somewhere—anywhere.

Cody guessed him to be about ten or eleven, but like a puppy that hadn't quite grown into his paws, the kid seemed a bit unsure and self-conscious. Sandy haired, with a dollop of freckles across his nose, he had blue eyes that at the moment were filled with awe and a bit of fear. His large hands were clenched at his sides, and his eyes were darting this way and that, trying to avoid Cody's but not quite succeeding.

"Something I can do for you, son?" Cody asked quietly.

Joey took a hesitant step closer, not certain what to say. He wished Louie were here; he'd know what to say. Joey glanced around again, realizing everyone was staring at him. It made him even more nervous, and he wiped his damp hands on his jeans, swinging his gaze back to the big man sitting in the booth, staring at him. He'd had no trouble recognizing Cody Kincaid. He was the only stranger in the B and G.

"Louie says..." Joey swallowed. Hard. He wasn't going to worry, he'd promised himself. And he was doing this to protect his mother and their home. He had to remember that. "Louie says you're a renegade and you're gonna want your house back and then we'll have to move." The words tumbled out in a rush, one on top of the other.

Cody banked down a smile, then popped a french fry in his mouth.

"Who's Louie?" he finally asked, surprising Joey.

Relaxing a bit, he grinned and his fists opened.

"My best friend." Joey took a hesitant step closer. Remembering he'd forgotten his lunch this morning, he stared longingly at Cody's french fries. His stomach rumbled. "Louie's my bestest friend in the whole wide world."

Cody gave another nod. He understood and remembered how important best friends were at that age. "So, how come Louie knows so much about me?" Cocking his head, he popped another fry into his mouth.

Caught off guard, Joey scrubbed at his nose. "Uh, well... Uh, his pa's the sheriff...and..." Afraid to say more, Joey let his voice trail off.

"Got it," Cody said with another nod. So Louie was Judd's son. Cody filed the information in the back of his mind. Sipping his coffee, he leaned back in the booth, resting his arms across the back. "Guess we should have a talk, then." Cody waited for the hesitant nod. The kid looked at the booth, then at him. "Have a seat," Cody offered. Obviously the kid had something on his mind.

Joey scrambled into the booth, setting a flurry of tongues wagging around them. Cody ignored them. The ever-interested waitress bustled over, chomping on her gum.

"Can I get you something, honey?" she asked, blowing a big bubble and smiling at Joey, who stared at her unashamedly. He'd never actually been in the B and G before. His ma always made him come right home after school every day. The B and G wasn't anything like he'd thought it would be, and he couldn't help staring at the waitress in her too-tight uniform with her bright red, glow-in-the-dark hair and her painted eyes and mouth, to say nothing of the wad of pink gum that kept popping out of her mouth. Awed, Joey stared, amusing Cody.

"Bring him a cheeseburger and fries." Cody glanced at Joey. "A soda?" Joey nodded, touching his pocket to see if he still had the five-dollar bill his mother always made him carry for emergencies. He figured a burger and fries with Cody Kincaid probably counted as an emergency. He sure hoped so.

"Coming right up." The waitress snatched the menus off the table, then sauntered away, popping her gum.

Wide-eyed, Joey watched her. "I never saw hair that color," Joey said with the pure honesty of a ten-year-old, "and I thought only kids chewed gum." Still staring, Joey dragged his gaze back to Cody's, amazed to find him chuckling.

"Can't say that I've ever seen hair that color before, either."

Joey frowned, wrinkling his nose. "My ma won't let me chew gum, says it's bad for my teeth." He sighed enviously. "Louie chews gum all the time."

"He does, does he?" Cody pushed his plate away. "So, now I know what Louie does and says, but I don't know anything about you." Folding his arms on the table, Cody waited.

Joey shifted his weight. The plastic booth was hot and sticky, and he wished his legs would stop twitching. "I'm . . . I'm . . . Joey Duncan."

It took a moment for the name to register. This was Savannah Duncan's son. Looking at him, Cody could see the resemblance. Wiping his hand on his napkin again, Cody extended it. "Joey. It's nice to meet you."

Joey stared at Cody's hand for a moment before taking it and shaking it. He hoped Cody didn't notice his palm was sweaty 'cause then he'd know he was nervous. Real nervous. He wished he would have swiped his hands down his jeans first.

Remembering his manners, Joey lowered his gaze. "I'm sorry about your pa, Mr. Kincaid.

"Cody," he corrected automatically. "And thank you." His eyes narrowed a bit as he studied the boy. "You knew my father?"

Lifting his head, Joey nodded, then offered a gap-toothed smile. "Yep. He was real nice to me and my ma."

"My father was a very nice man." Cody waited a moment.

"He was *real* nice," Joey confirmed. "I ain't got a pa, but..." Joey's voice trailed off, making Cody study him curiously. So he'd been right about Savannah; she was a woman alone.

Averting Cody's gaze, Joey shifted uncomfortably in the booth. He didn't want to admit to Cody that sometimes he'd pretend that Mr. Kincaid was his pa, just 'cause he was so nice to him, the way a real pa would be. He didn't mind not having a pa like the other kids, 'cause he had his ma and all. But sometimes he wished his pa were still alive so they could do stuff together—guy stuff—stuff his mother tried but just couldn't do.

"How long's your pa been gone, Joey?" Cody asked gently, watching the boy. A cloud seemed to descend over his face, and his fingers moved quickly, tearing bits of a paper napkin apart.

"He died before I was born," Joey finally muttered, not looking up, still shredding the napkin. He didn't like talking about this. It made him feel all funny inside. All he knew was what his ma had told him, which wasn't much. Whenever he asked questions about his pa, his mother got real sad, and sometimes she even looked as if she was going to cry. And he hated when his mother cried. It scared him.

"I'm sorry, Joey." Cody sighed. "Not having a pa is hard on a boy." He knew from experience, knew how much he'd missed his own father the past seven years. Cody glanced at Joey again. The boy was obviously shy and very self-conscious, and he wondered how much not having the benefit of a male's influence had been responsible for his lack of confidence. It touched something inside of Cody because he remembered how difficult growing up could be especially when you didn't have a man's hand in your life and you were consumed by feelings of fear and inadequacy.

He suddenly remembered how much his own father had been there for him—always—so that he'd never had to go through those awful, awkward periods. At least not alone. He couldn't prevent the rush of remorse that rolled over him. Pushing the feelings away, Cody sipped his coffee, watching Joey. Obviously the kid had something on his mind. Cody figured he'd get to it in his own good time.

The waitress slid Joey's meal on the table, then refilled Cody's coffee again. Aware that most of the assembled diners were still staring at them, Cody banked down a smile. If Miss Tulip didn't quit straining her neck to see what was going on, she was going to end up in a neck brace.

Eyeing his burger, Joey took a long, greedy sip of the soda, relishing the coolness, almost draining it in one gulp. His throat was so dry and the day was so hot, the ice-cold liquid felt good going down.

"Bring him another soda," Cody told the waitress with a smile, watching Joey dig into his food. The kid was eating as if he hadn't had a meal since birth. Cody grinned.

"Forget your lunch?" he asked, surprising Joey, who nodded with his mouth full.

"Yep." Popping a fry into his mouth, Joey rolled his eyes. "My ma's always saying I'd forget my head if it wasn't attached."

Cody laughed again. "My mother used to tell me the same thing."

Awed, Joey's head came up, and his eyes widened in surprise. "She did?" He didn't think a renegade would have a mother.

"Yep." Cody's grin slid wider. "And she always used to tell me to do my chores and my homework. Mind my manners and my mouth. Always wear clean underwear, and always carry a little extra money for emergencies." Leaning back, Cody dug deep in his pants pocket and extracted his wallet. Opening it, he pulled loose a bill folded into a small piece. Laughing, Cody tossed it onto the table. "See that twenty? That's my emergency money." Even after all these years, he still carried it around with him. He hadn't thought about it in years.

"Jeez, you're kidding." Astonished that someone so big and cool would listen to his mother, Joey hurriedly wiped his hands, then dug in his own pants pocket, extracting the five-dollar bill *his* mother had folded up and pinned into one of her handkerchiefs so he wouldn't lose it. He tossed his bounty on the table next to Cody's.

Joey nodded toward his bounty. "Mine makes me carry that everywhere." He rolled his eyes again. "For emergencies." He always wondered what kind of emergency could cost a whole five dollars, but sitting here having a cheeseburger and fries with Cody, now he knew. His brows crunched together. "How do you figure mothers know so much?" Joey took another bite of his sandwich. "I mean, my ma always knows *everything*." Still chomping on his sandwich, he frowned. "Says she's got eyes in the back of her head, and ears that hear miles away."

Cody smothered a laugh.

"Do you think they really do?"

The kid's eyes were so wide, so sincere, Cody figured he'd better handle this one judiciously, lest he have one pint size blonde coming after him. Absently he rubbed his jaw.

"Well, Joey, I don't know about that, but I do know my mother always knew everything I did, too." He shook his head, remembering. "She knew I was in trouble usually fifteen minutes before it happened."

"I know," Joey exclaimed in disgust, shoving the last of his hamburger into his mouth. "Mine's the same way." He shivered. "It's spooky."

Cody couldn't contain the chuckle that escaped him. "Guess mothers are pretty much all the same, don't you think?"

Grinning, Joey nodded, realizing he liked this man, renegade or not. And if he had a mother, he couldn't be all bad. Certainly not as bad as vampires.

"Can I ask you something, Joey?"

"Sure." Shoveling fries in his mouth, Joey reached for his glass of soda. Leaning forward, Cody grinned, glad to see the kid was finally relaxing.

"Why on earth did you name a bull Miss Sophie?" He was dying of curiosity.

Joey's hand froze in midair, and he looked up at Cody as if he'd just sprouted fins. "H-how...?" He swallowed. Hard. "H-how did you know about Miss Sophie?" His startled gaze was fastened to Cody's. Maybe a renegade meant you knew things and saw things. Joey's eyes widened. Oh, boy, wait until he told Louie! This was even better than vampires!

Laughing, Cody dragged a hand through his dark hair. "I, uh, sort of had a run-in with your mother *and* Miss Sophie this morning."

Joey tensed, his fingers tightening on his glass until his knuckles were white. "Did you scare her?" he asked hesitantly. The fear in his eyes was quick and genuine.

Cody frowned, not certain he understood. "Miss Sophie?"

"No, my ma." The boy's intense gaze searched his.

Cody could almost feel the tension and the fear coursing through the boy. He sought to quickly reassure him. "I didn't scare her, son," Cody said quietly, his voice gentle and low. He grinned suddenly. "But I can't say the same about her."

Joey's relieved smile was quick, and he gulped his soda before popping a few more fries in his mouth. "Yep, sounds like my ma," he said around a mouthful of food, nodding. He glanced at Cody. "She's not real partial to strangers."

Cody laughed, remembering Savannah's reaction to him. "I figured that." Wanting to know more about Savannah, but deciding now wasn't the time to press, Cody steered the conversation back around. "So, what about Miss Sophie?"

"Oh, that." Finished, Joey pushed his plate away. "My ma read me this story once when I was a little kid, and there was a dog named Miss Sophie in it." Shrugging his shoulders, he glanced around, wondering why everyone was still looking at them. "Since I don't got a dog, I figured I'd name ma's new bull Miss Sophie."

Looking a bit skeptical, Cody nodded. "I see." He didn't see anything of the kind, but figured it wasn't the time or his place to give the kid an anatomy lesson.

"What'd she do?"

"Who?"

"Miss Sophie." Joey drained his soda.

Cody smiled. "Broke through the fence."

"Again?" Joey rolled his eyes. "She's always doing that."

"He."

"What?"

Cody spoke slowly. "Miss Sophie isn't a she, Joey, it's a *he*."

Joey grinned. "I know that." He scrubbed at his nose. "Ma told me all about the bulls and the calves, and how Miss Sophie will be worth lots of money to us someday." He shrugged again. "I don't much care about the money." He grinned. "I just like Miss Sophie, even if she does have a mind of her own."

The waitress refilled Cody's coffee, scooped up Joey's plate and laid down the check. Cody reached for it and slid it under his cup.

"So, tell me, Joey, what's this about my house?"

"Oh, that." The boy suddenly looked crestfallen. "Louie says that now that your big house burned down, you won't have nowhere to live so we'll have to move out of our house so you could have it back and I don't want to move out of my house." The words tumbled in a rush, and Cody frowned, trying to follow the train of this convoluted conversation.

Eyes bright with expectation, Joey leaned forward in excitement. "But Louie and I, we got a plan, a real good plan."

One dark brow lifted in amusement. "You do, do you?"
Cody sat forward. "Well, let's hear it, then."

"Since I don't got a pa, I'm the man of the house and I
get to make the deals." Joey stopped to take a deep breath.
Whenever he talked real fast, he lost his breath. "Anyway,
we figured you'd need somewhere to stay, and me and ma,
well, we don't take up too much room, so Louie and I figured if you come and live with my ma and me, we could
keep our house and you'd have somewhere to stay." Gathering steam, Joey grinned. "It's perfect. Absolutely perfect. And maybe you could even help out with the chores,
'specially with Miss Sophie 'cause she's got a mind of her
own." Seeing the concern on Cody's face, Joey rushed on.
"You won't have to do *all* of the chores," he assured him.
"Just some. And I would even let you share my bedroom."
Satisfied, Joey grinned. "So what do you think? Is it a
deal?"

There was a long, pregnant pause while Cody tried to find
his tongue.

"Does your mother know about this...plan, Joey?"
Struggling not to laugh, Cody realized he already knew the
answer. If his mother knew her son had just invited him to
move in with them, she'd probably hog-tie and gag him.

Joey shook his head furiously. "Nope." He grinned
again. "I wanted it to be a surprise."

"A surprise," Cody repeated thoughtfully. Well, there
was no denying it certainly was going to be that. Cody was
quiet, wondering how to handle this. Carefully. Very carefully. Even at this age, a boy had pride. "I think, Joey, that
before we agree to anything we'd have to discuss it with your
mother." He rushed on at the look on the boy's face. "Just
because it's her house, too, and I don't think it would be fair
to invite someone to come and live with you without at least
asking her."

"But why?" Joey asked with a frown. "It's *your* house,
why wouldn't she want you to live there, 'specially if it
means we get to live there, too, and we won't have to
move?" He grinned. "We'll just...share."

He was in over his head, Cody realized. Way over his head. His mind went on search, trying to think of a logical reason to give the boy without hurting his feelings or his pride. Obviously the kid was too young to understand the complexities of male-female relationships. Hell, he wasn't even sure *he* understood them. But one thing he did know; living under the same roof with Savannah Duncan was about as remote as a July snowstorm in Texas.

"You know, Joey, this might not be too practical. You yourself said your mom wasn't real partial to strangers."

"But you're not a stranger," Joey protested, unnerving Cody with his logic. "You said you met my ma this morning."

"Yes, I did." Why did he have to open his big mouth? "But that doesn't mean that your mother is going to want to share her house with me." Or anything else, except perhaps some arsenic.

"But if it means we get to stay in our house, I'll bet she would." Dejected, Joey lowered his chin onto his hand, wondering if Louie had another plan. This one didn't seem to be working so good. "I don't want to move," he said quietly.

"Son." Cody reached out and touched Joey's hand, wanting only to reassure him and wipe the fear from his eyes. He'd find somewhere else to stay. The house wasn't that important to him, especially now, knowing how much it meant to Joey. "You're not going to have to move. I promise."

Joey's head snapped up, and he grinned. "Then you'll do it?" He didn't give Cody a chance to answer. Joey bounded from the booth, dancing from foot to foot in excitement. "I did it! I did it!" Clasping his hands tightly together, he spun around, pride shining in his eyes. "Wait till I tell Louie!"

"Joseph Aaron Duncan, you have some explaining to do," Savannah called the moment she heard the back door open. Down on her knees to wash the kitchen floor, she blew a tumbled wad of hair out of her face and continued scold-

ing and scrubbing. "You know the rules. Home right after
school. What was this nonsense today about you calling to
say you had business in town? What kind of business?
Monkey business, no doubt. You and Louie better not have
been getting into mischief. You know how..." Her voice
trailed off when she spotted a pair of well-worn, familiar
sneakers resting next to a pair of elegant, expensive, hand-
tooled black leather boots. Unless Joey had grown twenty
inches and two additional feet, he wasn't alone.

She looked up and groaned. It was *him*. Oh, Lord, Cody
Kincaid was standing bold as brass in the middle of her little kitchen. Well, he wasn't exactly *standing*. It was more
like he sort of filled her kitchen with his huge, intimidating
presence.

What was he doing with her son?

A flash of nerves had Savannah jumping to her feet, her
gaze going from Cody to Joey.

"What's wrong?" Her eyes moved back and forth again.
Neither said anything, making her even more nervous.
Without thought, she stepped forward and took her son
gently by the shoulders.

"Are you hurt?" Her worried eyes searched him from
head to toe in a matter of seconds in the manner only an
anxious mother could do. There was no blood evident anywhere, and she relaxed fractionally.

"I'm fine, Ma," Joey said, embarrassed she was fussing
over him in front of Cody. He didn't want him to think he
was a baby. Joey tried to shrug free of his mother. "I'm not
hurt and I'm not in trouble."

He glanced up at Cody, and Savannah didn't miss the
look of adoration in his eyes. She wanted to groan again.

"We don't gotta move," Joey announced with a big, gap-
toothed grin, turning to her, pleased and proud of his accomplishment.

"W-what?" Her gaze went back to Cody, who merely
shrugged before searching out her son's eyes. "What do you
mean we don't have to move?" Savannah took another step
forward, not caring that she was barefoot, had on her rat-

tiest pair of short shorts and one of her son's T-shirts. "Joey, what on earth are you talking about?" Where would Joey have gotten the idea that they might have to move?

Savannah blew another tumble of hair off her face. She'd pinned and piled it atop her head to do her cleaning, but now it was escaping like prisoners on a three-day furlough.

With a frown, she shook her head in confusion. "Joey, honey, would you please tell me what's going on?"

"Me and Cody, we made a deal." Joey's grin slid wider. "It was Louie's idea, Ma, and it worked."

"Oh, Lord," Savannah muttered, rolling her eyes and wondering just what kind of mischief Louie had conned her son into this time. Trepidation raced through her as she looked at Cody, who appeared far too amused for her peace of mind. "Exactly what kind of a deal, Joey, honey?" She was speaking to her son but looking at Cody. From the expression on his face, she had a feeling the other shoe was about to drop.

And explode.

Dancing from foot to foot, Joey tried to contain his excitement. "Cody is gonna come live with us. Isn't that great, Ma? Then we don't gotta move. He'll have somewhere to stay, and we won't have to move, and we'll even get help with the chores and Miss Sophie. Isn't that super?"

Savannah merely stared at her son in dumbfounded silence, certain her ears were deceiving her.

"W-what did you say?" Her gaze went back to Cody, who had crossed his arms across his broad chest and was smiling a bit too smugly for her comfort.

"Cody is gonna come live with us," Joey repeated, wondering why his ma was acting so weird. He leaned forward. "Are you all right, Ma?" he asked worriedly, his eyes going over her. She was white as a ghost. He thought she'd be thrilled that he'd handled this problem all on his own. But she didn't look too thrilled, he realized.

Wanting nothing more than to reassure her son, Savannah banked the sudden fear his words brought on to the back of her mind and forced a smile she didn't feel. No sense letting either her son or this . . . stranger know exactly what she was feeling. Or more important, why.

"I'm fine, honey, just fine." She brushed Joey's hair off his forehead with trembling fingers. "But I think Cody and I need to have a little chat."

She smiled, but there was a chill in her eyes that Cody didn't miss.

"Why don't you get changed and go feed the chickens?" she suggested.

Joey glanced at Cody, then at his mother. She had that look on her face, the "mother's look," he called it, the one that said he'd better do what he was told. Or else.

"Could I talk to Cody for a minute first, Ma?" Joey's eyes pleaded with her, and although she wasn't certain exactly what was going on, she nodded.

Joey tugged on Cody's arm, dragging him out of the kitchen and into the hallway and out of range of his mother's hearing.

"If she asks," Joey started in a conspiratorial whisper, "tell her you're not hungry."

Cody frowned, wondering what the kid was talking about now. "What?"

Rolling his eyes, Joey sighed heavily. "She's been baking again. Did you see the plate of brownies on the stove?" Cody nodded. "She can't bake," Joey said with a sad shake of his head. "She tries real hard, but everything she bakes tastes like cowcakes."

Cody wondered how the kid knew what cowcakes tasted like, but not enough to ask.

"I just pretend to eat the stuff she bakes, then I feed it to the chickens or Miss Sophie later when she's not looking." Suddenly sheepish, Joey shrugged. "I don't wanna hurt her feelings. So if she asks, you're not hungry."

"Got it." Cody nodded, pleasing Joey. "No brownies. I'm not hungry." Cody ruffled the boy's hair. "Go feed the chickens, I'll go talk to your mother."

"And remember," Joey called in a soft whisper as he headed upstairs to change, "we've got a deal."

Nodding, Cody turned and headed back into the kitchen, fully expecting to be met by a loaded shotgun. Instead, he was met by a frowning, pacing Savannah who barely offered him a glance.

He stood there a moment, watching her. Most women caught in their old clothes scrubbing floors would be primping and fussing right now, knowing a man was in the house, but not her. Seemingly unaware of how she was dressed, Savannah was just chewing on her lower lip, scowling. Not that he minded the way she was dressed. The shorts she had on revealed a long, creamy expanse of mouth-watering legs. The T-shirt she wore was a bit small for her, and lovingly caressed the curves of her breasts. Watching her, Cody felt his blood thicken.

"Just what the blazes is going on?" Hands on hips, Savannah suddenly whirled on him. Maybe Joey didn't have a clue how inappropriate what he'd done was, but that was certainly no excuse for Cody. How on earth could he even have entertained or encouraged such a ridiculous, preposterous idea?

She didn't even know the man, and the chance of her letting him live in her house with her and her son was about as remote as her learning to jump rope in high heels, backward. The thought of having him living in her house, under her roof, was enough to cause her to break out in hives. She was trying to get rid of him, and stay away from him, *not live with him.*

"What on earth do you think you're doing?" Still pacing, she glared at Cody, wondering why he was just... watching her.

Cody smiled a slow, lazy smile that set her heart thundering in her breast. He didn't think she'd be pleased if she knew exactly what it was he'd been doing: thinking about how she'd be in bed. Some women would lie passive and docile beneath a man, but remembering the way she'd fought him this morning, he had a feeling this feisty, independent woman would be anything but docile and passive. The thought made him ache. Still watching her, he had a feeling it might be wise to keep his thoughts to himself, but she was obviously waiting for some kind of answer.

He held up his hands in supplication. "None of this was my idea." That slow, lazy smile was back. "Blame Louie."

"Louie again," Savannah muttered, dragging a hand through her hair and sinking down into the closest chair.

Her hands were shaking, he noticed, and he wondered why.

Savannah shook her head. "I'd like to strangle that boy sometimes."

"I'd just like to meet him," Cody quipped with a laugh, leaning back against the refrigerator.

Pushing a wad of hair off her face, she glanced at him. "Do you want to tell me exactly what's going on?"

Moving closer, he pulled up a chair, turned it around, then straddled it, leaning his arms over the backrest. He glanced around; he hadn't really noticed the room before or what she'd done to it. He remembered the foreman's house as being cold and austere. Now it was decorated in varying shades of blue and white, and definitely had a homey, woman's touch. He realized he liked it.

"I was in the B and G minding my own business when Joey came to see me."

"He was in the B and G?" Savannah asked with a frown. Joey knew better. He wasn't allowed in town by himself.

"He started out by saying something about Louie and the house, but he was talking so fast I didn't really understand him."

Savannah couldn't help but smile. "He does that when he's nervous."

"So do you," Cody commented, remembering their verbal battle this morning.

She flushed but ignored his personal comment. The man seemed to make a lot of personal comments about her, she noticed.

"So what did Joey want?"

"Evidently the kid got it in his head—from Louie—that now that my father's house burned down, I was going to want you to move so I could live here." Shrugging, Cody glanced around. He wasn't one for making long-range plans, but tended to take things as they came. He was certain he'd have no trouble staying on at the hotel for as long as necessary. There was a lot of work to be done in clearing up his father's estate, not to mention taking care of all the livestock and the rest of the ranching assets. He had his work cut out for him, but even more important, he had a job to do: find his father's murderer. And he didn't plan on leaving Silver Creek until the job was done.

Cody brought his gaze back to Savannah's. "Joey said he had an idea. He invited me to move in here with you, so that you wouldn't have to move and I'd have a place to stay." Cody shrugged, trying not to grin at her harassed and horrified expression. "He thought it was a perfect solution."

"Oh, Lord," Savannah muttered, dropping her chin to her chest with a weary sigh. Her head came up suddenly. "You didn't agree to this, did you?" Aghast, she watched the slow, lazy smile spread across his features.

"Not exactly," he said carefully.

Her eyes cooled. "What do you mean...*not exactly?* Surely you can't possibly think I'd even consider the idea?"

"No," he said honestly. "In fact, I asked him if you knew about this... plan, and he said no, he wanted it to be a surprise."

"Wonderful," she said drolly, making him smile. "No wonder I don't like surprises."

"He obviously had his heart set on this being a solution to what he thought was a very real problem." Cody shifted his weight. "He's been worried about you having to move and wanted to handle the situation on his own...as the man of the house, he told me." Cody smiled that heart-stopping smile again. "I didn't have the heart to crush his idea or his surprise."

Touched by his concern for her son, not to mention the delicate way he'd apparently handled the situation, Savannah found some of her anger and discomfort dissipate. "Joey's a champion worrier," she explained with a smile.

"I didn't realize he even knew about my concerns about us having to move." She dared a glance at Cody; it was the first time she'd openly broached the subject of moving with him. Holding her breath, she waited for his answer.

"I never had any intention of asking you to move," Cody said quietly, seeing the fear shimmering in her eyes and wanting nothing more than to dispel it. "I went to my father's safety-deposit box this morning and found a letter he'd written to me with instructions in case anything happened to him. He wanted you to stay as long as you like, and I have no intention of going against my father's last wishes. You're welcome here as long as you want to stay."

Laying a hand over her heart, Savannah let out a relieved sigh. She felt as if the weight of the world had just slid off her shoulders. "Thank you," she whispered, feeling more gratitude than she believed possible. She could never explain and he would never understand how much this little house and the security it provided meant.

Smoothing her hands over her shorts, Savannah stood up, anxious to make amends now that he was being so kind. "Would you like some coffee?"

At his nod, she moved across the room to begin filling the pot before plugging it in. "I just baked some brownies, would you like one?" Moving to the stove, she set the plate of brownies on the table. Cody looked at the misshapen lumps, then reared back a bit. Apparently the kid was telling the truth. He eyed the brownies suspiciously, wondering why they had a sickly gray color to them.

"No, uh, thank you. I'm, uh, not much for sweets." He said a silent prayer of thanks to Joey as he inched the brownies farther away from him. He owed him one.

Watching her bustle around the kitchen made him realize she was nervous. He wondered how long it had been since she'd had a man in her kitchen. In her life? In her bed?

When she set two mugs on the table, he reached out and captured her wrist. She jumped as if she'd been scalded, her gaze flying to his. Fear, clear, bright and unmistakable, shone from her eyes, and he could feel her sudden trembling.

Cody met her gaze, and he saw that aching vulnerability again. It touched something deep inside of him in a place where nothing or no one had touched in a long, long time, a place he thought closed off to everyone.

"I'm sorry, I didn't mean to startle you." Still, he didn't release her, but held her gently. Most women revealed their true selves through their eyes; eyes never lied. He suddenly found himself very, very intrigued by her—because he didn't particularly like what her eyes were saying to him. Unless he'd lost his touch, she was obviously very wary of him and just a bit scared. Again he wondered why. She'd worn that look this morning, too, he remembered.

Gently, slowly his thumb stroked her wrist in a sweet, caressing manner. She was close enough for him to smell her intoxicating scent. He wondered if she smelled like that all over.

His fingers continued to stroke her. Her skin was unbearably pale and soft, like the finest silk. He wanted to taste that scent-sweetened skin, to caress it, to bury himself in it.

Trying to drag in a breath, Savannah attempted to pull her wrist free, but found she couldn't. His touch *had* startled her—scared her, really, yet not because of his touch alone, but because of her reaction to it. The moment he'd touched her again, she'd felt a riot of feelings. Her heart was thudding wildly in her breast, and the heat of him, the masculine warmth of him, seemed to slide from him into her.

Unable to drag her gaze from his, Savannah licked her suddenly dry lips.

Cody's gaze followed the movement of her tongue, and he felt his body ache and tighten. He wanted to taste her. She was so close, all he had to do was give her wrist a gentle tug and she'd be sprawled in his lap, wrapped in the protective warmth of his arms.

But he couldn't—wouldn't—do it. Not with that look in her eyes, on her face. As much as he wanted to touch her, he wanted more not to frighten her. Slowly he released her wrist. "I think the coffee's done."

Letting out a breath she hadn't known she was holding, Savannah nodded, grateful for something—anything—to do. Her breath was still a bit shaky as she crossed the room and picked up the coffeepot. She didn't know if she liked being cooped up in a room with him simply because any room seemed smaller with him in it.

She glanced at Cody. She was going to have to try harder to keep him at a distance; she couldn't afford to let him get close to her. He made her feel things, long for things, things she knew better than to want. She'd learned a long time ago not to wish for things she couldn't have.

Her hands were still trembling slightly as she poured them both some coffee.

"Savannah, how well did you know my father?"

Savannah paused, the coffeepot suspended in midair for a moment. "Not very well," she admitted with a sigh, filling his cup. "He was my friend," she said carefully. "I saw him every week at church, and then he came around about every two weeks to check on us, or to give Joey and me a hand with something, but I didn't know him socially or anything, if that's what you mean."

Sipping his coffee, Cody was thoughtful. He needed some information, but he didn't want to alarm her. "Have you noticed anything . . . unusual going on lately?"

"Unusual?" Savannah frowned as she sat. "No, nothing unusual that I know about." Cocking her head, she looked at him carefully. "Why? What's going on, Cody?"

"I don't know," he answered honestly.

"Is it because of the fire?" She didn't believe John Kincaid had been careless, but she hated to think of the alternative. "Do you think someone deliberately set it?" The thought was far too frightening to consider.

"I'm not sure," he hedged, not wanting to frighten her. He sipped his coffee thoughtfully. She might not know how to bake, but she made one good cup of coffee. "I heard a rumor that someone tried to buy my dad out. Know anything about it?'' He'd picked up that little tidbit at the B and G this morning.

"Hooper. Paul Hooper." Savannah made a face. "I don't like that man. Or his son, James," she added with a scowl. The thought of James Hooper gave her the creeps. There was something very, very odd about that man, something she couldn't quite put her finger on.

Cody's brows rose. Hooper was the neighbor nearest to the Kincaid ranch. He'd never liked the man, either, but had no reason for his feelings except that he thought the man a little sly and underhanded. As for his son, James, they'd had a run-in years ago when they were both still in high school. James had been odd even then, Cody remembered. There was just something about James Hooper, something he couldn't put his finger on, that stuck in his craw. It had all these years.

Cody sipped his coffee thoughtfully. "Why don't you like them? And how do you know Hooper tried to buy my dad out?" He watched her carefully.

Savannah absently rubbed her hands up and down her arms, then took a deep breath, vividly aware of how close Cody was and how intent his eyes were on her. It was making her skin itch as if it were too tight. Taking a deep breath, she tucked up a loose strand of hair. "I don't usually gossip, but your dad mentioned to me he was having a meeting with Hooper. He said Hooper had been trying to buy him out for quite a while, each time upping the offer. It seemed to amuse your father."

"What a fool," Cody said with a sad shake of his head. "Everyone in the county knows my father would never sell Kincaid land. It's been in our family for generations."

Savannah smiled slowly. "I know. But I don't think it was the land he was after, so much as the water from Silver Creek."

Nodding thoughtfully, Cody sipped his coffee. What she said made a lot of sense. He put Paul Hooper on the top of the list of suspects.

"So why don't you like him or his son?" he probed.

Savannah avoided his gaze. It made her nervous to look into those emotionless eyes. "Paul Hooper is just...I don't know." She shrugged. "He just seems a bit evil to me. And James gives me the creeps." She shivered suddenly, fiddling with the handle on her coffee cup. "There's just something about James I don't like."

She didn't add that a few months after she'd moved in here, James had begun hanging around, for what purpose she hadn't been certain until he'd boldly offered to ease what he politely called her "widow's needs." He didn't particularly like her answer, and had in fact acted extremely hurt, not to mention annoyed, as if it were a foregone conclusion that she would be interested in a relationship with him. He kept persisting until she'd finally lost her temper and sent a frying pan sailing through the window of the back door, just missing the back of his thick head.

"Was there any trouble with any of the ranch hands?" Cody asked, wanting to explore all possibilities. He drained his cup, and Savannah rose to refill it, shaking her head.

"Nothing that I know about, but I keep to myself, Cody. I don't exchange pleasantries or gossip. Besides, I don't think—"

"Oh, my God!" Cody was on his feet. "Savannah, call the fire department."

Savannah whirled. The henhouse was on fire! Her son was in there feeding the chickens! Her heart seemed to leap into her throat.

"Joey!" she screamed, dropping the coffeepot and racing out of the house right behind Cody. "Joey," she screamed again, stumbling in her bare feet in an effort to keep up with Cody. He was already at the door of the henhouse. Thick black smoke was billowing out through the roof, and the anguished cry of scared fowl echoed through the air.

"Joey!" Cody laid his palm against the door an instant before yanking it open. The smoke was thick, heavy, but from what he could see, the fire was contained to one small corner but had quickly ignited the hay scattered about, spreading more smoke than anything.

Savannah raced to the back of the house, near her little garden where the hose was. Nearly tripping over her bare feet, she flipped the spigot on, then tugged on the hose, dragging it behind her as she stumbled and ran toward the burning shed.

"Cody!" She couldn't see him for the smoke. "Joey!" she called, sobbing. Her heart was ready to pound through her chest, and she felt as if someone had injected her legs with adrenaline. She was so scared, she couldn't stop, couldn't pause. She had to get Joey out of there.

Swiping at her tears and suppressing a cough, Savannah aimed the hose into the open door, praying she was doing the right thing. A moment later, a drenched Cody emerged through the curtain of smoke, carrying a limp Joey in his arms a moment before the roof caved in, sending a flurry of screeching hens flying.

"Joey." With a sob, Savannah ran to them. Still holding Joey in his arms, Cody sank down on the ground. She followed him, reaching out to touch her son's face.

"Joey?"

He coughed and tried to sit up, but Cody held him firmly. "Sit for a minute, son," Cody said quietly. Joey nodded, then looked at his ma. She looked as if she were about to cry, and he didn't like it when she cried.

"Don't cry, Ma, I'm okay." He tried to smile, but he couldn't quite pull it off. He started coughing. His forehead hurt, and when he tried to breathe, it hurt inside. He'd been so scared. *Real* scared. He snuggled closer to Cody.

"What happened?" Savannah asked, wiping her son's brow with shaking hands, terror etched in her features.

"I don't know, Ma." Scowling, Joey tried to hide the flood of tears that suddenly threatened. He didn't want Cody to see him cry and think he was a scaredy-cat. Rubbing his chest because it hurt, Joey sniffled, then swiped his nose with the back of his hand. "The door just shut behind me, and I couldn't get it open, then smoke was every-

where." Joey cuddled even closer to Cody. "I got kinda
scared." His adoring gaze shifted to Cody. "Cody saved me,
Ma. He saved me."

"I know, honey," Savannah said, brushing away her own
tears. "I know." Now the blood-pounding fear was gone,
replaced by numbing, strength-stealing relief. Her son was
safe, but for a moment, she'd been more scared than she'd
ever been in her life. She looked at Cody, saw his strength
and his kindness and felt awash with gratitude. Right now,
all she wanted to do was lay her head on his chest just as her
son was doing and cry until she was all cried out.

She felt Cody's arm steal around her, as if he'd read her
thoughts, and she stiffened, her gaze going to his.

"Relax," he said quietly, drawing her closer. His shirt was
wet and cool, but she didn't care. "You've had quite a
scare." He was too close, and she was feeling too vulnerable at the moment to resist. The avalanche of tears came
from nowhere, and she laid her head on his shoulder and
sobbed. She felt Cody's hand, large, warm and comforting, stroking her back, drawing her closer until both she and
her son were wrapped in the protective shield of his arms.
Like this morning, she was once again astounded that a man
so big could be so gentle.

Safe.

It hit her like a hammer. For the first time in a long, long
time, Savannah felt . . . safe. Reaching up, she clutched the
front of Cody's wet shirt, holding on to him as if he were a
lifeline. She'd been so scared, so very, very scared.

What would she have done if he hadn't been here?

She began to tremble in earnest, and Cody's arm tightened around her. Damning her pride, she gratefully snuggled closer to his warmth.

The tears kept coming, and she couldn't seem to stop
them. It felt good to have someone to lean on, to feel com-
forted for a change. She couldn't remember the last time
someone had held her in comfort, and for a moment she
decided to indulge herself, to be selfish, to take this mo-

ment simply because she needed it. Until now, she'd never realized how much.

She was so tired, tired of being and doing everything by herself. So tired of having all the responsibilities in life but none of the pleasures. Right now she wanted nothing more than to bury herself in Cody's arms, to feel the warmth of his body pressed close to hers, to feel his huge arms holding her, *protecting* her. She'd never had this...this...male protection before, and realized how much she'd missed. How comforting it was to have someone hold you, comfort you, protect you.

It had been a long, long time since a man had wanted to hold her, and she found it was an amazing feeling. A glorious, wondrous feeling that made her feel alive and very, very feminine. She knew she was being selfish, but surely she was entitled to a few moments of blissful peace. What were a few minutes in a long, lonely lifetime?

With a world-weary sigh, Savannah buried her face in Cody's chest, savoring his warmth, his touch, his scent. He was calm and strong, so strong she needed his some of his strength at the moment, but just for a moment, because she knew anything more was impossible.

Watching her, holding her, Cody felt her tense body finally relax. She was clutching the front of his shirt tightly in her clenched fist. Her head was tucked just under his chin, and he could smell her hair; it was more intoxicating than the most expensive perfumes. Feeling her pressed against him, feeling her delicate feminine curves, he realized she was just as small, just as delicate as he thought. But strong. So strong.

She didn't fall apart when she'd thought Joey was in the henhouse; she had merely acted on instinct. He had a feeling she did a lot of things on instinct, and on her own. It amazed him, and he found his admiration for this proud, spirited, headstrong woman growing.

With Joey tucked in one arm and Savannah in the other, Cody realized how unbearably strong his own protective instincts were. For some reason, the two of them had touched him, moved him in a way that no one ever had. He wasn't a man who examined his feelings, but now he found himself wondering how a feisty, independent woman not big enough to make spit in a well, and an insecure little boy trying so hard to be a man had unutterably touched his guarded, wary heart.

Unable to stop himself, Cody kissed the top of Savannah's head, then turned to brush his lips against Joey's forehead. Joey's eyes widened for a moment, then he grinned, a big, tooth-gapped grin, as he wrapped his arms securely around Cody's neck and buried his head closer to his warmth. Something passed between them—boy to man, man to boy, and each understood the other.

"Ma?"

Savannah felt a small hand touch her hair, and she sniffled, trying to compose herself. She never let Joey see her cry. It upset him too much.

"Please don't cry." His voice sounded scared, and with great effort, Savannah lifted her head, brushed away her tears and forced a smile. She was his security, all he had in the world to hang on to. She had to be a rock—unshakable and indestructible—for her son's sake. Only she knew she wasn't. She was scared and vulnerable, and at times lonely. But those were human emotions a single mother wasn't allowed the luxury of—especially today.

"I'm not crying, honey," she lied, forcing her smile wider. Her son was frightened enough, and she didn't want to add to it. She brushed at his hair again, noting how Joey was snuggled against Cody. It pained her to see how desperate he was for male attention. Guilt rolled over her. She'd tried to be both mother and father to him, but knew it was impossible. A young boy needed the benefit of a man's hand. No matter how much *she* did for him, he was still missing a very important part of life. Watching the way he looked at Cody, adoration in his young eyes, she finally realized just how much her son had missed because of her self-imposed exile.

Sniffling hard, Savannah wiped her eyes, trying to steer her mind back to the ordinary to take her son's mind off of what had almost happened. "What do you say we get you cleaned up, sport, and then I'll make some dinner?"

Reluctantly Joey nodded, glancing at Cody. "Ma?"

"Yes, honey?" The crisis was past, and she began to get her strength back. She was embarrassed now at how she'd clung to Cody, showing her need. She wasn't a woman who wanted anyone's sympathy, especially his. Inhaling deeply, she slid out of Cody's embrace and rose, extending her hand to Joey and helping him to stand. He still seemed a bit shaky.

"I guess it's kinda good that Cody was here, huh?" He looked up at her with hopeful eyes.

Her gaze slid to Cody's, and she felt her cheeks go warm, but she couldn't look away. "Yes, honey, I guess it was good that Cody was here." She watched Joey slide his hand into Cody's and felt a little piece of her heart ache for her fatherless son.

"Guess it's gonna be a good thing to have him living here, too, huh?"

Joey's eyes were steady on her. Her gaze shifted to Cody's. She expected to see amusement, mischief, but she didn't. What she saw shook her. There was possessive male intent in his eyes, the kind a man gets when he sees something he wants—badly. Savannah shivered, knowing that no matter what, she had to keep him at bay—and away from her battered heart. But, oh Lord, it surely would help if he didn't look at her like that.

"Ma?" Joey shifted his feet. "Cody can stay, can't he?" he asked worriedly. "We made a deal."

"Joey..." She didn't know what to say. To tell Joey that Cody couldn't stay with them now would seem ungrateful. Savannah bent down until she was at eye level with her son. "Honey." Savannah chose her words carefully. "You know how small the house is, and I'm not sure Cody would be...comfortable."

"But he could share my room," Joey reasoned. "I don't need all that space."

Savannah placed a hand on her son's shoulder. "Joey, listen to me." She looked at him for a long moment, and Cody watched them, wondering again why Savannah wore such a leery look around him. Was it just him she was wary of? Or all men? His lips thinned. He didn't know, but he damn well was going to find out. In the meantime, he was just going to make sure they were safe.

"Joey," Cody interrupted, "why don't you go on in and get cleaned up so your mother and I can talk?"

"Are you gonna leave?" Squinting against the setting but still-hot sun, Joey looked up at him, his face a mask of concern.

Cody smiled and ruffled his hair.

"No, son. I promise I won't leave, not until I find out what's going on here." His gaze shifted to Savannah's, and he saw the determination glinting in her eyes. Well, she was simply going to have to learn that he could be just as determined when the need arose.

"All right." Dejectedly Joey started walking toward the house, kicking up dust along the way and glancing back at them.

"Cody." Savannah dragged a hand through her hair, which had fallen in a tumbled heap to her shoulders. "I think—"

"Don't think, Savannah, just listen." Taking her by the shoulders, he turned her to face him. She had to tilt her head to look at him. "I'm going to tell you something I haven't told anyone else." Her eyes widened in surprise, but she didn't say anything, just let him continue. "I think my father was murdered."

"Oh, my God, Cody." Instinctively her hand went to his chest in comfort. Cody covered her small hand with his own, holding her hand against the not-so-steady beat of his heart. "I'm so sorry. But why—?" Stunned, she shook her head.

"I don't know why or who, but I'm damn well going to find out." He glanced over her head to the shed, which had rapidly burned itself out. "Two fires in one week is a bit too much coincidence for me."

She glanced back over her shoulder at the charred ruins of the henhouse. "You mean you think..." Her voice trailed off, and she shivered. He held her hand tighter. "Oh, God." Fear crisscrossed her face. "You think someone did that deliberately?" She shook her head. "Why would anyone want to hurt me or Joey?" She shivered again, and he resisted the urge to wrap her in his arms until that fear was gone.

Cody sighed heavily. "I don't know, but I don't like this, any of it." He glanced down at her for a moment. "Savannah, I know you don't like the idea of me staying with you, and I admit it is rather strange, but after what happened here this afternoon, I can't just go off and leave you and Joey to fend for yourself, not until I'm certain there's no danger to either of you."

"Cody." Her chin angled defiantly. The last thing in the world she needed was for him to think she was some needy, clingy, helpless woman who wilted at the first sign of trouble. Or, God forbid, needed a man to look after her and protect her. She was perfectly capable of looking after herself and her son, not to mention protecting them. She'd had plenty of experience at it.

Watching her, Cody sighed. He knew that look; it was the same look of fiery determination she'd worn this morning. It was trouble. Definitely. He sighed again.

"Cody." Her eyes had darkened into fierce pools. "Joey and I have been taking care of ourselves for a long time." The chin went higher. "We don't need anyone to look out for us."

"Tough." He caught her chin and forced her to look at him. "What if it's the house next time? What if you're out in the pasture and Joey's home alone? Or what if you're sleeping and you don't smell the smoke in time? Are you

willing to take a risk with your son's life?'' His words made
her tremble.

Oh, God. He had her there. Being a single parent was a
24-hour-a-day, 7-day-a-week, 365-day-a-year responsibility, with no time off for good behavior, illness or anything
else. Joey relied on her for everything. She had to run the
ranch, and couldn't be with her son like a shadow every
moment of every day. It would be impossible.

"See what I mean?" Cody said with a slight smile,
watching frustration streak across her features. "I don't
know who started this fire or why they've targeted you now,
but you're on Kincaid property and there's a lot more going on here than meets the eye. And I intend to find out exactly what it is. But I'm certainly not going to put you or
Joey in harm's way in the meantime. Whatever is going on
has to have something to do with this land. And as long as
you're on my land, I'm responsible for you. If you think I'm
going to up and walk away and let you fend for yourself,
you're crazy." He tapped her chin to close her mouth when
she opened it, no doubt to start spewing a string of epithets
at him. She could yell at him later. Much later.

"You were dragged into this mess through no fault of
your own, and I intend to stay until I'm sure that you and
Joey are safe." His mouth thinned into a flat line, and his
eyes hardened. "Someone else started this, but I sure as hell
am going to finish it. So you and Joey can either move into
town until I figure out what the hell is going on, or I can
move in here. It's up to you."

"You mean leave our house?" Stunned, she merely stared
at him as his words finally registered. "But... what you're
proposing is...is...blackmail," she sputtered, making him
smile. That smile almost took her breath away.

"That's right," he said smugly. "But since it's my game
and my land, I get to make the rules. You've got two choices
here. Either move, or let me move in—there is no other option, Savannah," he said, forestalling any objection she
might have.

Pulling her hand free, she glared at him for a moment. "You can't bully me," she said defiantly, tossing her hair. His grin widened.

"If that's what it takes to keep you and Joey safe, I'll bully you and more." His eyes softened as they went over her delicate features. "Nothing is going to happen to either of you, not as long as you're on my land and I think there's a danger to either you or Joey." He crossed his arms across his chest, his eyes defying her. "I don't see that you have any choice in the matter. I can't even imagine that you'd willingly put your son in danger." He'd go for guilt or whatever else it took to make her see reason.

"That's not fair," she countered, realizing instantly what he was doing. But he was right. She'd never put Joey in any kind of danger. And after what had just happened, she couldn't be certain they *weren't* in danger. Still, Savannah worried her lower lip, troubled at the thought of actually having Cody living with her. In the same house. Under the same roof. He'd be there...morning...noon...and night. Oh, Lord.

Cody watched the shadows of suspicion play along her face. "Do you doubt that I could keep you and Joey safe?"

Her gaze flew to his. "N-no," she stammered, shaking her head, wishing she could tell him that it wasn't him she doubted, but her own ability to keep her senses when he was around. Her eyes widened as Cody pulled something out of his pocket and held it up for her to see.

"What?" She squinted in the sun. "What is that? Your Commander Cody secret decoder badge?"

Shaking his head in amusement, Cody chuckled softly.

"Savannah, this is a badge, but I haven't been appointed commander—yet."

She stared at the badge for a moment, then her eyes widened. "You're a cop?" she fairly shrieked, her voice edging upward in shock. He clamped a hand over her mouth.

"Shh," he whispered. He glanced around as if the whole town were standing behind him, listening. "Not a cop. A ranger. A Texas Ranger." A grin claimed his mouth. "Let's just say I've had a little experience dealing with the bad guys, to say nothing about keeping damsels in distress safe.''

"Oh, Lord," she muttered, letting her head drop again and ignoring the damsel-in-distress line—for the moment. A Texas Ranger. This was all she needed. If Joey ever found out Cody was a badge-carrying, certified ranger, she'd *never* be able to get rid of him. Joey thought the rangers were the be-all and end-all of heroes. Her head came up suddenly. "How many people in town know about this?" She nodded toward the badge he was still holding in the air.

"Not many," he said grimly, slipping his badge back in his pocket. "And I'd like to keep it that way. It's going to give me a definite edge." He studied her face for a moment, trying not to be amused by her obvious dismay. Obviously this changed the picture for her. "So, Savannah, now that you know this isn't really personal—technically it's business—what's it going to be? Are we moving or staying?" Grinning, he rocked back on his heels and waited.

We.

She scowled up at him, wishing the man didn't have to be so damn infuriating. Logic was something not even she could argue with, let alone with a badge. This might be business, but that little badge didn't make her feel any better *personally.* Not as long as she had to deal with Cody on a personal level.

Muttering a few pithy oaths under her breath about men and their intellectual capacity, Savannah finally realized she simply had no choice. She couldn't move; it was out of the question. Where on earth would she find somewhere to live on such short notice? And she wasn't about to disrupt Joey's life—again—never mind hers. She had livestock to deal with, a garden to take care of, not to mention Miss Sophie, a new henhouse to see to, as well as the day-to-day tasks of merely living on a ranch.

But more important, she thought with a hint of temper, she was not about to let anyone—*anyone*—scare her out of her home. Not some unnamed stranger, nor some unknown danger.

And especially *not* Cody Kincaid.

She could handle him—he was, after all, just a *man*.

Looking up at him, Savannah felt some of her determination falter. Well, there were men and then there were *men*. And Lord have mercy, he was one of the former, not the latter. But she could handle him, she reassured herself. If only she just wasn't so tired.

And frightened.

She hated admitting such a weakness. But the thought that someone might want to deliberately hurt her or Joey was more than she could take at the moment. As much as she hated the idea of having Cody in her home—in her life—she knew it would be foolish and irresponsible to just ignore the very real threat of danger.

And the honest-to-goodness protection he offered.

He *was* a ranger, she reasoned. It wasn't as if she was just letting some stranger off the street move in with them.

Engulfed in his arms just a few moments before, she had felt so safe, so secure, it was as if nothing in the world could harm her.

Or Joey.

It had been ages since she'd felt that way—a lifetime, really.

And she couldn't, in all good conscience, do anything to jeopardize Joey's health or welfare. She wasn't about to throw caution to the wind now just because she was worried about her own reactions to Cody. She glanced up at him, and felt the wicked beat of her heart. She could handle him, she assured herself once again. Couldn't she?

Mystified, Savannah sighed. There was no denying Joey was crazy about him. In spite of his size, and his deceptively dangerous appearance, Cody Kincaid was a kind, gentle, caring man. Although she was quite certain he wouldn't want that information passed around town. Bad for his image. No wonder her son had taken to him so quickly. Her son, who was never really comfortable around men, had practically attached himself to Cody. Children were inherently honest; they could see through people as if

they were made of glass. Obviously Joey could see exactly
what Cody was: a kind, decent, moral man.

And there were darn few of those left anymore.

"It won't be forever, Savannah," Cody said, wondering
what was going on behind those vivid blue eyes. "Just until
I find out what the hell is going on." He smiled that heart-
stopping smile of his, and she thought the ground might
have shifted a little under her. It didn't, but Lord, when he
looked at her like that, smiled at her like that, it sure felt as
if it had. Something in her heart shifted at his words.

She hesitated for a moment, then sighed, realizing he was
right. As a parent, she had a responsibility to protect her
son, and she was not above using any means available. And
she had no doubt Joey would be safe with Cody around.
They'd both be safe. She wasn't certain she found the
thought as comforting as she'd like.

"All right, Cody," she finally conceded, a hint of resentment in her voice and her heart.

Pleased, Cody dropped his arm around her and guided
her toward the house.

"But it's just for a little while," she insisted fiercely, "and
just until we find out what's going on."

One dark brow lifted. *"We?"*

She poked him in the side. "Yes, *we.*" Her eyes flashed.
"If you think I'm going to sit by like some helpless twit after someone tried to harm my son, you've got another guess
coming." She came to a halt, hands on hips, challenging
him.

He grinned. "Now, why aren't I surprised?" He gave her
a quick hug. "Think you said something about dinner?"

"Dinner," she muttered, wondering how he could even
think about food. Trying to relax, Savannah took a deep
breath, pushing her hair off her face as she let him guide her
toward the house. She could feel the warmth of his arm at
her waist, weakening her knees.

She could handle this, she assured herself. And him.
She'd just have to fortify her defenses and batten down and

dead-bolt the locks and gates that she'd erected to protect herself so that he couldn't sneak through.

Piece of cake.

Savannah glanced up at Cody again, and another thought occurred to her, nearly stopping her in her tracks.

Oh, Lord, she groaned.

What was she going to do if he had the . . . key?

Chapter Four

"Can I go, Ma? Please, oh please?" Standing in the doorway of the kitchen, Joey turned soulful, pleading eyes to his mother, who was clearing the dinner dishes from the table. "I ate my dinner and did my chores. I even finished all my stupid homework."

"Even your math?"

"Uh-huh," Joey confirmed with a nod of his head. He grinned, suddenly exposing a missing front tooth. "Cody helped me while you were making dinner." Awestruck, he shifted his gaze to Cody's. "He's *real* good at math."

Savannah's glance shifted from her son to Cody. He was calmly sitting there, just watching the interplay between her and Joey. She'd wondered where they'd gone off to while she'd been making dinner. The last time she'd seen them, Joey had his hand tucked snugly in Cody's as he led him toward the living room.

Savannah sighed. Joey's homework was usually a task she tackled after dinner. And it wasn't a particularly pleasant task, since Joey hated doing his homework—math in particular—so she usually put it off until after the evening chores and meal were over.

Savannah tried to conjure up some resentment at having Cody suddenly usurp her parental territory, but she was far too weary and tense to conjure up anything but gratitude. At the moment, she could definitely see the benefit of having another adult in the house, another head and hand to help with her son and the myriad other chores and tasks a single parent had to do.

She'd never realized until today just how difficult it was doing everything by herself, maybe because she'd always done it and just took for granted it was part of life. Or maybe because she'd never had that helping hand before, had never known what a luxury it was to share the chores and burdens of everyday life. Since Cody had ridden into her life this morning, unannounced and certainly unexpected, he seemed to be easing her burdens a bit, whether she wanted him to or not. It would be selfish not to be appreciative, particularly after the day she'd had.

"Come on, Ma, *p-lease?*" Joey tried another tactic. "Louie's dad said it was all right. And we'll be good." He crossed his fingers behind his back—just in case. "Please, oh please?"

Worrying her lower lip, Savannah shifted a stack of dirty dinner plates to her other arm. Without a word, Cody stood up, took them from her, carried them to the sink, then returned to the table to continue clearing it. She watched him in silence for a moment.

"Do you do windows?" she asked with a smile as Cody made quick work of the table. He looked up at her with that heart-stopping crooked grin.

"Windows?" He appeared to give it some thought. "Nope." He shook his head. "No windows. Not in my contract." His eyes suddenly twinkled mischievously. "But maybe we could . . . negotiate a new contract?"

He wiggled his brows at her, and she flushed scarlet. She had a pretty good idea what kind of negotiations he was talking about. She may not have had a man in her life in a long time, but it hadn't been so long that she didn't recognize male interest when she saw it.

Intense male interest.

A flutter of feminine nerves had her chewing her lower lip again. She had to remember this was merely business to him; he was simply protecting his property, and she and Joey just happened to live on that property. She had to remember that and keep Cody at arm's length. She couldn't afford to get involved with him on any level, not just for her sake, but for her son's, as well.

"Ma?" Joey's impatient voice brought her back to their conversation and the problem at hand. "Please can I go to Louie's?"

He was *dying* to tell Louie everything that had happened today. How his plan had worked and Cody was going to live with them now, and how they wouldn't have to move. And wait until Louie learned Cody had rescued him from a fire, just like a real TV hero! Boy, Louie was going die, just *die.* Not since the vampire nurse had anything so exciting happened. And if he had to wait until tomorrow to tell Louie, he was going to bust! "I'll come home early," he wheedled, bending to scratch a mosquito bite.

"But it's a school night," Savannah protested. "You know you're not supposed to go out on school nights." She fought back the fear and panic that letting her son out of her sight brought on. She'd come so close to losing him this afternoon, so close that the idea of keeping him within earshot and eyesight—at least until he was about forty—seemed infinitely appealing. Particularly since they still had no idea who had started the fire in the henhouse or why. Or who exactly was the target. The thought made her shiver, and she rubbed her hands up and down her bare arms, trying to banish her thoughts and her fears.

If she could lock Joey in his room in order to keep him safe and sound until he was grown, she'd do it.

But she knew for her son's sake she couldn't do that. She couldn't coddle, spoil or smother Joey, even though it was part of her nature to do so. Those she loved, she loved without hesitation or reservation, and with every fiber in her being. And she'd never loved anything or anyone the way she loved her son. He was the center of her world, and it was her job to protect him and keep him safe.

Savannah sighed. But he was still a boy, and boys needed their freedom and independence, *especially* from their mothers.

But she didn't have to like it.

"But we don't got school tomorrow," Joey informed her with an exasperated sigh. "Teachers' institute day, remember? I told ya last week."

"I forgot," she said lamely, realizing this morning she'd forgotten to check the big wall calendar she kept posted in the kitchen with every day's activities and appointments on it. It was the only way she could keep track of their schedules.

"So can I go, huh? Please, Ma?" Eyes shining in excitement, Joey was bouncing from foot to foot. He was making her queasy with all that movement.

Savannah rubbed her temple where an ache had suddenly begun to throb. Her shoulders and neck ached with tension, and now her head was getting into the act.

"I'll be happy to drive him over, Savannah." Cody cleared the last of the dinner dishes from the table and set them on the counter by the sink before turning to her. "I'm sure he'll be perfectly fine," he added, as if he'd just read her worried thoughts. He smiled gently when her gaze flew to his in surprise. "Besides, I'd like a chance to talk to Judd for a few moments. The sooner the better." The look in his eyes said more than words, and she knew he was being circumspect because Joey was in the room and he didn't want to alarm him.

Cody had confided that Sheriff Judd Powers, Louie's father, was an old classmate of his and one of the only people in town who knew he was a Texas Ranger. She knew, too, that Cody wanted to report the fire in the henhouse as soon as possible before the trail got cold. He'd gone out to investigate what remained of the henhouse while she made dinner and Joey changed. She had no idea what he'd found, since they hadn't had much of a chance to talk.

"All right." She let out her breath and tried to relax. "You can go." Excitement increased Joey's bouncing. "But I want your word that you and Louie are not going to get into any mischief." Savannah almost smiled. Asking Louie to stay out of mischief was like asking flowers not to bloom.

"Yes, ma'am," Joey said solemnly, lowering his eyes.

"I mean it. No monkey business." She tried to make her voice stern, something she'd been practicing since his birth ten years ago. She still hadn't quite accomplished it. Maybe by the time he was eighteen, she'd manage it.

"Jeez, Ma," Joey complained, rolling his eyes again. "Louie doesn't even got a monkey." He shoved his hands in his pockets and found a precious piece of contraband gum. He planned to chew it on the way to Louie's. Maybe he'd even learn how to blow those real big bubbles.

"And stay inside," Savannah cautioned. "Don't go anywhere." She glanced out the window with a frown. Night had fallen, and for the first time since she'd moved to Silver Creek, she found the dark and the desolation a bit eerie. "I don't want you mucking around Louie's tree house in the dark." Taking a deep breath for calm, Savannah pushed her hair off her face. "And don't give Mr. Powers a hard time."

"I won't, I won't," Joey grumbled.

"I'm sure the boys will be fine, Savannah." Cody crossed the room, dropping an arm around Joey's shoulder.

The boy turned adoring eyes to him, and Savannah almost groaned. She knew it wasn't good for Joey to get so instantly attached to Cody. He was only going to be in Silver Creek temporarily, and when he left, Joey would no doubt be hurt, which was one of the myriad reasons she'd never dated. She would never introduce someone into their lives who wasn't going to become a permanent member. And the chances of *that* happening, of her ever allowing a man to get that close to her physically or emotionally, were about as good as her playing starting quarterback in the next Super Bowl.

Still, she was going to have to talk to Cody—alone—about the problem. He had to be aware that just his presence had the power to hurt her son. The thought brought on a sick feeling in her stomach. Maybe she could work up a schedule for Joey. She always worked from one, or else she'd never get done all the things she needed to do each day. That way, Joey would stay busy and out and away from Cody. It was for his own protection, she reasoned, fighting back a bout of guilt.

"Come on, kid, let's go." Cody steered Joey toward the back door. "While we're gone, Savannah," Cody called over his left shoulder, flashing her a smile, "why don't you take something for that headache?"

Unconsciously Savannah's hand went to her throbbing temple, and she stood staring after him openmouthed, wondering how he knew she had a headache.

Probably because he was the one who'd given it to her!

Joey had never ridden in a Jeep before. He liked it 'cause it was bumpy and it was high; he could see forever, even into the cars next to them. Craning his neck, he peered curiously into the car that had pulled to a stop beside them. Yuk. Disgusting. Two teenagers were smooching each other.

"You like her?" Turning his head, Joey looked at Cody across the dark interior.

Glancing in the rearview mirror as he waited for the light to change, Cody frowned in the darkness. "Who?"

"My ma." Joey slipped the piece of contraband bubble gum in his mouth and the wrapper in his pocket. Goofy Grape. His favorite. He chomped noisily.

Caught off guard, Cody cleared his throat. He'd never spent much time around children, but they did seem to have a propensity for speaking their minds.

"Y-yes," Cody said hesitantly. "I like your mother."

Joey grinned. "I like her, too." He blew a small bubble, then frowned, wishing he could blow the real big ones like Louie. Maybe he'd get Louie to teach him. "She likes you," he commented offhandedly, causing Cody to glance at him.

"Your mother?"

Joey nodded, crossing his eyes so he could look down his nose to see how big this bubble was.

Cody flipped on his directional signal, then eased the Jeep around the corner. "What makes you think your mother likes me?" He felt ridiculously like a teenager prying information from a younger brother or sister.

"'Cause."

Cody sighed. "Did your mother tell you she liked me?"

"Nah." Joey shook his head again. "I could just tell. She didn't throw a pan at you."

A small smile played along Cody's lips. Obviously this was a dating ritual he was unfamiliar with. "Has she thrown many pans?"

Joey shook his head furiously, almost swallowing his gum. "Nah, just once."

"At who?" Cody tried not to smile. This was getting interesting.

Joey blew another bubble, not quite as big as he wanted, but pretty good. "Old man Hooper's son." Instantly Joey clapped a hand over his mouth, and his eyes widened in horror.

"What?" Cody glanced from the road to Joey. "What's wrong?"

"I'm not supposed to call him old man Hooper," Joey whispered. "I forgot." He checked out the car next to them before turning back to Cody. "You're not gonna tell, are you?"

Cody shook his head. "Not me. I didn't hear a thing." He waited a moment. "So your mother threw a pan at old man—Mr. Hooper's son?"

"Yep."

Cody frowned, wondering what on earth James Hooper could have done to Savannah to cause her to do such a thing. Not that it surprised him. "Why?"

Joey shrugged. "Dunno. But boy, she was mad." Shaking his head, he rolled his eyes expressively. "*Real* mad." Joey shifted in his seat. "Did you like your pa?" he asked abruptly, and Cody blinked, trying to keep up with this shifting conversation.

"Of course. I liked him very much."

"Then how come you didn't live with him?" Joey blew a little bubble, let it pop, then carefully peeled the gum off his lips so there'd be no telltale signs. "If I had a pa, I'd like him a whole lot and I'd live with him always so I could see him every single day."

He heard the yearning in the boy's voice and felt it touch his heart. The kid was getting to him every which way. His answer, when it finally came, came slowly. "Sometimes fathers and sons don't get along, Joey. That doesn't mean they don't like or love each other. Sometimes it's better if they live apart."

"But why?"

Good question. Cody was thoughtful for a moment. "When you grow up, Joey, sometimes you and your parents have different ideas about things." From the look on the kid's face, he had a feeling he could have been speaking Swahili for all he understood. Cody tried again. "When you grow up, you're going to live on your own, with your wife and kids, aren't you?"

Joey's brows drew together. He'd never thought about being a grown-up. Probably because it seemed like a forever time away.

"Nope." He shook his head. "I'm never getting married." He'd have to kiss a girl then. Yuk. He gave a self-satisfied smile and crossed his arms. "I'm gonna live with my ma and take care of her and Miss Sophie always." He looked at Cody carefully. "Do you got a wife?"

Cody laughed. "Nope."

"How come?" Joey blew another bubble. Pleased at its size, he popped it with his finger.

Cody grinned to himself. Because no one had ever run fast enough to catch him was probably *not* the answer the kid was looking for.

"Maybe because I've never found the right woman." He didn't think he still believed in such a thing.

"My ma's a woman."

"So I've noticed," Cody said mildly. It was, in fact, all he'd been noticing since he'd laid eyes on Savannah. It would have been hard *not* to notice she was a woman with those skimpy shorts that revealed a long, mouth-watering length of legs and the well-worn T-shirt that revealed as much as it concealed. He'd never had a doubt Savannah was a woman.

"Is she right?" Joey asked, not quite certain what *the right woman* meant. He knew it meant something. He brightened. "My ma writes with her right hand. Is that what you mean?"

Cody grinned in the darkness. "Not quite, son."

Joey frowned. He still didn't understand, but maybe Louie would. Louie knew everything. "You got kids?"

Cody shook his head. "Nope."

"How come? Don't you like 'em?" Joey's brows scrunched into a worried frown.

"I like kids, Joey," Cody assured him, "but it's kinda hard for a single man to work and take care of kids by himself."

"My ma works and still takes care of me all by herself."

"Yeah, I know."

Joey cocked his head. "Do you want kids?"

Cody was thoughtful for a moment. He'd never really given the matter much thought before. He glanced at Joey, thought about the impact the kid had had on him in just a few hours.

"Yeah," he said softly, "I'd like to have kids."

Joey's grin was huge. He was a kid. His ma was a woman. A plan began to form in his mind. He'd have to ask Louie about it. He frowned suddenly. "How come the henhouse started on fire?" His frown deepened. "Did someone do it on purpose?" He got kind of scared thinking about it.

Cody was quiet as he eased the vehicle up the long, winding driveway to Judd Powers's house, trying to figure out how to answer the kid without lying. Cody sighed. He was grateful they'd reached their destination. He was getting dizzy from all the questions, not to mention the abrupt change in subject matter. He switched off the engine and turned to Joey.

"I'm not sure, but I promise you I'm going to find out before I leave." Cody threw open the door and climbed out, coming around the front to meet Joey.

"What if you don't find out before you gotta leave?" Joey asked, gazing up at him. The thought of Cody leaving made him sad. He liked him, *really* liked him. He was even nicer than his pa, Mr. Kincaid.

Cody's eyes hardened. "I'm not going anywhere until I find out."

"Promise?"

Cody looked down at him and saw a shadow of sadness and hope in the boy's eyes. "Promise." Smiling, he gave Joey's hand a squeeze as they started up the walk.

Joey grinned in the darkness. Maybe, just maybe, Louie could come up with a plan, a *super-duper* one that would make Cody want to stay forever. His grinned widened. He'd ask Louie about it tonight.

"Need any help?"

Standing at the sink, her elbows deep in sudsy water, her mind on the chores yet to be done that night, Savannah nearly jumped out of her shoes at the soft, masculine voice so close to her ear. The pot she was scrubbing nearly went airborne.

"Touchy, aren't we?" Cody commented with a smile, laying a hand on her shoulder to calm her. She had wariness in her eyes and a puff of soap suds on her left cheek. He itched to touch her, to glide his finger along the curve of her cheek. And a few other places, as well.

Instead, he leaned his long frame back against the cabinet, crossed his arms and proceeded to merely...watch her, making her more nervous than she already was.

"I am *not* touchy," Savannah declared fiercely, trying to ignore the warmth of his touch as she nearly scrubbed the finish off the pot. For the first time since moving to Silver Creek, she found herself jumpy at being alone, perhaps because of what had happened this afternoon. It was hard to imagine that someone had deliberately set the henhouse on fire. Crime in their small county was negligible. The most exciting thing that had happened in the six years she'd lived here was when Miss Tulip accused someone on the school board of stealing her umbrella—until she found it at the Silver Creek Supermart, where she'd left it in a shopping cart. But knowing someone had deliberately set out to hurt or frighten her and Joey was incomprehensible, not to mention downright scary.

Savannah sighed. She'd been jumpy and on edge ever since Cody and Joey had left for Louie's. Maybe it was because while she did the dishes, she couldn't help but look out the window over the sink. The huge pile of ashes where the henhouse had once stood was a constant reminder that they might be in danger. It was an eerie feeling.

When she heard Cody's Jeep in the driveway, she'd let out a sigh of relief, grateful he was back, grateful just for his presence. But she wasn't about to admit such a thing to him.

She glanced at him now, aware his hand was still on her shoulder. Warm. Strong. Gentle. Making her pulse jump and her heart pound, not in fear, but something far more powerful. And frightening.

"I'm just not used to... to... having someone sneak up on me, that's all." She wasn't used to having a man in her house, at her table or underfoot. It was totally unnerving, helpful at times, she reluctantly added, but no less unnerving. Especially since *this* particular man had the power to make her heart and pulse do world-class gymnastics.

One brow rose mildly, and Cody chuckled. *"Sneak?"* He couldn't resist. He lifted a finger and traced it down her left cheek, removing the puff of suds. Immediately she drew back, and wariness leapt in her eyes again, intriguing him.

"I hardly think someone my size is capable of . . . sneaking anywhere, Savannah."

She scowled, not certain if she was more annoyed with him or herself for her ridiculous reactions again. And he was back to using logic again. How was she supposed to understand logic, when she couldn't think clearly with him so close.

She darted a glance at him. "Well, let's just say I'm not used to having anyone in my kitchen," she said, her voice prim.

Still watching her, Cody picked up an apple from the fruit basket on the counter and began tossing it from hand to hand. He felt restless for some inexplicable reason. "So, uh, tell me . . . how long has it been since you've had someone . . . in your kitchen?" Grinning wickedly, he bit into the apple and waited, watching as her face turned scarlet.

Savannah scrubbed the pot harder, avoiding his mischievous gaze. He wasn't inquiring about her kitchen or anything else in it, and she knew it.

And so did he.

Infuriated and embarrassed, she avoided his gaze, afraid he might see the truth. "How long it's been since anyone's been in my . . . kitchen is none of your business."

Chewing thoughtfully, Cody nodded. "I know." He flashed her a grin. "But it doesn't hurt to ask." He took another generous bite of his apple, then glanced out the window. The pile of gray ashes where the henhouse had been was a sudden reminder of why he was here. With her. At least part of the reason.

"I spoke with Judd when I dropped Joey off." He paused, pretending to examine his apple as she glanced up at him.

"And?" She waited, rolling her shoulders in an effort to ease some of the tension snaking through her.

Watching her, he took another bite before speaking. She was incredibly tense, and he didn't know if it was the traumatic events of the day or his presence. "Judd thinks it's too much of a coincidence, as well." Cody shook his head. "Two fires in one week. Not very likely."

"So he thinks someone set both deliberately?" She tried to keep the fear out of her voice. But he heard it. It made something tighten in his gut.

"Definitely."

"But why?" Savannah asked with a frown, still scrubbing the now-clean pot so she wouldn't have to look directly at him. Those blue eyes of his were far too disconcerting. "Why would someone deliberately set those fires?" She shook her head. None of this made sense.

"Good question." Tilting his head, he studied her for a moment. A few stray strands of her hair lay curled against her cheek; a few others curled along the long glide of her neck. Her scent was sweet, intoxicating. He wanted to kiss the strands of hair from her cheek, then slide his mouth down the gentle slope of her neck. Instead, he took aim at the wastebasket across the room and tossed the core of his apple into it. Knowing she was wary, he'd have to go slow. "One I hope to have an answer for very soon. Judd's going to start looking into things. Quietly, of course. If someone did set both fires deliberately, that means they murdered my father."

His eyes flashed for a moment and his lips thinned. Savannah saw and heard the pain in his voice and ached for him. After all that had happened today, it was hard to remember that he'd just buried his daddy this afternoon.

"We don't want to spook them, nor do we want to tip our hand." Cody rubbed a hand across his stubbled chin. He had big hands, strong but gentle. She remembered the way he'd held her this afternoon, making her feel safe, protected. Cody shrugged. "But it sort of stands to reason it's someone in town. The only stranger that's been noticed lately is me."

Savannah took a deep breath. "And the only connection to the fires is that they were both on Kincaid land?" He nodded, shifting slightly so that he was closer to her. Savannah shook her head. "I can't imagine anyone in Silver Creek doing such a thing, let alone deliberately." And not to his father. Her eyes met his. "Everyone seems so...nice, so...normal." Lifting a hand, Savannah rubbed a particularly sore spot at the back of her neck.

"I know it's not a pleasant thought, Savannah, but everything seems to point to it." She had incredible eyes. Huge and blue, they reflected her every emotion. At the moment, she looked a little wary and frightened. He wondered which of those emotions he had caused. "So until we get a handle on what's going on, I want you to stick as close as possible to the ranch." *And me,* he wanted to add, but didn't, knowing she'd probably take *extreme* umbrage not only at the idea, but at the fact that he'd *told* her to do it. In just a few hours, he'd learned that Savannah Duncan could be as stubborn and headstrong as a rattler with a buzz saw in its belly. And he wasn't certain how good his pot-ducking abilities were anymore. So it was probably best not to rile her.

"Judd's going to start checking into some things on his end, and I'll handle some things on this end." His smile was gentle. "Together we should be able to come up with something to smoke this guy out."

"Smoke him out?" Savannah fairly shuddered. "Do you mean you're going to deliberately bait whoever it is?" When he nodded, she realized she didn't like this idea at all. "But won't that be dangerous?"

"Could be," Cody acknowledged with such nonchalance she wanted to whack him. How could he be so blasé about the whole thing?

"But, Cody, you suspect this person has already killed your father." She didn't like the edge of fear in her voice.

"Yeah, so, what's your point?"

She wanted to whack him again. "What's my point?" she repeated incredulously, struggling to hold on to her patience. "My point is that this person is either crazy or dangerous, possibly both, and deliberately baiting or antagonizing him does not sound like a particularly bright idea to me." She was beginning to think Cody was the one who needed looking after.

"Bright or not, it's the only way to make him crawl out of the shadows."

Savannah frowned. "Why do you keep saying 'him'? It could be a woman, you know. Criminals aren't limited by gender."

That stopped him cold, and he merely stared at her, his mind whirling. "I just assumed it was a man," Cody admitted reluctantly, realizing she might have a point. "I never even considered a woman."

"Well, consider it. Maybe it's an old flame, or some woman whose heart you broke."

He couldn't help the grin that broke free. Absently he rubbed the stubble of his jaw. "Now that you mention it, there have been a...few, uh, ladies that might have a slight—mind you, I said *slight*—grudge against me for one reason or another."

"Now, why doesn't that surprise me?" Savannah asked, trying not to smile. She had a feeling Cody Kincaid had left a string of broken hearts all across the state. Which was just another reason to keep him at a distance. She wasn't interested in becoming one of a crowd.

"A woman, huh?" Cody rubbed his jaw again. He'd have to think about that one. It shot all of his theories to hell. Well, he'd just have to rethink the situation when his mind was a little clearer. Right now the only thing on his mind was the woman standing next to him.

He watched Savannah roll her shoulders again. He shifted his weight until he was standing directly behind her. He moved too fast, too smoothly for her to be alarmed. Sliding his arms alongside hers, he effectively trapped her between him and the sink, then covered her hands with his.

Savannah tried to step back, but found she couldn't. He was standing too close. She could feel the warmth of his body heat, smell the clean male scent of him. If she moved even slightly, her back would be pressed against his chest.

She tried to take a deep breath to calm herself, but every nerve was screaming in alarm.

"I've heard about your propensity for throwing pots," he whispered, taking the soapy pot from her hands and dropping it with a plop back into the water. He was close. Too close. His warm breath was buffeting her skin, making a rash of goose bumps rise. "Relax, Savannah. You're so tense I could bounce a quarter off your shoulders." His soft, warm voice was suspiciously close to her ear. "Anybody ever tell you you worry too much?"

She opened her mouth to speak, but no words came out. Her pulse was galloping, and her knees suddenly felt a bit weak. She fought it, resisting the urge to lean back and rest against him. A mere man wasn't going to make her behave like a mindless female!

"Cody, I don't think this is a good—"

"Then don't think," he whispered, lifting his hands to her shoulders to knead the tense muscles. "Just relax."

How was she supposed to relax when he was crowded behind her, his voice teasing her ear, while his hands seduced her skin? But it felt so good, her eyes slid closed and she couldn't stop the soft, appreciative moan that slipped through her lips.

He smiled as he kept kneading. "Feel good?"

She murmured her approval. One form of tension lessened, another increased.

"You smell good," he whispered, bending to plant a soft kiss on her neck.

She started to tremble.

"Cody..." Her voice sounded slightly breathless.

"Shh," he whispered, moving his hands in a soothing, circular motion. "Try to relax for a few minutes." He kept kneading, rubbing, smoothing away the tension that had tightened every muscle in her neck and shoulders. His hands gently slid to the slender column of her neck. Her skin was soft, like silk. It warmed under his touch, releasing more of a sweet feminine scent, drawing him in deeper and deeper.

His fingers moved to her shoulders, and he turned her to face him.

Her eyes opened dreamily, and she looked at him. Panic set in at the look on his face. Need and desire clashed like cymbals, darkening his eyes. Tightening his hands at her shoulders, he slowly drew her closer. Savannah swallowed hard.

He was so close, the fabric of his jeans was brushing against the skin of her legs. Her bare feet were trapped between his booted ones, reminding him again of how small and delicate she was.

They stood staring at each other, pummeled by a tumble of feelings and emotions neither wanted but neither could ignore. She wanted—tried—to look away, but found she couldn't. It was as if she were mesmerized by him. A hot knot of desire tightened her stomach, making her palms sweat and shake. Absently she rubbed her hands down her shorts, anything to keep from reaching out and touching him, pulling him closer.

"Savannah." He lifted a hand to her cheek, his thumb softly stroking, moving down to trace the outline of her mouth before gliding softly over her lower lip. Her eyes widened, and he saw the wariness again, and something else: vulnerability. He could sense her trembling.

"I won't hurt you," he whispered, still tracing her lower lip with his thumb. "I promise." Bending his head slightly, he gently nipped the corner of her mouth.

She lifted her hands to his chest, in protest, she thought, but the thought died on a sigh when he continued nibbling and nipping her mouth, lighting a line of fire and need, and she clutched his shirt to steady herself.

With his hands still on her shoulders, he moved her closer to him, then closer still, sliding his arms around her slender waist to gather her up until she was pressed against the long, hard length of him.

"Cody—" She was saying one thing, but her eyes were telling him something else. He much preferred the message in her eyes.

Her protest was absorbed by his mouth. Shock nearly knocked the wind out of her. His mouth was soft, patient, gentle, allowing her to get used to the touch and feel of him before deepening the kiss. She'd have sworn the floor tilted. Or perhaps it was just the world—*her* world—and she slid her hands from the hard expanse of his chest to his shoulders, standing on tiptoe to reach, clinging to him, drawing him closer in wonder.

His fingers splayed along her spine, stroking, caressing, soothing much the way he'd soothe a nervous filly. She wasn't what he'd expected. He'd kissed many women, and none had surprised him.

Until now.

Savannah wasn't shy or tentative, as he'd expected her to be. She was warm, and generous, giving back whatever she received. There was passion and need. She was like a storm that had been repressed and suddenly was struggling to be freed.

He wanted to be the one to free her, to free the storm clouds of her passion until they finally exploded in a shower that engulfed them both.

But he knew he had to go slow. He couldn't scare or overwhelm her, or she'd crawl right back into her shell, like a threatened turtle who hid its head whenever danger approached.

She was smart enough to know he was dangerous. But not nearly as dangerous as she was turning out to be.

She was pressed intimately against him, and his desperate hands slid to tangle in her hair. Slanting her mouth, he tasted, sipped from her lips as if she were his life source, wanting more, unable to bear the thought of letting her go.

A silent warning went off in his head, reminding him of who he was, but more important, who *she* was.

She was patience and permanence; he was wild and a wanderer.

She needed roots and ties; he needed to be free.

She was day; he was night and all the darkness that came with it.

She had a child, a family; he was a loner—always had been; always would be.

She wore her emotions on her sleeve for the world to see; those who knew him would swear he'd never *had* a real emotion and wouldn't recognize one if he did.

She loved openly, honestly, wholeheartedly.

He couldn't—wouldn't—love anything or anyone. His experience with women, specifically one woman, had taught him how dangerous women could be. Dangerous to his emotions and his heart, which was off limits to everyone. He could handle his physical desire, sharing his body simply because it was as natural as breathing to him, but he'd never let another woman get close enough to entangle him emotionally.

Never again.

But still, some things about Savannah surprised him, and he'd thought he was far too old to be surprised by any woman. But she had. He hadn't realized his life had been dull and boring until she'd come along and added a spark of something. What, he wasn't even sure. All he knew was that being with her and her son made him happier than he'd been in years. Funny, he'd never even realized he *wasn't* happy. But she added something to his life, something that made him want to smile, or pet puppies, or dance a jig.

But it was only temporary.

He knew it, had to remember it. He wouldn't hurt her by letting her think that it could be anything more. He had nothing to offer her, nothing of permanence anyway.

The warning clanged louder, and Cody shifted her in his arms, indulging himself, letting his mouth take all that she gave. His hands slid the slender length of her, caressing her, before coming to rest on the curve of her hips, dragging her closer until there was no denying her effect on him, then he slowly let her go.

Dazed and breathless, Savannah merely stared at him, clinging to his shoulders for balance, stunned by his kiss, her reaction. He touched her cheek in a movement that was clearly meant to calm the riot of feelings inside of her. It didn't.

Cody sought to put some distance between them. He needed time to think and put things in their proper perspective. He couldn't do that with her standing in front of him, looking slightly dazed and tousled with her full mouth slightly red and pouty from his kiss. At the moment, all he wanted to do was haul her back in his arms, but this time he wouldn't let her go. And that wasn't good for either of them.

"Why don't you finish up in here?" He nodded toward the last of the dishes. "I'll go pick up Joey." He glanced at his watch. "It's about time."

Afraid she couldn't find her voice, she merely nodded, watching as Cody stepped away from her. Without moving from where she stood, Savannah watched him, unable to do anything else until the back door shut softly behind him.

Finally she took a deep breath, pulling a great gulp of much-needed air into her lungs. Frightened and unsettled, Savannah rubbed her hands over her face. Her lips still tingled from Cody's kiss. His masculine scent seemed to be everywhere, teasing her, reminding her of him. She wondered what on earth had happened to her.

Cody had happened to her. And as much as she tried to deny it, she couldn't deny the fact that he'd maneuvered his way into her life. But she was bound and determined not to let him maneuver his way into her heart.

Chapter Five

Savannah and Joey had a deal: she could sleep as late as she wanted on the days he didn't have school, and he could stay up as late as he wanted on the days he didn't have school. So she couldn't understand why he was now pounding on her bedroom door with what sounded like a hammer.

Dragging her head out from under the pillow, Savannah opened her mouth to protest, then realized the pounding wasn't on her bedroom door, but outside. Hopping out of bed, she shoved a sleep-tangled wad of hair out of her face as she went to the window to investigate the commotion. Scowling, she craned her neck, but realized she couldn't see a thing, at least not anything that would account for all the racket. Whatever was going on was behind the house. Still frowning, she dragged some clothes out of her bureau, hoping Joey hadn't already gotten into mischief this morning. He knew he wasn't supposed to leave the house when she was sleeping. It was one of her cardinal rules.

Discarding her silk nightshirt, she took a quick shower before slipping into a pair of denim shorts and a T-shirt. It was probably going to be another scorcher; it was already getting warm in the house.

Padding downstairs, she yawned, pushing her hair back again. She hadn't bothered to fix her hair; she was far too concerned with what Joey was up to. She'd braid it later, after she'd had some coffee. And some answers.

The kitchen was empty, but there was a note on the table, as well as a full pot of fresh coffee. According to the note, Cody and Joey were out back rebuilding the henhouse.

Rebuilding the henhouse? Savannah frowned. She hoped Cody knew how to build, because neither she nor Joey did. She couldn't tell a hammer from a hammock. And neither could her son. Carpentry wasn't listed under mother's chores, at least not *this* mother's chores. And where on earth had Cody gotten the materials?

Deciding this needed further investigation, Savannah crossed the kitchen and dug her favorite coffee mug out of the cabinet. It was an ugly brown and chipped in several places, but she was far too sentimental to ever discard it. Joey had made it for her on Mother's Day when he was in kindergarten. The white lettering had been washed nearly off, but ugly or not, it would always be her favorite.

The fresh-brewed coffee made her smile in genuine gratitude. What a treat to come downstairs and have coffee made. And she definitely needed a strong cup to get her going this morning. She'd had a miserable night's sleep, tossing and turning. It had almost been dawn before she'd finally drifted off, her thoughts a constant tangle about Cody. She was exhausted and had a slight headache, but she supposed she could forgive Cody for unintentionally ruining her sleep; fresh-brewed coffee in the morning was her weakness, and gratitude instantly improved her mood.

She glanced at the sink, which was full of dishes. An assortment of pans decorated the range. Frowning, she went over to investigate. Cody not only had made coffee, but if the dishes and pans were any indication, he'd apparently made breakfast, as well. The man obviously had many talents, she thought with a smile.

After filling her mug, Savannah wandered outside, following the direction of the noise. Squinting, she glanced up at the sun. It was high and hot in the morning sky, already radiating an intense heat that would guarantee a fast burn.

"Good morning," she said, coming around the back of the house and nearly skidding to a stop. Her mouth instinctively opened to protest, but quickly shut again. Cody was holding a piece of lumber up, while Joey, who was wearing some kind of belt around his waist with an assortment of lethal-looking tools in it, tried to maneuver a hammer. She started to panic, fearing the board might come down and conk her son right on the noggin, or he'd hit himself with the hammer. But she banked her fear, knowing her son would be mortified if she said anything. Besides, Cody was standing right there, almost as big as the board. Instinctively she knew he wouldn't let anything happen to her son.

Appeased a bit, Savannah sipped her coffee and tried to settle her nerves. Cody was dressed for the heat and the work. Stripped to the waist, he wore a pair of faded denim jeans and work boots. She tried not to stare at his bare, broad, sun-bronzed chest. Looking at him now, she couldn't help but remember what it felt like to be pressed against that broad chest.

Safe.

Last night, when Cody was holding her, it was the only thing she could think of—how safe she felt. How protected. It was an unusual feeling, one she'd never felt, but one she was afraid she just might get used to.

But she knew she couldn't allow herself such indulgences. The sense of safety she felt was illusory. She knew, too, that a man's arms were the *last* place a woman would find safety or security. Safety and security could only come from within, not from someone else, especially a man. If you allowed yourself to need, lean or depend on a man, the minute he moved, you'd fall.

And she'd already learned the hard way how hard and how long the fall could be. She couldn't lean, she couldn't need and she sure as hell couldn't depend on a man. To allow herself to do so would be a sure path to heartbreak. She'd learned her lessons well and she wasn't a woman who made the same mistake twice. Ever.

Cody was here merely to protect his land and investigate what had happened to his father. Once they got to the bottom of this mess, Cody would be on his way, and she'd go back to her life.

This was merely a temporary arrangement.

She couldn't—wouldn't—forget that, because she had no intention of becoming a temporary playmate. Not for Cody. Not for any man.

Banishing her thoughts, she sipped her coffee as her gaze shifted to Joey. She tried not to grin. The tool belt he was wearing had to belong to Cody; it drooped around Joey's slender hips like a drunken ballerina's tutu. And he wore protective glasses that were clearly too big for his face; he looked as if he had fish bowls over his eyes. On his head he wore a construction hard hat in a shade of yellow so loud it could have woken the dead. It, too, was too big for him, but a thick chin strap held it firmly in place. Dressed as he was, Joey looked as though someone had just dropped him from a spaceship.

Spotting her, Cody flashed her a grin but didn't let go of the board he was holding. She held her breath as Joey tried to hit a nail with the hammer. Her eyes never left her son. She could hear Cody talking to him, instructing him, gently correcting him, helping him until the nail was in the board—crookedly—but it was in, and the look on her son's face was complete and utter satisfaction.

Savannah felt an ache in her heart. Watching her son absorb every word Cody said, staring at him in rapt attention, she realized once again how starved for male attention her son really was.

Usually she didn't trust anyone with her son; his care and welfare were far too important. But for some reason, she trusted Cody with him. Perhaps it was because of the way he'd behaved yesterday, charging into the burning henhouse without regard for his own safety. It took a lot of courage to do that, and instinctively she knew her son would always be safe when Cody was around.

Watching Cody, and the way he acted and interacted with her son, made some of her natural caution about men—or rather, this specific man—dissolve. There weren't many men—especially a man who didn't have children of his own—who would have the patience to deal with a curious and inquisitive ten-year-old, one who was full of mischief and questions. But Cody seemed to not only take it in stride, but even to be fairly amused by it.

And she found that Cody's treatment of her son had melted some of her own reserve and wariness toward him. A man who treated a child with such regard and respect was a man worthy of *her* respect. And there hadn't been many men like that. Maybe because Joey's own father had abandoned him sight unseen, she found Cody's actions so endearing.

All in all, she was beginning to have a sneaky suspicion that Cody was an honorable man, the kind of man a woman could count on no matter what. And Lord have mercy, she'd always been a sucker for an honorable man. Simply because in her experience, there were so few of them around. Men who cared about hurts and hearts, men who honored their commitments and didn't run for cover when the going got rough. The kind of man a woman could respect and lean on, knowing he'd never let her fall or hurt her. The kind of man a woman could fall in love with.

Stunned, Savannah blinked, wondering where that thought had come from. It wasn't like her to daydream; she was far too busy and much too practical for such nonsense. But then again, she'd never met a man like Cody before. He was proving to be the antithesis of everything she believed men to be.

She thought about the way she'd felt in his arms last night. She never let men get close to her, not physically, and especially not emotionally, because once you let a man close to you emotionally, you gave him the power to hurt you. And she'd never give anyone that power again, but she was heartily afraid that somehow, in the past twenty-four hours, Cody Kincaid had managed to sneak past all her natural reserves on both levels.

For a moment, the thought brought on a flare of panic, but she quickly banked it. It was only natural, she reasoned, that she have some...attachment to Cody, as well as some feelings. After all, he *had* saved her son's life. Satisfied that was all it was, Savannah smiled as Joey spotted her.

"Ma!" He came rushing over. "Look, look." He grabbed her hand and all but dragged her closer to the still-in-progress building. "Look what me and Cody are doing."

She pretended to examine it closely. They must have been up for hours. Two walls were almost complete, filled with an abundance of crooked nails, compliments of her son, no doubt, and the yard was piled high with different-sized boards and an assortment of work tools.

"We're building a new henhouse. We even cleaned up all the yuk from the old one."

Turning her head, she saw that the only thing left of the old henhouse was a dry patch of scorched earth.

"Pretty good work, son," she said with a smile, leaning down to peer into his face. "Looks like you've been working hard."

"We been up forever." Rubbing his itchy nose, Joey grinned. "Cody's a real good teacher. He even made breakfast. I helped."

Joey's eyes were dancing with excitement, and he couldn't seem to stand still. She couldn't remember ever seeing her son so animated or quite so happy.

"Morning." Taking a step toward her, Cody slid her mug from her hands, frowned at the brown mug, then took a long drink of her coffee.

"You made breakfast?" One delicate blond brow rose as she retrieved her coffee. He nodded, grabbing his shirt off a post to mop his damp brow.

"Don't look so surprised," he chastised with a smile, dropping his shirt to the dry ground. "I've been known to scramble a mean egg." He tried not to stare at her, but she smelled fresh and clean; with her hair a sleepy, tousled mess, she looked sexier than hell. He desperately wanted to kiss her but resisted, knowing Joey was watching his every move. Instead, he gently chucked her under the chin, but it didn't do much to appease the growing need inside.

"On your way, woman, we've got work to do." If she kept standing here, in his line of vision, he wasn't going to get any work done. As it was, she'd haunted his dreams, making for a lousy night's sleep, knowing she was just a few feet away. If Joey hadn't been in the house, he knew there was no way he would have been able to keep himself from going into her room.

"Yeah," Joey agreed, grinning. "We've got work to do."

She laughed, letting Cody drain the last of her coffee before giving her back the empty mug. "I know when I'm not wanted." Her glance took them both in. "Can I get you anything before I start the morning chores?"

"They're done, Ma."

She blinked in confusion. "What?"

Joey's grin slid wider as he glanced at Cody. "They're done. Me and Cody did all the chores before breakfast. He works real fast, and even Miss Sophie listens to him."

She didn't know which surprised her more: the fact that Cody had done all her chores, or that Miss Sophie had actually listened to him. Each was a first. And she didn't know if she should feel grateful. Or resentful. Cody had once again usurped her, taking over her responsibilities, lifting some of the burden from her shoulders.

Her gaze went from Cody to her son. "Why didn't you wake me up?" They always shared the morning chores, feeding the hens, gathering eggs, feeding and tending Miss Sophie, watering the garden. Even though her land was small, there was always work to be done.

"Cody said to let you sleep. But you missed a really good breakfast." He rubbed his stomach and rolled his eyes.

"I'm sure I did," she murmured, her glance focused on Cody. "Thank you," she whispered, letting gratitude win.

Grabbing another board from the ground, he merely shrugged away her appreciation. "You made dinner last night, I made breakfast. All works out in the end."

"Well, as long as the chores are done and you two are going to be occupied for a while, I think I'll go into town and do some marketing."

Cody's eyes darkened as he propped the board he was holding against one of the newly built walls. "Joey, why don't you run in the house and get us something cold to drink?" Eager to please, Joey took off like a shot, leaving them alone.

"Savannah." Cody placed his hands on her shoulders, and the riot of nerves his touch evoked started immediately. She tried to ignore it.

"Remember what I said last night?" he said. "About sticking close to the house?" Her stubborn little chin went up, and he recognized that look in her eyes. He shook her gently. "Listen to me. I don't want to scare you, but I also don't want you being careless."

"You are scaring me," she grumbled, tilting her chin to look at him.

"I'm sorry." Pushing a tumble of hair back off her face, he smiled gently at her. She tried not to be touched by his endearingly gentle gesture. "But I don't want you to be caught off guard. Until we have a better handle on what's going on, maybe you shouldn't be going into town by yourself."

Her spine instantly stiffened, and Cody sighed, knowing instinctively what was coming. Her chin lifted a quarter of an inch higher, and he swore under his breath.

"I don't need a guard, Cody, and I have no intention of hiding out in the house. That's the most ridiculous thing I've ever heard. I have a life to lead and a child to take care of. I have to shop and work and tutor. I simply can't lock myself in the house until this mess is settled."

He didn't tell her that's exactly what he wished she'd do. For *her* safety and *his* sanity. It made him uneasy to just let her go off into town by herself. He wanted to go with her, but knew if he even suggested it she'd resent it and probably give him an earful.

"I know." The look in her eyes told him he was wasting his breath. "All right, go, but be careful." He dragged a hand through his hair. "And stop by the sheriff's office to let him know you're in town."

Her eyes narrowed suspiciously. "Why?"

Cody shrugged, trying not to be amused by the indignant look in her eye. "Just to be neighborly."

"I don't think so, Cody." She studied him for a moment. "I've been in town hundreds of times and never stopped in to see Judd." Her mind raced, and she looked at him steadily, recognition straightening her spine again. "What you want me to do is *check in* with the sheriff, isn't that right?" She tried to keep the resentment out of her voice. She was not accustomed to taking orders. Giving them was more her style.

"Now, don't go getting yourself in an uproar," Cody cautioned with a smile.

Savannah's eyes glittered with a mixture of frustration and fury. She resented the fact that he thought she couldn't take care of herself. Tilting her head, she met his gaze, her eyes unwavering. "Do I look like Heidi the little goat girl to you?"

Cody was caught off guard for a moment, then he threw back his head and laughed, making her smile in spite of herself.

"Well, do I?" she asked, planting slender hands on her hips.

"No," he admitted. "You don't look like Heidi the little goat girl." He reached out and tugged on a wayward strand of her hair. "Heidi had braids, as I recall. And she had goats. Lots and lots of goats." Amused, he glanced around. "No goats around here, far as I can tell."

"Exactly. So stop treating me like I'm some addle-brained female who doesn't have enough sense to take care of herself."

"I never said I didn't think you could take care of yourself." His words were measured, his tone cool.

"You didn't have to say it," she countered, her voice heated. "You implied it. I've been taking care of myself by myself for a long, long time, Cody, *without* anyone's help."

"Then maybe it's time to let someone else take care of you for a change. It's not a crime, you know. Everyone needs someone to lean on once in a while."

She opened her mouth to say something, some snappy little retort, no doubt, but he didn't give her a chance. Giving in to the need that had surfaced the moment he'd laid eyes on her, his mouth swooped down and covered hers, smothering any word, any thought.

Standing with the heat of the blazing sun beating down on her, Savannah didn't think—she just reacted. Instinctively. Honestly. Her hands came up to clutch his bare shoulders, and she went up on tiptoe to cling to him. His hands ran the length of her back. Strong hands. Gentle hands. She had never imagined a man's mere touch would set her skin on fire or set her heart to racing. His did.

As she strained against him, her breasts were crushed against his bare chest and she moaned softly when she felt the sleek softness of his tongue tangle with hers. Her hands slid to the back of his neck, warm and heated by the sun, savoring the feel of him. Her lips clung to his, her tongue as searching and playful as his.

The sound of running footsteps had Cody swearing softly under his breath. The words were muffled against her mouth as he slowly withdrew and set her away from him.

Savannah touched her mouth, still amazed at the impact the man's kiss had on her. He'd taken her by surprise this time; she'd been totally unprepared. Getting kissed senseless first thing in the morning wasn't usually on her agenda, and it left her mind just a little scattered. Her pulse was still beating erratically, and her palms were damp, her legs shaky.

Cody watched her. Her eyes reflected everything. He could see the smoldering passion that had been banked and buried for too long, could see the wild wanting and need his kiss had brought on. But he saw something else, as well: wariness. What had brought that on he wasn't sure. But he suddenly wanted to know everything—every single thing about her, but especially why she wore her wariness like a cloak.

"I brought us some colas," Joey announced, skidding to a halt between his mother and Cody. His head swiveled from one adult to the other. His mother had a funny look on her face. Uh-oh. "What's wrong?" he asked with a frown.

Savannah forced a smile through lips that felt bruised from Cody's. "Nothing, Joey." Her glance shifted to Cody. "Cody and I were just discussing the lumber. Weren't we?" She waited for his nod. "Now, where did you say you got it?"

"Fred."

"Fred," she repeated as if the one word explained everything. She tried not to be exasperated. "Fred who?" she asked with deliberate patience.

Cody took the cola from Joey, popped the top and took a long pull before answering. "Fred as in Fred's hardware and lumber. Last night on my way back from Louie's, I stopped at Fred's house, told him what I wanted and he said he'd have it delivered first thing this morning." He grinned, taking another pull on his soda. "And he did. That's one of the advantages of living in a small town and knowing everyone."

Savannah frowned. "I've lived here over six years and I never even knew Silver Creek had a hardware or lumber store, let alone an owner named Fred."

Cody laughed. "No need for you to, I guess. I assume my father handled all maintenance and repairs?"

She nodded. Good thing, too, because if she'd had to, nothing would be working properly. Mechanics and woodworking were not her forte.

"How did you pay...Fred?"

Cody drained the last of his cola in a long swallow, crushing the can in one hand as he shrugged. "Same way I pay everyone else."

"Which is?"

"Put it on the Kincaid account."

She stared at him in disbelief. Aware that Joey's head was swiveling between them, she banked her temper and decided to measure her words.

Doing her chores and pitching in to give her a hand was one thing. Paying for her goods was a different matter entirely. One she was not particularly crazy about. She may not have much money, but she had pride, and she wasn't about to start mooching off of him or anyone else. She never wanted to feel indebted to anyone.

"Do you mean to tell me you paid for *my* lumber for *my* henhouse on *your* account?" There was just a hint of temper in her words that Cody immediately responded to.

"It's *my* land," he stressed with a bit more emphasis than necessary. "And unless you plan on knocking the henhouse down and taking the lumber with you when you move, I believe it will remain on my land long after you're gone, which makes it *my* henhouse and *my* responsibility. Now, doesn't it?" He had her there. He could see the defiance slowly ebb from her eyes. "So, if there's nothing else, we'd like to get back to work."

Patting Joey on the shoulder to get him moving, Cody signaled to the box of nails sitting on the ground. "Remember, son, we need the long ones." He glanced over his shoulder at Savannah, who was just standing there watching them. Probably fuming, he decided, amused in spite of himself. She started to walk away, but he called to her, bringing her to an abrupt halt.

"Hey, *Heidi*, throw this out for me, will you?" He tossed her the crushed cola can, his eyes dancing in mischief. "And don't forget what I said about stopping to say hello to the sheriff." She started to say something, to protest, no doubt, but the look on his face stopped her. "Please? Just do it." He glanced at her son as if to say, *Do it for his sake.*

"All right, all right," she grumbled, turning her back to him. Head held high, she marched back around to the front of the house muttering under her breath about pushy men.

Grinning, Cody shook his head as he went back to work. They'd just nailed up another board, when a sudden, eerie feeling swept over him. His head came up and his eyes narrowed the way an animal's might when he sensed danger. Shading his eyes from the sun, Cody slowly, carefully scanned the horizon. There was nothing but land. Not even a bird flew overhead. But *something* had caused the hair on the back of his head to stand on end. As a ranger, he had relied on his gut instincts more times than not; they'd never been wrong before. And right now his instincts were telling him *something* was wrong. He scanned the landscape again.

"Sumthin' wrong?" Joey was standing right next to him, his face a mixture of curiosity and sweat.

Cody forced a smile. The last thing he wanted to do was alarm the boy. "Nope. Not a thing, partner." He glanced around quickly again. "It's getting hot out here. I think maybe it's time to take a break." He swiped his hand across his forehead, checking out the horizon again. The eerie feeling was getting stronger. If something was about to go down, he wanted Joey out of here and safely tucked in the house. He hoped Savannah hadn't left for town yet. She could go later. Right now he wanted her safe in her house, too.

"Okay," Joey said dejectedly. "But I can still help, can't I?"

"Absolutely," Cody assured him, patting his slender shoulder. "Why don't you run along inside? I'll just clean up a bit."

He waited until Joey rounded the corner of the house before breathing a sigh of relief. He'd deliberately set out to work outdoors this morning; he wanted to let whoever was interested know that he was here, staying on Kincaid land.

He and Judd agreed they had very little to go on, and until whoever was responsible for the fires made another move, they'd just have to bide their time. But that didn't mean he couldn't antagonize them, which was exactly what this little morning exercise in the sun was.

He just hadn't planned on having Joey help him, but the kid looked so hopeful, so expectant, he hadn't had the heart to turn him down. As he gathered up his tools, every nerve in his body was screaming in alarm, making him sorry he'd left his gun in the car. With one final look at the surrounding empty landscape, Cody headed toward the house, hoping whoever it was, was about to make a move.

Because he was more than ready, and waiting.

Cody Kincaid sure worked fast. Hadn't been home forty-eight hours, and he'd already hooked up with the pretty widow woman. But then again, Cody had always had a way with the ladies, ever since he was young.

Too bad the pretty widow didn't have such good taste. Thought she was too high and mighty for folks in town. She was always walking around with her nose in the air. She didn't even bother speaking to anyone. But he knew what she was. He saw her this morning, parading around in those skimpy clothes that showed everything. It was a disgrace. He saw, too, the way she was kissing Cody, pressing herself against him like an animal in heat right out in the open where anyone could see.

The bitch.

Had she no shame?

She could have had any man in town. Any one of them. Even him. But she thought she was too good for him. She had to go and pick Cody to warm her bed.

Everything would have been fine if Cody hadn't come home. He'd gone and ruined everything. Cody had been away so long, he hadn't figured on him returning. He thought for sure that with no one to claim the Kincaid land, it would go up for auction, and then finally it would belong to its rightful owner. The one man who needed and deserved it.

But Cody Kincaid had spoiled everything. Again.

A grim smile curved his mouth. Maybe it was time someone taught them both a lesson.

He'd just have to take care of him. And the pretty widow.

And he was just the one to do it.

The Silver Creek County Sheriff's Office was situated in the large, two-story, brick municipal building on Main Street right in the heart of town. Sheriff Judd Powers's squad car, a four-wheel-drive Jeep, was parked out front. Savannah waved as she passed, but didn't bother to stop; she still had lunch to make, dinner to start and groceries to unload. Besides, she'd be home safe and sound in less than fifteen minutes.

Her marketing had taken longer than she'd anticipated because it seemed as if everyone in town had picked this particular morning to speak to her. News about the fire in the henhouse seemed to have spread overnight. If she didn't know better, she would have sworn Cody had sent out some kind of SOS for the whole town to keep an eye on her. A small smile touched her lips. She hadn't realized how friendly the folks in town were, how much they truly cared. She'd had offers to help rebuild the henhouse from the men, and offers of food and just about everything and anything else from the women.

One of Judd's deputies had even carried her groceries to the car, after offering to escort her home. She declined the offer, knowing that Cody had probably called Judd to let him know she was going to be in town. She tried not to be annoyed at his high-handedness, and reasoned he was merely trying to protect her, but still she didn't like the feeling that she needed someone to look after her.

With a tired sigh, Savannah braked for the last stoplight at the edge of town, wishing she had time for a break. But her day, as usual, was jam-packed. She had three tutoring sessions scheduled for this afternoon and one for right after dinner.

"Mrs. Duncan?"

Savannah turned to glance out her open window and almost groaned. Miss Tulip. Just what she needed today. The grande dame of the county had a reputation for being nosy, cantankerous and not above giving someone a swat with her

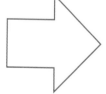

NO COST! NO OBLIGATION TO BUY!
NO PURCHASE NECESSARY!

PLAY "LUCKY 7"
AND GET FIVE FREE GIFTS!

HOW TO PLAY:

1. With a coin, carefully scratch off the silver box at the right. Then check the claim chart to see what we have for you—FREE BOOKS and a gift—ALL YOURS! ALL FREE!

2. Send back this card and you'll receive brand-new Silhouette Special Edition® novels. These books have a cover price of $3.99 each, but they are yours to keep absolutely free.

3. There's no catch. You're under no obligation to buy anything. We charge nothing—ZERO—for your first shipment. And you don't have to make any minimum number of purchases—not even one!

4. The fact is thousands of readers enjoy receiving books by mail from the Silhouette Reader Service™ months before they're available in stores. They like the convenience of home delivery and they love our discount prices!

5. We hope that after receiving your free books you'll want to remain a subscriber. But the choice is yours—to continue or cancel, anytime at all! So why not take us up on our invitation, with no risk of any kind. You'll be glad you did!

This beautiful porcelain box is topped with a lovely bouquet of porcelain flowers, perfect for holding rings, pins or other precious trinkets — and is yours absolutely free when you accept our no risk offer!

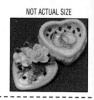
NOT ACTUAL SIZE

THE SILHOUETTE READER SERVICE™: HERE'S HOW IT WORKS

Accepting free books places you under no obligation to buy anything. You may keep the books and gift and return the shipping statement marked "cancel". If you do not cancel, about a month later we'll send you 6 additional novels, and bill you just $3.34 each plus 25¢ delivery per book and applicable sales tax, if any.* That's the complete price–and compared to cover prices of $3.99 each–quite a bargain! You may cancel at any time, but if you choose to continue, every month we'll send you 6 more books, which you may either purchase at the discount price…or return to us and cancel your subscription.

*Terms and prices subject to change without notice. Sales tax applicable in N.Y.

ever-present rubber-tipped cane if they did something to annoy her. Savannah couldn't possibly imagine what she wanted. She didn't really know the wóman and, in fact, had only met her once in all the years she'd lived in Silver Creek. But once, Savannah remembered, was enough.

Miss Tulip was standing in the middle of the street with a thin, white-gloved hand in the air to stop the already stopped traffic. Thin and frail as a dried reed, Miss Tulip was dressed in a billowing floral dress from another era. With her silver hair tucked under a matching sunbonnet that tottered precariously atop her head, and a flowered parasol to protect her from the harsh rays of the sun, Miss Tulip used her rubber-tipped cane to inch her way slowly across the street.

Not only was Miss Tulip the oldest living resident, but she was also the last member of one of the founding families, and the most respected, if not outspoken, citizen of Silver Creek. She was on every board and had her blue-veined, arthritic fingers in every bit of business that concerned the county. She kept an eagle eye on all matters from approving new teachers for the Silver Creek County Day School to the election of members to the Silver Creek Bridge and Garden Club. Because of her position, she was accorded a great deal of respect, not to mention leeway. A widow, she lived on a large, sprawling ranch right on the outskirts of town with a menagerie of pets she treated like children.

Although getting up in age—and her exact age was a closely guarded secret—she still made the rounds in town every single day.

Watching her, Savannah climbed out of the car and extended a hand to help Miss Tulip the last few feet. She received a swat in the air for her trouble. Savannah tried not to grin.

Huffing, Miss Tulip placed a white-gloved hand over her heart, ignoring the fact that the light had changed and she was now standing in the middle of the street blocking traffic.

"Mrs. Duncan." A tad deaf, if Miss Tulip had her hearing aids turned off, she had a tendency to screech at a level that was equivalent to a jet. A loud horn blared, and Miss Tulip's eyes widened in disbelief for a moment. Then her silver head whipped around, dislodging her bonnet so it sat atop her head like a crooked sail. Narrowing her gaze, she shook her cane at the honker. "Learn some manners, young man," she yelled, even though the driver had to be close to sixty. Savannah tried not to grin as Miss Tulip turned back to her, her bonnet still askew. "I understand you had a spot of trouble at your place last night?" Shrewd, assessing eyes went over Savannah's face carefully.

"Yes, Miss Tulip. The henhouse caught on fire." Why did she feel as if she were five years old and speaking to the principal?

"Your boy, is he all right?" A frown creased the older woman's delicate brows, and genuine concern lit her crystal blue eyes. Savannah was instantly touched. She didn't even know Miss Tulip was aware she had a son.

"Yes," Savannah said with a soft smile, cautiously laying a gentle hand on Miss Tulip's bony arm and hoping she wouldn't get a swat for her trouble. "My son, Joey, is fine."

"Good." Miss Tulip nodded her head. Her sunbonnet drooped forward, and she lifted a hand and shoved it back in place. "Never had a boy of my own." There was a soft sadness in her eyes. "Never was blessed with any children." She looked at Savannah carefully, her eyes full of questions. "Heard the Kincaid boy is staying at your house."

Caught off guard, Savannah tried not to smile at Miss Tulip's insinuation that Cody was a boy. And she wasn't at all certain how to answer her. Apparently everyone in town knew Cody was staying with her, and she wasn't certain how she felt about it. She had her reputation to think of, not to mention Joey's feelings. She never wanted anything to hurt Joey, and having a man living in the house with them could cause tongues to wag. Another flare of panic hit her, but she tamped it down.

Taking a deep breath, she chose her words carefully. "Cody Kincaid was at the house at the time of the fire and pulled my son out of the burning building."

Miss Tulip nodded, ignoring the snarl of traffic she was causing. "He's a good man, a bit of a rascal, but a good man nevertheless. Knew him since he was no bigger than a tadpole." She grinned suddenly, her eyes dancing wickedly. "Some folks said he was wild." She shook her head, making her bonnet bob as she rapped her cane soundly on the ground for emphasis. "Don't you believe it. Like his daddy, a finer man you'll never find." She rapped her cane on the ground again, her words gathering steam. "Honorable. That's what he is, just like his daddy was, and don't go believing all the stories you hear. Some folks ain't got nothing better to do with their time than tell tall tales."

Pursing her wrinkled lips, Miss Tulip was thoughtful for a moment. "Don't like all this nonsense that's been going on in my town. Some hellion on the loose, making trouble, scaring women and children, starting fires." She shook her head again. "It's time to put a stop to it. Don't want people afraid in their own homes, not in my town. It's not right." She looked at Savannah for a long moment. "Tell young Kincaid to come see me." Miss Tulip paused to glare at another honker before turning back to Savannah. "And tell him to be quick about it."

Savannah was trying not to grin. She could just imagine Cody's face when she passed on this little dictate. "I will, Miss Tulip."

Glancing at the backed-up traffic, Miss Tulip finally smiled. "Well, guess I've had my excitement for the day." Mischief lit her eyes as she leaned close to Savannah, shoving her bonnet back again. "Folks expect me to act a little dotty, so I always try to oblige. Keeps life a bit interesting." She patted Savannah's arm. "You take care of that boy of yours, *and* that young Kincaid." She shook her cane at Savannah. "And don't forget what I said." With that, Miss Tulip turned around and inched her way slowly back across the street, ignoring the aggravated motorists.

Still smiling, Savannah climbed back into the car, knowing within an hour everyone in town would know she and Miss Tulip had stopped traffic in order to converse in the middle of Main Street. No doubt, tongues would be wagging. For a woman who had kept to herself for the past six years, Savannah realized she'd sure made an impact this morning. Amused, she found herself still smiling as she pulled away from the light. She couldn't help but wonder what Miss Tulip wanted with Cody. She had a feeling it might be interesting to find out.

Once Savannah turned off Main Street, the secondary streets were less crowded, although a lot bumpier. Once you were out of town, the area surrounding Silver Creek was typical Texas ranching territory. Ranches were separated by acres and acres of land, so you didn't see many pedestrians or cars unless someone had a purpose. You could drive for miles without seeing another moving vehicle or a person. This particular road was winding and pretty, the rolling bluff below protected by a metal guardrail that ran along the edge of the road. In the winter, or during bad rainstorms, this stretch of road could be very treacherous. Today it was just peaceful and beautiful.

Opening her window wider, Savannah inhaled deeply of the warm spring air. Although she'd barely had any sleep last night, she suddenly felt energized. She loved spring and all that came with it. The blooming of flowers, the signal of new life. Not a spring went by that she didn't wish she could have another child. She'd never intended to have an only child. Growing up, she'd always thought she'd have a brood. At least four, maybe even five. One was not something she ever considered simply because she felt that for all the advantages an only child had, there were far more disadvantages, not the least of which was loneliness.

Lost in her thoughts, she was startled by the loud popping sound. It sounded like a firecracker going off, or someone's car backfiring. Her car suddenly veered to the left, almost crashing into the guardrail, and Savannah's hands tightened on the wheel. Terrified, she slammed on the brakes, but that only seemed to make the car careen more out of control.

Swearing under her breath, she wrestled with the steering wheel, using all her strength in order to keep the car on the road. As she swerved madly, her heart was beating in double time and her hands were shaking. She pumped the brakes, but every time she did, it seemed as if she lost the power to steer. When the front end hit the metal guardrail, she felt the car crumple as metal tested metal. The jolt was violent and abrupt, vibrating all through her, knocking her head back and wrenching her neck. Thank God she had her seat belt on.

Frantic and a bit dazed, Savannah uttered a single prayer, and holding her breath, yanked hard on the steering wheel with all her strength. She could hear the gravel crunching under her tires and metal scraping against metal as the car skidded along the guardrail. If the car broke through the rail, she knew she and the vehicle would go sailing downward over the bluff, and she most assuredly would be killed.

Fear nearly paralyzed her, but she didn't have time to think, only to react. With her foot still pumping the brakes, and a silent prayer on her lips, she yanked the steering wheel hard to the right. The seconds seemed like an eternity as Savannah concentrated. Holding her breath, she somehow managed to steer the car, by strength, force and sheer will back onto the paved road, then quickly slammed on her brakes and threw the car into Park. The car came to an abrupt, shuddering stop.

She was shaking badly, her pulse skittering and her heart hammering, and the hot sting of tears filled her eyes. Savannah laid her forehead on the steering wheel and let the tears come, too frightened to stop them. She gave in to the sobs until the trembling slowed and the fear subsided a bit.

Sniffling, she dabbed at her eyes, then touched her forehead, wincing. She must have hit her head on the steering wheel. Her fingers had blood on them. Trembling or not, she couldn't sit here crying all afternoon.

Still sniffling, she got out to check the damage. The first thing she saw was her tire. The left front tire on the driver's side was completely flat. She must have had a blowout, although she couldn't understand why; she'd just put new tires on the car less than a year ago. The damage to the front end and driver's side was fairly extensive. No wonder her head was bleeding and her neck was throbbing.

Gathering her purse and keys, Savannah locked the car, trying hard not to cry. Sniffling, she started walking down the long, winding road toward town, cursing the thin-soled, strappy sandals she wore.

Chapter Six

Leaning back in his chair, his booted feet propped atop his desk, Sheriff Judd Powers sipped his coffee and listened carefully to Savannah. One of his deputies had found her bleeding and a bit dazed, and madder than a wet hen, as she limped into town, one shoe on, one shoe off, muttering about flat tires and spoiled groceries.

He'd called Cody the moment his deputy had radioed in. Glancing at his watch now, Judd figured the door to his office should probably be flying open and off its hinges in about three to four minutes.

With a sigh, Judd set his coffee mug on the desk and sat forward. His eyes were calm, his smile gentle as they met hers. "Savannah, let's go over this one more time."

"Judd, are you getting old or senile?" Savannah scooted forward in the chair and looked at him carefully. "Or are you just going deaf?" She was feeling surly and unsettled, and wanted nothing more than to go home and take a long, hot bath and forget the whole miserable afternoon. Her hands were still shaking, and her heart hadn't quite settled down to its normal rhythm. The bump on her forehead had caused a giant headache, and her neck felt as if it had been wrung several times.

At her words, Judd couldn't suppress his smile of amusement. Her eyes were flashing fire, and her chin was tilted up in a habit he remembered women had when they got their dander up about something. He was glad to see Savannah was back to her old feisty self.

When he'd first laid eyes on her, it had set his nerves on edge. She'd been pale as a snowstorm, her eyes huge. The only spot of color was a smattering of blood on her forehead. The first thing he'd done was assess her injuries—in spite of her objections. He didn't think the bump on her head was serious, but he'd left a message for the doc to stop by her house later, just to be on the safe side.

"Just one more time, Savannah. Sometimes in the retelling you remember something. Even something minor could be important."

Banking down her impatience, Savannah carefully refolded the damp towel Judd had given to her to stem the bleeding, then pressed the cool cloth to her forehead again. "Judd, I had a blowout. There's nothing much to tell, and I've repeated this about ten times already." Why he was making such a big deal about this and wasting their time was beyond her comprehension.

Nodding his head patiently, Judd smiled. He was stalling for time, waiting for Cody to arrive. He'd offered to drive her back to the ranch himself, but Cody had insisted on coming to get her. It was just as well. He had a stack of faxes for Cody that had arrived this morning from Austin. Mighty interesting information in them, information he knew Cody would be anxious for.

"I know, Savannah, but just once more, please?" Leaning back, Judd reached for his cup and sipped his coffee. "Maybe there's something you've forgotten or missed. After your conversation with Miss Tulip, in the middle of Main Street," he added in amusement, remembering the number of irate calls he'd had about that little fiasco. "You took

Main Street straight out of town, then turned onto Prairie, right?''

"Right."

"Did you see anyone?"

"No."

"Talk to anyone?"

"Just myself," she grumbled.

"What happened next?"

"I told you, Judd, the car started acting funny."

He frowned slightly. "Funny how?"

Savannah sighed. Maybe he *was* getting senile. She'd just told him all of this about ten times. "Funny in that something happened to the steering wheel. I couldn't seem to control it."

"Anything happen before that?"

Savannah was thoughtful for a moment. Suddenly she brightened. "Wait a minute, Judd. I just remembered something. Right before that, I heard a loud popping noise."

Sitting forward abruptly, he began jotting down notes on a yellow legal pad. "What kind of a popping noise?"

"Like a car backfiring. Or a firecracker."

His brows drew together. "And you're sure this happened *before* you had problems with the steering."

"I'm positive. In fact, almost as soon as I heard the noise, the steering problem began."

He nodded, saying nothing. "Anything else? Did you see anyone? Another car maybe? Maybe a rider on a horse?"

Shoving her hair off her face, she shook her head. "Nothing. There wasn't a car or anyone else around for miles." She flexed her ankle and grimaced at her ruined sandals. "I know—I walked nearly all the way back to town."

"Anyone know you were going into town this morning?"

"Just Cody and Joey."

"Do you normally do your grocery shopping on Friday mornings?" If she was a creature of habit, it wouldn't be hard to make her a target.

Savannah frowned, getting a bit worried and suspicious. "No, Judd. I shop when I need to."

"Never the same day or time?"

She sighed in exasperation. "Judd, I think you're making—"

The door to Judd's office burst open with such force Savannah jumped, scared it was going to come off its hinges. The cool cloth slid from her nerveless fingers.

Cody stood in the doorway, his eyes dark, his stance dangerous. His frantic, frightened gaze took her in. The sight of blood on her pale skin set his own to boiling.

"Jesus." His voice was dark with anger and fear. From the moment Judd had called, Cody couldn't think of anything but her. He'd burned rubber all the way from the ranch into town, and had hopped out of the Jeep even before the engine had been killed.

He was at her side in two long strides. He pulled her up and out of the chair. "Are you all right?" He didn't give her a chance to answer, but merely hauled her into his arms, nearly crushing her with his strength. He could feel her slender body trembling against him as she clutched the front of his shirt in her hands, clinging to him.

"Cody." His name came out half whisper, half prayer. She didn't think; she just reacted, burying her face against his chest and letting the tears come again. Soft little sobs escaped as she clung to him, wanting nothing more than to feel his strength, his calm, his warmth. She was a great deal more frightened than she'd realized, but she hadn't known it until she saw Cody.

"You're safe now," he said softly, stroking the silk of her hair. Her trembling went straight to his heart, and he protectively tightened his arms around her, cursing himself for ever letting her leave the ranch. "You're safe," he murmured.

Safe.

The word went straight to her battered heart, and she burrowed closer to him. When and how she began to equate Cody with safety she wasn't sure, but all she knew was right now, he was here, holding her. And for the first time since the moment the car had started careening out of control, she truly felt... safe.

In that moment, Savannah realized just how much she'd come to care for Cody. In just a short time, he'd become a tower of strength, someone for her to lean on, depend on. And now, she realized, she not only trusted Cody, but in spite of her resolve to remain independent, she found herself leaning on Cody and *needing* him. Worse, she felt her battered, lonely heart responding to him in a way it had never responded to a man before. At the moment, the idea of never moving out of the security and safety of Cody's arms sounded immensely appealing. But a sudden thought had her lifting her gaze to his.

"Joey...?" Her voice trailed off as he forced a grim smile.

"He's fine. I dropped him off at Louie's on my way into town. Judd's housekeeper, Mrs. Minor, is going to keep an eye on both boys until we get back."

Her eyes were clouded with worry. "You didn't tell him—"

Cody shook his head. "I told him you had a flat tire and I was going to pick you up. He didn't question it, and I didn't see any point in worrying him."

"Good." She nodded gratefully. "Joey's a champion worrier...." She touched a hand to her forehead, her thoughts trailing off. Her head was throbbing painfully.

Cody's eyes went over her. He didn't like her color. He didn't know if she was just scared or more hurt than she was letting on. Damn prideful woman. "I think we'd better get you home."

Judd cleared his throat. "I put a call in to the doc. She's out making calls, so I left a message for her to stop by Savannah's place when she's finished."

Cody nodded. "Have you got anything?" he asked. When Judd called, he knew immediately this wasn't just an accident. His gut feeling had told him there was more to this, much more.

Judd nodded. "Had Savannah's car towed over to the body shop. Frankie says he'll have something definite for us later." Judd shifted his weight, making his chair squeak. "But his first guess was that the tire had been shot out. From the way the rubber gave, he's guessing it was a high-powered rifle shot from a pretty good distance."

Cody's jaw tightened. "When will he know for sure?"

"Not until later this afternoon."

Savannah abruptly stopped crying. Anger replaced fear, and she tried to step out of Cody's arms, but he held tight. She glanced up at him. "Someone did this deliberately?" Her eyes searched his.

"Looks that way, Savannah."

"Oh, God."

He hated the look of fear that crept over her face, clouding her eyes, which filled with tears she desperately tried to hide. She was proud and stubborn, but she was also scared. And with good reason. Anyone would be scared.

"This is a nightmare." She laid her head on his chest, suddenly feeling scared and overwhelmed and more than grateful he was there. She clung tighter to him, unable to even comprehend this turn of events. Not at the moment, not when her head was throbbing and her knees were still shaking. To think someone had done this deliberately was unthinkable.

"This is getting out of hand," Cody said to Judd, who nodded in agreement.

"Have a look at these." Judd leaned forward, scrounging through a pile of papers on his desk. He extracted three and handed them to Cody, who shifted Savannah into his other arm. "These faxes came in for you from Austin early this morning. I think you'll find them interesting."

Cody's eyes scanned the papers, and his jaw tightened. "You read these?" he asked, looking at Judd.

"First thing. Checked the county records, too." Judd rocked in his chair. "It's all true. Paul Hooper's almost six months behind on his mortgage. The bank's ready to call in the papers on another loan he hasn't paid, as well." Leaning back, Judd scrubbed at his face and sighed. "He owes money to merchants all over town. Heard he's lost about half of his hands for back pay, too."

Cody frowned. "Doesn't make sense then that he'd be trying to buy my dad out. Where'd he plan on getting the money?"

Judd's smile was slow and cold. He'd never liked Paul Hooper or his son, James. They were both weird buckaroos as far as he was concerned. Hooper always operated right at the line of the law, close but not close enough for him to do anything about it. Maybe this time they'd get lucky.

"Why don't I ask him?"

Cody's jaw tightened. "I want to go with you—unofficially, of course."

Judd was thoughtful for a moment. He knew the strength and force of Cody's temper. "Think that's a good idea?" he asked mildly, letting his gaze stray to Savannah. Cody immediately understood.

"Best damn idea I've had all day," Cody growled. "This isn't business anymore, Judd, this is personal. Damn personal." His arms possessively tightened around Savannah. "Someone murdered my father and damn near killed Joey and Savannah. It's my land, and I'm responsible for them and their safety." He glanced down at Savannah, then back up at Judd. "I'm not about to sit back and let him get away with it. I want to get to the bottom of this before someone else gets hurt—or killed." His temper was simmering again, and he worked hard to keep it under control.

"I understand," Judd said carefully. "I plan on stopping by Hooper's place right after dinner. By then, Frankie should have something definite for us."

Cody nodded. "Fine. I'll be ready. We'll stop and get Joey on our way back to the ranch."

"Don't bother." Judd smiled. "Since it's Friday, why don't you just let Joey spend the weekend at my house? I

know Louie would love the company." He didn't add that
he thought it might be a good idea to have Joey tucked away
somewhere far away from the ranch. He didn't have to; the
look on Cody's face told him he understood.

Nodding, Cody glanced down at Savannah, who was still
curled in his arms. Her trembling had finally slowed, but
hadn't stopped completely. "I'm going to take her home and
put her to bed until the doc has a look at her. I don't want
to leave her alone."

Abruptly Savannah's head came up. Why were they talking about her as if she weren't there? She hadn't really been
listening to them until now. She didn't need to hear any of
the gory details of what was going on; just knowing someone had done this deliberately was more than enough.

Sniffling, Savannah thumped Cody's chest to get his attention. "Stop talking about me like I'm six. Or invisible,"
she added with a frown, feeling surly and resentful again. "I
don't need a baby-sitter in my own house and I don't need
to see a doctor. I'm fine."

"Tough," Cody said in a voice that brooked no argument. He drew back from her, his eyes glittering fiercely.
"Listen to me, you stubborn, hardheaded woman. Until we
get this settled, you're not going anywhere without me, got
it?" He stared her down, not bothering to hide his determination. On this, he wouldn't budge. Defiant blue eyes
warred with determined blue ones.

The look was so dangerous, if it would have been anyone
else, it would have sent her running in the opposite direction as fast and as far as her little legs could carry her. But
this was Cody, and she could never be afraid of him.

"Got it," she mumbled, reluctantly accepting that he was
probably right. There was a difference between being proud
and being stupid. If she'd had Joey in the car this afternoon... Her eyes slid closed. She couldn't even bear to think
of it, grateful Joey would be safe at Judd's this weekend and
away from harm. It would give her one less thing to worry
about.

Cody's fingertip gently touched her forehead. He was relieved to see the bleeding had finally stopped. She tried not to wince. "And as for the doc, you've got a royal-size goose egg on your forehead. I want the doc to check it out."

"I was jostled about when the car hit the guardrail. I must have banged my head on the steering wheel. It's nothing," she lied, absently rubbing the back of her neck. Every muscle and every bone was screaming in protest right now.

"We're going home." Swearing under his breath, Cody clasped her hand in his and started dragging her toward the door before she had a chance to protest.

"Wait." Savannah dug her heels in, pulling Cody to a stop as he tried to drag her through the doorway. "What about my groceries? They'll spoil in this heat."

"Groceries?" Shaking his head, Cody sighed in disbelief. For the first time since Judd's call, his heart had finally settled down in his chest. He'd never been so scared in his life, and he wasn't a man who got scared. Ever. By anything. "You were almost killed, and all you're worried about are your groceries?"

Her chin went up defiantly, and he knew there was no use arguing with her. "I just spent two hundred bucks on food and I'm not about to just throw it away."

Tightening his hand on hers, Cody sighed. "All right. All right. We'll stop at Frankie's and get your groceries out of the car. But then you're going straight home." He wasn't about to let her become a target again, not while he was around. If they wanted her, they'd have to go through him, and he intended to make it a very painful journey. It would give him a chance to have a look at her car for himself.

Her hands were still trembling as she gave him a shaky salute. "Yes, sir."

He grinned simply because the docile role did not suit her. Spitting and fighting seemed more her style. "Now, that's more like it, Savannah. See how easy life would be if you just followed orders?"

"Followed orders?" she repeated suspiciously. "Followed orders!"

He grinned, deliberately baiting her, grateful she was back to her usual stubborn, feisty self. It gave him hope that she was going to be fine.

"Yeah, Savannah, I expect you to follow my orders."

"In your dreams, Kincaid." She whacked him with her free hand. "And *only* in your dreams."

Judd's amused laughter followed them out the door.

Joey's brows were scrunched together as he stared at Louie. They were sitting Indian style on the bottom bunk bed in Louie's bedroom with a bowl of potato chips separating them, and a whole lot of mischief between them. "Are you sure this plan is gonna work?"

"Joey, Joey, Joey, you're worrying again." Louie grabbed Joey's shoulders and shook him, almost toppling him from the bed. "Absolutely positively this is going to work," Louie said with a confident grin, spreading his arms akimbo. "Would Louie the Magnificent ever let you down?"

Joey tried not to frown. "No, but—"

Louie rolled his eyes. "Didn't my plan work about getting Cody to come live with you so you wouldn't have to move?" Louie chomped noisily on a chip he'd stuffed into his mouth.

"Yeah," Joey said hesitantly, watching as Louie hung over the side of the bed to snatch his can of soda off the floor. "But this is different, Louie. Cody said he wasn't married because he'd never found the right woman."

"So it's simple, then. All we gotta do is convince Cody your ma is the right woman." Louie shrugged, then tipped his soda back and drank greedily. A dribble of grape soda slid down his chin, and he swiped at it with the back of his hand. "Once we do that, then they'll get married and Cody will be your new dad and never leave." Louie grinned. "See? Simple."

Joey was still frowning. "Yeah, but how we gonna convince Cody my ma's the right woman?"

Louie scratched his head, thinking. Suddenly he brightened. "I know. We'll do what my dad does when he goes to buy a horse. He's always yapping about how it's important to get the right horse. He makes lists of stuff that the horse's gotta have. He says when he finds one that's got everything on the list, he's found the right horse."

"Yeah, but Louie, my ma's not exactly a...horse," Joey declared, just in case Louie had forgotten.

"Horse. Wife." Louie shrugged. "Same difference." Grinning, he bounded off the bed. "The first thing we gotta do is make a list of all the good stuff about your ma. Then we just have to tell Cody, and he'll know she's the right woman." Louie grinned. "Works for me."

Scrounging through the pile of school papers, books and homework on top of his desk, Louie dug out a sheet of paper and held it in the air. "There. Now all we need is a pencil." Frowning, he kept scrounging until he found a stub of a pencil. He grabbed a book to write on, then climbed back on the bed, smoothing the crumpled sheet of paper out. "Now we gotta make a list of the good stuff about your ma."

"Like what?"

"I don't know," Louie admitted with a frown. "The first thing my dad looks for in the right horse is good teeth."

"Teeth?" Joey was frowning again. "Why?"

Louie shrugged. "Don't know. Guess it's important. If it's important for the right horse, it's probably important for the right wife. Does your ma got good teeth?"

Joey was thoughtful for a moment, then shrugged helplessly. "I don't know." He'd never really looked at her teeth. "She's always yelling at me about not chewing gum 'cause it will ruin mine." He grinned, rubbing his itchy nose. "She says if I don't take care of my teeth, I'll lose 'em." Joey absently ran a finger over the top row of his teeth just to be sure they were still there.

"I know." Louie frowned. "My grandma's teeth come out. She leaves them in a glass at night. It's neat. Sometimes I like to just stare at them or hide them. Does your ma's teeth come out?''

Joey frowned thoughtfully. "I don't think so."

"Too bad. I'll bet Cody would've liked that."

Joey inched up on his knees, trying to see what Louie was writing.

"Good teeth and they don't come out." Satisfied, Louie put it at the top of his list.

"What else?" Joey asked, warming to the idea.

Louie scratched his head again. "My dad's always checking out the hooves and shoes to see if they need to be replaced."

"Louie, my ma doesn't got any hooves."

"No, but she's got shoes, doesn't she?"

"Yeah," Joey said suspiciously.

"So?" Louie waited expectantly.

"So...what?"

Louie heaved an exasperated sigh. "Well, are her shoes good or what?"

"Can shoes be bad?" Joey asked in confusion. This was harder than he thought.

"Guess so." Louie chewed on the end of the pencil. "Do you think your ma's shoes need to be replaced?"

"I dunno."

"Let's just say no. My dad says replacing shoes can be expensive, and I don't think we want Cody to think your ma's expensive." He added good shoes to the list. "Now, what about legs? My dad says you always gotta get a horse with strong legs so they can run fast."

"Uh-oh." Joey looked crestfallen.

"What's wrong?"

"We're in trouble." Sadly Joey shook his head.

"Why?"

"My ma's legs ain't so good, Louie. She runs like a girl." A fate worse than death. Disappointed, Joey plucked at the bedspread. "And last month after the PTA meeting, I heard Mr. Marchant say my ma had skinny legs."

"Maybe we better skip that one." Frowning, Louie chewed on the end of the pencil again, thinking.

"What else?" Joey watched him carefully.

"Eyes." Louie brightened. "My dad says the right horse has clear, shiny eyes. That means it's healthy."

"Uh-oh." Joey chewed on his lower lip.

"What?"

"My ma's eyes ain't so good, either, Louie. She can't read without her glasses." A sudden thought almost had Joey panicking. "Do you think that means she's not...healthy?"

"Dunno. But, Joey, your ma's not doing so good here. We better think of some more stuff—good stuff—otherwise, Cody's never going to believe she's the right woman." He thought some more. "What about her coat?"

"What coat?" Joey's frown was threatening to become permanent.

"You know, like a horse's coat. My dad says it's gotta be nice and shiny, and you gotta brush it lots and lots."

Joey scratched his nose. "My ma doesn't got a coat, but she's got nice hair. It's real long, and she brushes it every night about a gazillion times."

"Okay. Nice hair." After jotting that down, Louie turned the paper over, then smoothed it. "Come on, we gotta think of some more stuff." He chewed the end of the pencil. "What about her hide? My dad says a horse's hide is real important."

"I don't think my ma's got a hide."

"Well, what about her skin, then? Has she got good skin?"

Joey shrugged. "Dunno. But it's real white, and she never goes in the sun 'cause she says it makes your skin all brown and wrinkly."

"Does not," Louie protested.

"Does too."

Louie bounded off the bed and checked his face out in the mirror above his dresser. "I go out in the sun all the time, and I'm not all brown and wrinkly." He touched his face just to be sure. "Maybe it's just your mom."

"Maybe," Joey admitted worriedly.

Louie hopped back onto the bed. "Okay, so what do we say about her hide—skin?"

Joey thought for a moment. "That's it's not all brown and wrinkly."

"Sounds pretty good. What else? It's gotta be something good," Louie warned, looking over the list.

"Like what?" Exasperated, Joey fell back against the bed. He stared at the ceiling. There was a smashed spider right over Louie's head. He wondered who smashed it.

"Dunno. She's *your* mother." Louie poked Joey with his knee. "Come on, think, Joey. Think! You want Cody to stay and be your dad, don't ya?"

"Yeah."

"Then start thinking."

They sat in silence for a moment. Suddenly Joey brightened, bounding up to his knees. "My ma smells good except for when she's been in the barn taking care of Miss Sophie."

"All right!" Louie added it to the list. "But we'd better not mention sometimes she smells like Miss Sophie."

Watching Louie write, Joey chewed his lip, thinking. "She doesn't eat a lot."

"Miss Sophie?"

"No, Louie, my ma!" It was Joey's turn to poke Louie.

"What else?" Louie was frowning. "You know, my dad was talking to Uncle Jack one day, and they said that real good horses had tattoos in their mouths and good chests so they get plenty of wind. Does your ma maybe got a tattoo in her mouth?"

"Nah, she doesn't got one."

"Maybe she could get one?" Louie asked hopefully.

Joey shrugged. "I could ask. But she doesn't like needles. They make her faint."

"Well, we ain't putting that on the list," Louie said with a weary shake of his head. "What about her chest?"

"Her chest?" Joey flopped back on the bed again, thinking.

"Yeah, does she get good wind?"

"Louie, I don't even know what that means."

"Joey," Louie wailed. "Come on, come on, I came up with the plan, the least you could do is think up the good stuff."

"All right, all right," Joey grumbled, thinking real hard. He didn't want to tell Louie his ma hugged real good, 'cause he figured he was probably too old to be getting hugs, so he just kept quiet. Besides, Cody was a lot older than him, and hugging probably wasn't important to him anyway.

"She's not scared of thunder."

"That's good," Louie said with a grin.

On a roll, Joey's mind whirled. "She's a good teacher and she knows just about everything."

"So does my dad," Louie said, adding it to the list. "How do you figure they know so much?"

"Dunno. Maybe it's 'cause they're so old."

"You think so?" Louie crossed his eyes and looked at Joey. There were two of him.

Joey shrugged. "I'm not sure. But I'll bet we could ask Cody. He says mothers are all alike, so he should know."

Uncrossing his eyes, Louie scribbled a note on the bottom of the page to remind Joey to ask Cody about it. "Can you think of anything else? There must be something else good about your ma."

"What have we got so far?"

Louie flipped the paper over. "Let's see. She's got good teeth and they don't come out at night, probably 'cause she doesn't chew gum. Good shoes that don't need to be replaced. She runs like a girl 'cause she's got skinny legs. Her eyes ain't so good, but she doesn't got any knots in her hair, and her skin's not brown and wrinkly. Sometimes she smells good, better than Miss Sophie, and she's not scared of thunder and she doesn't eat a lot. She's a good teacher and knows just about everything 'cause she's real old."

"Sounds pretty good, huh?" Joey asked hopefully, and Louie nodded slowly.

"Think so. Now all you gotta do is tell Cody all this good stuff, and then bingo—he'll know she's the right woman. Then he'll marry her and stay and be your dad forever." A huge grin split Louie's face. "Works for me." He folded up the paper and handed it to Joey. "I told you I had a plan."

Joey took the paper and tucked it in his jeans pocket, hoping Louie's plan was going to work. "Uh, Louie, I just thought of something."

"Are you worrying again?" Louie asked suspiciously.

"No, but—"

"But what?" Louie asked in exasperation.

"What if my ma finds out what we're doing?"

"How's she gonna find out?"

Not having a mother, Louie didn't understand that mothers *always* knew everything.

He shook his head firmly. "Nah, she'll never know a thing." He grabbed Joey's shoulders and shook him. "Would I lie to you? Trust me, Joey. Have I ever let you down? Your ma will *never* know. I'm Louie the Magnificent, remember?" A mischievous grin split Louie's face. "The Plan Man."

Chapter Seven

"Cody, you're being ridiculous."

"I've been called worse things."

"I'm perfectly capable of taking a shower by myself."

"Not with a nasty gash on your head, you're not. What if you got dizzy?"

"There's nothing wrong with my mouth. I could call you."

"What if you fainted?"

"I've never fainted in my life."

"There's a first time for everything."

"You're making too much of this. You wouldn't even let me carry in a bag of groceries. I'm not made of glass, you know."

"Good thing, too. After that accident you had, you would have been busted up into little pieces. Think of all the time and glue it would have taken to put you back together again." Even though he was joking, the thought had his gut unexpectedly tightening.

"First you treat me like Heidi the little goat girl. Now you're treating me like Humpty Dumpty. What's next?" she wondered aloud. "Little Red Riding Hood?"

Leaning against the open bathroom door that connected to her bedroom, Cody crossed his arms across his chest and chuckled. "Only if I get to play the wolf."

"Just what I need in my life—another wolf," she grumbled from behind the glass shower door. The glass was frosted, and she could barely see his outline through the fog of steam, which meant he could barely see hers—she hoped. The man made her nervous enough as it was—with her clothes on—but standing under a steaming stream of hot water, naked as a newborn babe and knowing he was just inches away on the other side of the glass, hadn't exactly done anything to calm her jagged nerves. "Cody—"

"Are you going to shower or argue?" he challenged, not giving her a chance to answer. "You might as well give it up, Savannah. You're wasting your breath. I'm not budging on this point," he insisted firmly, shifting his weight. "Until the doc gets here and checks you out, no showers or anything else by yourself. So just stop grumbling."

She'd given him enough of a scare for one day. His heart had finally settled back down to a normal rhythm. It had stunned him to realize all the emotions that had swept through him from the moment of Judd's call until the moment he laid eyes on her and held her in his arms, assuring himself she really was safe.

Sighing, Cody shifted his weight and glanced at the shower stall. All Savannah had wanted to do when she got home was take a hot shower to ease some of her aches and pains. He hadn't objected, but he wasn't about to let her do it alone. She was still far too shaky and pale, and he wasn't sure just how serious her head injury was. So just to be on the safe side, he insisted—no, demanded—she leave the bathroom door open so he could hear her if she got into trouble. He grinned suddenly.

He'd volunteered to go right into the shower with her, but she hadn't exactly been crazy about that idea. In fact, his ears were still burning a bit from her rather low opinion of that idea. He couldn't help the smile that slid over his features. Obviously the bump on her head hadn't dampened her streak of stubbornness.

Now, as he leaned against the doorjamb, heat and steam filled the room, almost obscuring her outline completely. But he knew she was in there. The scent of her perfumed soap filled the air and swirled around him, intoxicating him, ensnaring him.

His eyes slid closed, and he inhaled deeply of the sweet, sensuous scent, trying to fight off the burning ache of desire that had suddenly leapt to life. It had been like this since the moment he'd laid eyes on her, and the ache had only intensified with each passing moment.

Desire was nothing new to him. He'd desired many women over the years. Since the age of sixteen, he'd never had any trouble satisfying those desires. But that was all it ever was—a physical need mutually satisfied. He willingly shared his body, but that was all he had ever shared, had ever wanted to share. Occasionally a woman posed a challenge, and that tended to keep things interesting, but no one had ever touched anything more than his body. He wouldn't—couldn't—allow it. He'd learned early in life what happened when you let a woman crawl under your skin and burrow her way into your heart.

He was never going to let another woman get to him emotionally. He'd allowed it once, and was left at the altar like a chump, with his insides torn up and into pieces. He'd *never* allow another woman the power to do that to him again.

In spite of his resolve, it didn't stop the ache that rushed through him now, reminding him how powerful desire could be, how easy it was to blind a man. For the first time in a long time he realized that *this* ache, *this* desire, could only be satisfied by *one* woman. One very specific woman.

Savannah.

It had been a long time since that had happened to him. Years. And it scared the living hell out of him.

In spite of himself, his eyes slid closed and he inhaled
deeply, letting her fragrance entice him. He knew he would
always remember that scent, like a haunting memory at the
corners of his mind. He would never again smell it without
thinking of her. He wanted to drown himself in it, to bury
himself deep inside of her until nothing but her filled his
starved senses. He wanted to assuage the need and desire
that was tearing through him, making his body harden and
his blood run thick and slow.

Still grumbling, Savannah snapped off the water, and the
sound had Cody straightening, cursing himself softly under his breath. He saw one slender hand reach for the fluffy
terry-cloth towels she'd draped over the top of the shower
door.

With her muscles finally beginning to relax from the heat
of the water, Savannah breathed a weary sigh as she lifted a
hand to nurse her sore neck before wrapping one towel
around her wet, tangled hair, and the other around her
damp body.

She slid the door open and found Cody's gaze on her. She
froze for a moment at the look in his eyes. The intensity of
his gaze made her pulse jump. She'd never taken a shower
with a man in the room with her. It seemed incredibly intimate and made her unbearably taut nerves tighten further
in alarm. Even though she'd had a child, in some ways she
was still naive, still innocent. She'd only known one man
intimately, and that was so long ago as to practically be
forgotten.

Cody was looking at her now the same way he had looked
at her last night the moment before his mouth had covered
hers. The towel covered her from breast to thigh, but she
suddenly felt naked and exposed and very, very vulnerable.
A tremble slid over her tender skin.

Mesmerized, Cody watched as a rivulet of water slid with
agonizing slowness down her neck, inching a sensuous path
along her collarbone to disappear quietly in the soft cleft
between her breasts. He swallowed hard, his throat suddenly bone dry. He ached to trace his tongue along the same

path, to taste that creamy, satin skin, to let his tongue nuzzle aside the towel to taste and savor the soft, feminine breasts beneath. He longed to bring her to heat, to taste her honey.

With her eyes still on his, Savannah started to step from the tub, but he extended his hand. She stared at his hand uncertainly, breathing deeply, making the towel expand dangerously, not certain she trusted herself to touch him right now. She was feeling much too vulnerable. Too needy. In spite of her protests that she was fine, she'd been more shaken today than she wanted to let on.

Standing stock-still, she continued to stare at his hand uncertainly. "Cody—"

"Take my hand." The words came out a husky whisper.

Heaving an exasperated sigh, Savannah hesitantly took his hand, and Cody felt the jolt of her touch like an electric current all through him. Her hand was small, delicate and very, very soft. He wondered if the rest of her was as soft.

Holding his hand, Savannah stepped out of the shower, bringing her scent with her. It wrapped around him, beckoning him closer. She tugged to free her hand, but he didn't release her until both small, bare feet were planted safely on the mat on the floor.

"Cody, this is ridiculous," she protested, totally unnerved. "I'm fine...really," she stammered, looking everywhere but at him. Finally she turned to him. She knew immediately it was a mistake. The room was too small; he was too close. The way he was looking at her made her feel as if the towel had melted away. Her skin warmed, and her face flushed. She lifted a hand to check the tuck of the towel, and his hand covered hers. Her eyes flew to his.

The wariness came so quickly, it stunned him. He ached to touch her, to pull her into his arms and assuage the need and desire tearing through him, but that wariness stopped him. Was it just him she was wary of?

Or all men?

Women who were used to the company of males usually weren't wary around them. They didn't skitter in alarm every time a man came near them or every time a man touched them.

Unless they weren't accustomed to being touched by a man.

"Savannah."

He didn't know what to say, and thought again of how little he knew about her or her past. Joey had said his father had died before he was born. Other than that, he knew nothing about her, but suddenly realized he wanted— needed—to know everything. Surely Savannah hadn't been . . . alone all this time? She was a beautiful, desirable woman; it was hard to imagine that she'd spend all these years alone. But if she had, it might explain her wariness around him.

There were so many questions he wanted to ask, things he wanted to know, but right now none of that mattered. All that mattered was that he wanted her. Desperately. In the past, that had always been enough, more than enough, but he knew it wasn't enough, not this time. Not with her. He had nothing to offer a woman like her, nothing to give but a few pleasurable moments and perhaps a lingering memory.

Growing increasingly uncomfortable, Savannah shifted her weight nervously. She wasn't sure what to say, how to respond to that look in his eyes. All she knew was that look made her body yearn for things, things she had long ago given up hope of ever having.

Eyes wide and innocent, she just stood there . . . waiting, not knowing what else to do. His hand still covered hers, connecting them in a way she'd never felt connected to anyone. It wasn't just a physical connection, but something far more powerful and frightening. She couldn't stop looking at him, drawn to his mesmerizing gaze, which seemed to be saying more than mere words ever could.

Abruptly Cody averted his gaze and dropped his hand from hers. "Get dressed," he said curtly. He saw the hurt fill her eyes a moment before he turned and headed out the door. He felt like a heel, but knew it was for the best. For both of them. He wouldn't let a woman mean anything to him. And as much as he desired her, wanted her, he knew he couldn't indulge himself simply because the combination of emotions and desire packed a powerful punch, one he wasn't certain he could handle. So it was best to leave it alone. To leave her alone.

Savannah stood there a moment, staring after him, wondering what had happened. She had thought... she was almost certain he was going to kiss her, to touch her, to... The thought trailed off. Something had happened. She may not have had much experience with men, but she wasn't an idiot. She could tell when a man was interested in her, could tell, too, when he looked at her with desire. And Cody had been looking at her like that from the moment they'd met. So what had happened?

Confused, she shook her head, then a familiar feeling swept over her.

Rejection.

It was a feeling she'd never forgotten. It was too strong, too powerful, far too hurtful for her to forget. She didn't need to hear the words; she had seen it in Cody's eyes. It was a look a woman never forgot.

A hot rush of tears filled her eyes, and she swallowed hard, cursing herself for her stupidity. She had no idea what had just happened or why.

All she knew was that it hurt.

The Hooper ranch, like most of the ranches in Silver Creek, was set back far from the road, surrounded by acres of land. As Judd's Jeep bumped its way down the gravel road toward the house, Cody's eyes carefully scanned his surroundings. He didn't know what—if anything—he was looking for, but he was just looking.

"Does he know we're coming?" Cody asked, turning to Judd, who shook his head.

"No." Judd glanced in the rearview mirror to be sure no one was behind him. "I thought it best not to give him any warning."

Cody nodded in agreement. It was the way he would have handled it. Even though he was a ranger and technically had jurisdiction over all of Texas, he had to allow Judd a measure of respect, because he was the Sheriff. He didn't want to go stepping on the man's toes or going behind his back or over his head. Judd was more than competent and had been more than helpful, so there was no need to take over the investigation himself. Besides, he also didn't want everyone in the county knowing what he was up to, at least not until they had some more concrete answers.

"How's Savannah?"

Cody couldn't control the smile that sneaked up on him. "Fine. The doc checked her out this afternoon. Other than some pretty sore muscles, she's fine. The bump on her head looked more serious than it was. No concussion, just a whopper of a headache. The doc advised her to take it easy for a few days."

Judd laughed. "Think she'll do it?" He glanced at Cody. "She doesn't strike me as the type of woman who takes or follows orders very well."

"She doesn't have much choice," Cody countered. "I called and canceled her tutoring appointments, then did her afternoon chores. Her car's still in town at Frankie's, so she can't go anywhere, and Joey's at your house, so there wasn't much left for her to do *but* take it easy." Cody glanced out his window. "She was resting when I left."

He'd deliberately avoided her all afternoon. He needed some time to think and put things in perspective. The past few days, so much had happened he needed some time away from her to think, since he wasn't certain he could think clearly while he was with her. And right now he needed a clear head to solve this mystery. For the first time in memory, he found his judgment clouded on a professional level. He wondered if he'd been so wrapped up in Savannah and Joey that he'd missed something, something important. They were counting on him to protect them, and so far he hadn't exactly been doing a stellar job.

Her image floated through his mind. The hurt look in her eyes had haunted him all afternoon. He knew he'd put that look there, knew he'd hurt her. He thought about yesterday, the first time he'd pulled her into his arms, when he'd promised he *wouldn't* hurt her. Savannah was turning out to be a bigger complication than he'd ever anticipated. He wasn't good for her, couldn't be good for her. They were two different people from two different worlds. And he instinctively knew Savannah wasn't like the other women who had flitted in and out of his life over the years. She was different, very different. She deserved more than he could offer her, more than he was willing—or able—to give.

It had taken a supreme effort to walk away from her this morning, when all he'd wanted to do was tug her into his arms, strip off that towel and make love to her. But with Savannah, it wasn't that simple, would never be that simple. He had no right to be thinking about her, wanting her, when he had nothing to offer her, nothing to give. The place where his heart had once been was empty and desolate.

"Did you find out any more from Frankie?" Judd asked, turning back to Cody.

Cody's mouth thinned. "When we went to pick up Savannah's groceries, I had a look at the car myself. No doubt about it. Her tire was shot out. From the angle and shape of the tear, I'd say it definitely was a high-powered rifle. Looked like it had been shot from a hell of a distance." His lips thinned. "Which means that whoever it was is a hell of a shot, and that someone knew exactly where she was going to be."

Judd was frowning. "Do you think someone was following her?"

"Might be." The thought sent a chill through Cody, and he suddenly questioned whether he should have left her alone at the ranch or not. Even though Judd had posted a deputy near the house just to be on the safe side, he would have felt better had he been there himself. But it couldn't be helped. He wanted to see Paul Hooper himself. And he'd checked the house and all the buildings before he left to make sure everything was secure.

They'd only be gone a little while, he assured himself, hoping she'd be all right until then. He didn't like the idea of Savannah being all alone in the house. She may have been accustomed to taking care of herself and Joey, but that was before they'd become a target for someone. "Damn," he said again.

Judd braked to slow the Jeep. "The only connection I can see to all of this is the Kincaid land. But what Savannah and Joey have to do with it, I don't know."

Cody frowned thoughtfully. "Maybe we're missing something. Maybe the attacks on Joey and Savannah aren't related to my father's death or the land."

"But why would anyone want to target them?" Judd asked with a frown.

Cody shook his head again, unable to answer Judd.

"It just doesn't make sense, Cody."

Cody stared out the window a moment. "How much do you know about Savannah?"

Judd's smile was grim. "About the same as everyone else, I guess. She and Joey moved here about five, maybe six years ago. She keeps pretty much to herself, although she's not unfriendly or anything. From what I hear, she's a very dedicated teacher to her students and always willing to lend a hand if she's asked. She's real active in Joey's life, and I see her in church every Sunday but other than that—" Judd shrugged "—there's not much else." Judd frowned. "Why?"

"Just curious," Cody mumbled. "What about men? Has she been seeing anyone regularly?" He was asking purely for professional reasons, he assured himself, knowing it was a damn lie.

"You thinking it might be a rejected suitor or something?"

"Might be."

Laughing, Judd shook his head. "Not hardly. From what I hear, Savannah hasn't been seen in the company of a man in all the time she's lived here. She's either alone or with her son. In a town this size, gossip travels fast. I'd have heard about it from one of the townsfolk or from Louie." Judd laughed again. "Louie and Joey are as tight as twine. If Savannah had a boyfriend, trust me, I'd have probably been the first to hear about it. But the only thing I've ever heard is that she's made it pretty clear she just wants to be left alone."

Cody digested the information. Satisfied what he'd suspected about Savannah was true, his only thought was why had she deliberately chosen to remain alone?

He didn't know, but he intended to find out.

Judd braked the Jeep to a halt right in front of the Hooper house and checked his gun. "Are you armed?" he asked. "I don't know what we're gonna find when we get in there."

"I'm armed." Cody checked his own holstered gun.

"Things might get...dicey," Judd warned, and an unholy glint lit Cody's eyes.

"That's just what I was hoping for," he said, throwing open his door and climbing out. He had a gut feeling about Paul Hooper, nothing concrete, but just a feeling that somehow, some way, he was behind all of this, and if he was...

Cody let the thought trail off as he and Judd approached the house. Lights were burning brightly, and through the sheer white curtains they could see movement at the table inside.

"Probably caught them during dinner," Judd said, ringing the doorbell.

"Or caught them doing something else." Cody glanced over his shoulder, then all around him. That eerie feeling was back. The same one he'd had this morning when he'd been building the henhouse with Joey. It made his nerves sing in alarm and the hair on the back of his neck stand on end, as if someone was...watching him.

The front door to the house was slowly pulled open. Standing in his pants and undershirt, Paul Hooper squinted in the darkness. "Sheriff?" Hooper's voice was surprised, and his gaze shifted to Cody. He studied him for a moment. "Kincaid? Is that you, Cody Kincaid?"

"It's me," Cody admitted, realizing the man had aged and spread a great deal since the last time he'd seen him.

"We need to talk to you, Paul. May we come in?" Judd removed his hat. Paul Hooper looked at them for a long moment before stepping back to allow them to enter.

Standing in the foyer of the house, Cody removed his Stetson, then glanced around. He could see clear into the living room and dining room. The house had a worn, cluttered look, and the dust on the furniture was almost an inch thick. Obviously Hooper didn't employ a housekeeper any longer.

Tucking his thumbs into his frayed suspenders, Paul Hooper looked at them curiously. "What can I do for you, Sheriff?" Cautious and a bit wary, Hooper's gaze went from one man to the other.

"Paul, I'm investigating some unusual occurrences at the Kincaid ranch, and I'd like to ask you some questions." Judd fingered his Stetson, watching the man carefully.

Hooper nodded silently, never taking his eyes off the sheriff. "I don't know much about what's been going on lately, other than the big fire last week." His gaze shifted to Cody. "Sorry about your daddy, son. He was a good man."

"Paul, where were you this morning, around eleven?"

Hooper blinked several times, clearly surprised by the question. "This morning?" He shook his head, then smiled. "Sitting in the waiting room of Doc Wilson's office. Had me an appointment at ten, but the doc was called out on some emergency and I sat there waiting until well after two."

Nodding, Judd slowly digested the information. It would be easy enough to verify. He remembered being told the same thing when he'd called the doctor's office about Savannah. "Having some health problems?" he inquired casually.

"A few," Hooper said slowly.

Not wanting to pry into the man's personal health problems, Judd let it go for the moment. He'd check it out with the doc. "What about your son, James?" Judd's gaze swept past Hooper and around the house. "Is he here? I'd like to ask him a few questions."

"James?" Hooper seemed genuinely surprised. He shook his head. "Afraid that's not possible, Judd. Sent James to Austin early this morning to see about selling off some of our cattle. He won't be back until morning." He shook his head. "Times have been hard." He rubbed his grizzled chin. "This drought has taken its toll on everyone."

"Mr. Hooper," Cody finally spoke, choosing his words carefully. "I understand you spoke to my father about buying our land."

Hooper laughed, shaking his bald head. "Yeah, Cody, but that was a while back. I knew your daddy was having a hard time handling the ranch all alone, even with all the help he had."

The words went through Cody like a knife. If circumstances had been different, he would have been—should have been—home helping his father out.

"I thought he might be interested in selling," Hooper explained.

"And was he?" Cody asked carefully, knowing the answer before he even asked the question.

Hooper laughed again. "No, son, can't say that he was." His smile seemed genuine and he shrugged. "But I figure it sure didn't hurt to ask. Kincaid land's mighty valuable 'round here. Only land with a natural water supply. Without Silver Creek, your daddy would have been in the same boat as the rest of us. Guess it was just the luck of the draw that his land encompassed the creek. Even talked to him about combining our ranches, maybe starting some kind of partnership, but he wasn't interested." Hooper shrugged, scratching his balding head. "And why should he be? As long as he had the creek, he wasn't in any difficulty."

Judd shot Cody a look, absently fingering his Stetson. While the information was interesting, it wasn't anything they could use. He figured they'd gotten as much as they were going to get—for the moment. Judd held out his hand, and the old man took it. "Well, Paul, thank you for your time. Tell James to give me a call when he gets back tomorrow."

"No problem. I'll be happy to." Hooper's gaze went to Cody. "You take care, hear son?"

Nodding, Cody shook the man's hand before following Judd out the door and pulling it closed softly behind them. They stood on the front porch for a moment, letting the warm, dark night wrap around them.

"What do you think?" Judd asked, adjusting his Stetson atop his head.

Cody shrugged. He still had that eerie feeling, the one that had plagued him this morning. His narrowed gaze swept the horizon. Someone was out there...watching...he could just *feel* it. His fists tightened. He wished the coward would come out in the open and show his face like a man.

"Looks like we've hit a dead end here," Cody reluctantly admitted. "I have a feeling the man was telling the truth."

Judd sighed heavily. "Yeah, so do I." Digging in his pocket for his keys, he headed toward the truck. "I'll check out his story first thing in the morning."

"How about if I talk to James?" Cody asked, fingering his own Stetson as he glanced around the dark property. "I'd like to know where he's been and what he's been up to the past few weeks."

"Good idea," Judd said, his brows drawing together thoughtfully. "But I don't think he had anything to do with any of this. He's not that bright, and besides, he's always been a little strange. Not really in touch with reality. I think Paul's kept him close to home all these years because he knew the boy wasn't all there." Judd glanced at Cody, wondering why he was suddenly so quiet. "What are you thinking?" he asked, opening the door to the Jeep.

Cody's lips thinned. "Something or someone's out there." His gaze swept the horizon again, the feeling getting stronger. "Now we just have to find him before he tries to harm anyone else."

"We will," Judd assured him, climbing in the Jeep. "We will. I promise, Cody. Come on, I'll take you home."

Someone was in bed with her.
Sleeping soundly, Savannah awoke immediately.

She tried to curb the rush of panic that washed over her and keep her breathing level and her eyes closed. When you'd slept alone for years, the sudden presence of someone else in your bed was startling. The mattress bounced and shifted, which was what probably had woken her up.

"Savannah?"

She felt his hand on her shoulder at the same moment she recognized his voice. The breath rushed out of her in a relieved whoosh as she bolted upright into a sitting position.

"Cody!" She whacked him. Hard. Her hand instinctively went to her pounding heart. "You scared the life out of me." The room was bathed in darkness except for a small shaft of light from the hallway. But she could still see his features, feel his presence. Her heart was pounding wickedly, not in fear, but something else, that unfathomable something that always started the moment he was near.

He looked drawn and tired, she realized, watching him nestle his head deeper into the pillow in order to get comfortable. She wanted to stroke the gentle tumble of dark hair that had fallen over his forehead, but remembering what had happened this morning, she resisted, not knowing how he'd respond to her touch.

She'd never been so unsure of herself in her life.

This morning, after her shower, she'd been certain he'd wanted to kiss her, to touch her. But then something had happened—what, she wasn't certain—and he'd walked away from her, clearly rejecting her. He'd wanted to touch her, she was almost certain, but what she didn't know was why he hadn't. With the memory fresh in her mind, and fearing another rejection, she didn't know how to act or react around him.

"What are you doing in my bed?" she demanded, making a belated attempt to grab the sheet that had fallen to her waist, leaving her dressed in a nearly transparent silk night-gown that didn't really cover as much as it enticed. He was stretched out comfortably atop the covers, his booted feet crossed, his hand absently rubbing his tired face.

"Trying to rest," he mumbled, adjusting his feet again. With a frown, he toed off his boots, letting them fall haphazardly to the floor before resettling his long legs more comfortably in the big bed. With a tired sigh, he glanced at her, felt his gut tighten. The pale puff of silk she had on was the same color as her hair and clung lovingly to her breasts, dipping low to reveal just a hint of the soft curves.

She continued to stare at him. "But why are you in my bed instead of your own—or rather, Joey's?"

Cody yawned. Turning on his side toward her, he propped his head in his hand to study her. Her hair was sleep tumbled and fell in wicked abandon over her shoulders. Her eyes were soft and drowsy, and her pale skin looked like porcelain in the dim light.

"Yours was closer. Besides, I wanted to check on you." He touched the shadowed, puffy bruise on her forehead, relieved that she didn't wince. But she did draw back from him, her eyes flashing in the dark. He sighed again, wondering what he'd done now.

Savannah glared at him. He was back to treating her like Heidi the little goat girl again. "I'm perfectly fine," she said a bit stiffly, clutching the sheet tighter as his gaze traveled over her bare shoulders. She leaned back against the headboard, still clutching the sheet. "You're the one who looks like he needs a doctor."

"Just tired," he assured her, trying to stifle another yawn. "After Judd and I went to see Paul Hooper, we stopped by Miss Tulip's." He couldn't help the grin that slid across his tired features.

Savannah found herself smiling as well. She would have loved to have been a fly on the wall to see how Cody dealt with the cantankerous woman. Not to mention her trusty cane.

"And what exactly did Miss Tulip want?" she asked, trying not to be amused.

"Me."

"Excuse me?" She knew his reputation with women, but surely a woman Miss Tulip's age was immune to him. Wasn't she? Oh, Lord. Savannah wanted to groan. If he was still able to charm a woman Miss Tulip's age, how on earth could she hope to resist him?

Cody laughed suddenly, dragging a hand through his hair. "She wanted me to know that she thinks it's time I came home." He glanced at her. "To Silver Creek."

"And what did you say to that?" Savannah asked softly, trying to ignore the sudden pounding of hope in her heart. She knew Cody was planning on leaving as soon as he got to the bottom of this horrid mess, but she hadn't even considered, hadn't wanted to hope, that there was a possibility he would stay. She had to keep things in perspective, had to remember why he was here.

And that he'd be leaving.

He merely shrugged but didn't answer, stifling a yawn again. He couldn't take his eyes off of her. "After that, Judd dropped me off, and I did the evening chores and locked up for the night." He reached out and brushed a strand of hair off her bare shoulder. He'd told himself he had to stay away from her, do his job and get the hell out of here. So much for good intentions, he thought as he looked at her.

"Thank you," she said in an excruciatingly polite voice, wishing he'd stop looking at her like that. When he'd touched her bare shoulder, she'd almost jumped out of her skin.

"We have to talk."

"Talk?" she said in surprise. Talk? He wanted to *talk?* Unless things between the sexes had changed dramatically during the past ten years and someone forgot to tell her, when a man climbed into a woman's bed it generally wasn't to . . . talk.

"You want to *talk?*" she repeated, looking at him in bewilderment.

He nodded, amused by the look on her face. Obviously talking wasn't exactly what she thought he was after.

"About what?" she continued.

"You."

Now she was really confused. "Me?" Savannah shook her head. He'd climbed into her bed to talk about her? The man was definitely weird. "What on earth do you want to talk about me for?"

Stifling another yawn, Cody adjusted his legs on the bed. "Savannah, is it possible that you've got a rejected suitor somewhere and he's gotten it in his mind to extract a little revenge?"

She looked at him as if he'd taken leave of his senses. And she wasn't entirely certain he hadn't. "Cody, what on earth are you talking about?"

She shook her head, sending her hair flying about her like a halo. He itched to feel the silk of it, to let it drag through his fingers.

"Are you saying you think all this nonsense is about someone who's after me?"

Cody was thoughtful for a moment, stroking a finger along the soft skin of her hand. "I don't know, Savannah," he replied honestly. "Judd and I went to see Paul Hooper tonight. I'd bet my badge he was telling the truth. I don't think he had anything to do with my father's death or with the fire in the henhouse or shooting out your tire." He shrugged. "It's possible that we're just assuming my father's death and the attacks on you and Joey are related."

"And you're saying they're not?" Her heart began to thud at the possibility that someone could be after her and Joey for some unexplained reason.

"No, I'm saying we have to consider it." He studied her for a moment, still stroking her hand. "So, is it possible it's a rejected suitor?"

She shook her head. "No."

"You're positive?"

"Absolutely positive." She tugged the sheet up higher, trying to ignore the fact that his stroking finger had now traveled to her arm and was sending a flurry of goose bumps over her.

"How can you be so sure?" His gaze was steady on hers.

She was quiet for a moment. "Because," she said softly, glancing down at the sheet so she wouldn't have to look into those knowing blue eyes. She suddenly felt very vulnerable. "There, uh, haven't been any suitors. Rejected or any other kind." In light of what had happened this morning, she wasn't sure she wanted to divulge this information, but realized she had no choice.

Cody took a moment to absorb the information, then sat up and leaned against the headboard right next to her. Now he understood why she was so wary. She *wasn't* accustomed to being around a man, to having one near her, touching her, loving her.

She'd stiffened the moment he'd asked her about this, and he had a feeling she was uncomfortable, but why?

"For how long?" he asked softly, watching her. He draped an arm around her shoulder, pulling her close. She stiffened a moment, and the wariness leapt to her eyes, then faded away. Relenting, she leaned against him, snuggling against his warmth, his closeness. "How long, Savannah?"

"Is it important?" She risked a glance at him.

"Very."

She took a long, deep breath, fiddling with the sheet. He covered her hand with his free one to stop her fiddling.

"Ten years," she said. "Not . . . not since Joey's father."

A million questions sprung to his mind, none of which had anything to do with the investigation but had everything to do with what he was feeling. She hadn't been with anyone since her husband had died, hadn't let a man near her, by choice obviously. No one had touched her in all these years. No one.

Except him.

He couldn't help the surge of pure masculine pride and possessiveness that shot through him.

"Why, Savannah? Why haven't you been with anyone since your husband died?"

She turned to look at him, and he didn't understand the stricken look on her face. It was as if she'd grown even paler right before his eyes.

"Cody." Savannah swallowed hard. "There's something you should know." She never thought she'd have to tell him this, didn't want to tell him now. But she had no choice. She *had* to tell him. Had to trust him, trust him in a way she hadn't trusted a man in years, because if what he suspected was true, he had a right to know the truth.

Licking her suddenly dry lips, Savannah allowed her gaze to drift toward the open window. A soft breeze blew, moving the drapes in a gentle rhythm. She hoped she was doing the right thing, hoped Cody truly was an honorable man, worthy of her trust, because if he wasn't, she didn't think she could handle another betrayal.

She brought her gaze back to his. "Cody," she began slowly, "Joey's father is not dead."

Chapter Eight

For long, silent moments, Cody could do nothing but stare at her in stunned silence, trying to grasp the enormity of what she'd just told him. A flicker of anger raced through him.

"I think you'd better explain," he said quietly. "Everything. I want the whole truth, Savannah, and I want it now." He should have remembered that women weren't to be trusted, that they lied to suit their purposes. He just hadn't expected it of her. But that was part of the problem; maybe he shouldn't have been expecting anything. He knew better.

Savannah saw the look in his eyes and felt the pain of it shoot right through her heart. She'd somehow hurt him with her admission.

"Cody." She splayed her hand across his chest, wanting him to understand. Taking a deep breath, she started slowly. "Joey's father is alive and well, and the last I heard, living in Chicago."

His eyes narrowed as they went over her. He tried to bank down his anger. "Why, Savannah? Why would you lie about something like that?" He shook his head. "It doesn't make sense."

She forced a grim smile. "It does if you know the whole story. His name was Gary, and I thought I was in love with him. We planned to marry, but I got pregnant. He didn't want a child, thought it would interfere with his life-style." Daring a glance at Cody, she tried to smile but found she couldn't. His arm tightened around her, drawing her closer. "When he realized I was going to go through with the pregnancy regardless of what he said, he . . . just up and disappeared. Last I heard, he'd married some long-legged blond model and moved to Chicago."

Cody felt everything slowly still inside of him as he absorbed her words. "Do you mean to tell me he left you alone and pregnant?" Cold fury tinged his words.

"Yes." She glanced down at the sheet, and he couldn't bear the look on her face. He lifted her chin, forcing her to look at him. Her mouth was trembling, and she was biting her lower lip, trying not to cry. The instinct to kill the man who had caused those tears and her pain came quickly, but he fought it back.

"You've got nothing to be ashamed of, Savannah," he said softly, impulsively pressing a kiss to her temple. Her scent drifted toward him, infiltrating his breathing space, clouding his thoughts. "The man was an idiot."

"We were never married," she continued softly, ignoring the fact that she was pressed firmly against him so that she could feel every hard, muscled inch of him. One thin silk strap of her gown had dipped low on her shoulder, near where his hand rested, stroking the tender skin. "It never bothered me, but when Joey was two, I confided to someone about the true circumstances of his birth and word got out." Chewing her bottom lip, she tried to bank down the memory. "It was a small town like Silver Creek, and you know how small towns can be. I was a teacher. But as soon as word leaked out that I had never been married and my son was illegitimate, I lost my tutoring business since people didn't want their kids associating with me."

"Damn narrow-minded fools," Cody said with a shake of his head.

She couldn't help but smile.

"That's when I decided to lie. I never wanted Joey to know the truth. Kids can be cruel, and I was a single parent to begin with. I didn't want Joey to feel any different than anyone else. That's why I told him his father died before he was born."

"So he wouldn't know that you'd both been rejected before he'd been born?" She merely nodded. "Or that you and his father had never married?" She nodded again.

"Is that why there haven't been any men in your life?" He knew the answer but had to be certain. It would be difficult to trust anyone after that kind of betrayal, that kind of brutal rejection. He knew, for he had also suffered the same gut-cutting betrayal, knew what it had done to him. It explained a lot about her.

"Yes," she admitted quietly, unable or unwilling to tell him that she'd lost the ability to trust when Gary had betrayed and rejected her. She couldn't tell him that she'd never trusted another man enough to let him close to her, either physically or emotionally.

Until now.

"You're . . . you're not going to tell anyone, are you?"

Her eyes searched his, and Cody felt a small stab of pain. It hurt that she'd even ask, that she didn't know the kind of man he was or how much he valued the trust she'd placed in him. A long time ago, he'd learned that trust was a treasured thing. When someone gave you their trust—whether you asked for it, whether you wanted it or not—you had a responsibility not to abuse it or misuse it. He'd *never* do anything to betray her trust in him, especially knowing what she'd been through. To do so would be like a double betrayal. Not even he could be that much of a bastard.

"No," he said quietly, drawing her closer and wrapping both arms protectively around her.

Savannah let loose a sigh of relief, then gave in to temptation and laid her head against his chest, absently rubbing her cheek against the soft fabric of his shirt. He felt solid and strong and . . . safe.

"No reason for me to tell anyone," Cody whispered. "If he walked out on you, I doubt that he'd come looking for you now." He stroked her hair for a moment, just enjoying the feel of her. No wonder she was wary of men. The only experience she'd had with them had left her devastated and betrayed.

"Gary made it very clear he wanted nothing to do with me or his child. He turned his back on us without a backward glance. I never heard from him again. All of this stuff that's been happening couldn't be connected to Gary. He doesn't even know where we're at. And besides, it was his choice to walk away. He made it clear he never wanted to see or hear from me again."

"His loss," he said simply. Satisfied he could eliminate the man as a suspect, Cody began to relax as her hand slowly stroked his chest. Now he understood why she was so fiercely independent, so proud, so stubborn. She'd had no choice but to do for herself by herself. It must have been hard to face the future alone, pregnant, but she'd done it. Not many women would have had the courage to do what she'd done. She could have given the child up—then gone on with her life as if nothing had happened.

But she hadn't. She'd chosen to go forward and make a new life for herself and her child, to put the past behind her. He couldn't help but feel his admiration for her growing. He glanced down at her just as she glanced up at him. Their gazes held.

Cody never took his eyes off of her, and Savannah swallowed hard. She was sprawled across his broad, hard chest, and his arms were wrapped protectively around her. Heat burned through her, warming her skin, increasing her heartbeat. The silk of her nightgown offered little protection, and in fact, was another source of arousal as it slid erotically over her heated skin while his hand absently drew circles on her back.

He brushed the hair off her face, trying to fight down the need and desire building inside of him. He should get up and off this bed and away from her as fast as his long legs could carry him. He knew it, but he also knew it was a lost cause. Her mouth, so soft, so full, so inviting, was just inches from his. Too close for comfort, but not nearly close enough.

Savannah saw the same look on his face that she'd seen this morning and started to pull away. He held her tight, unwilling to let her go. His vision filled her gaze a moment before his mouth settled over hers. Savannah moaned softly in welcome, sliding her hands up his chest to circle his neck and draw him closer.

The moment her mouth opened under his and he felt her surrender, Cody knew he'd lost the cause. Her soft moan nearly did him in as she tried to bring him closer. She'd brought something to life in him, something that was more powerful than all his good intentions. He was drunk on the taste of her, his arms felt empty without her and his body ached for her, an ache that he knew could never be satisfied by anyone *but* her.

He tightened his arms around her, drawing her closer until she was lying fully atop him. The thin silk of her gown had crept up her thighs, baring them. His hands slid down her back, slowly caressing his way over her hips, fitting her snugly over his hard, aching arousal. She shifted her hips against him, and it was his turn to groan. Her hands, as frantic as his, tunneled their way through his hair, her mouth hot and hungry as he dragged her deeper and deeper into the pool of passion.

His hands slid the length of her bare thighs, so soft, as soft as the silk that had once covered them. His mouth drifted from hers, sliding to her throat where her scent was hot and strong. He could feel her pulse thudding wildly, as wildly as his, and his tongue snaked out, touching the beat, making her moan again.

His name tore from her lips, half prayer, half plea, as she moved against him. He was frantic, desperate to take what she so generously offered. But reality reared its ugly head, and he remembered what he was taking and from whom. He had nothing to offer her, nothing to give but a few moments of his time and his body. And it wasn't enough. Not this time. Not with her.

Abruptly he dragged his lips away, his breathing jagged and uneven. He shifted his weight and slid her off him. She stiffened, but he kept his arms tightly around her.

"Cody?" Her head lifted and she looked at him. There was confusion, bewilderment and pain. He would have died a thousand deaths not to see that look in her eyes, a look he'd put there, but it couldn't be helped. Swearing softly, he shook his head, dragging a hand through his hair, trying to get himself back under control.

Disgusted with himself, Cody knew he had to explain; he couldn't bear to let her think what she was thinking. He shouldn't have let things go so far.

"Savannah. We—I...I...don't want to hurt you."

Blinking back the tears of humiliation before they could fall, she merely stared at him, trying to control the sudden fury that ran through her. "You don't want to hurt me?" she repeated, wondering what he thought he'd just done.

He blew out an exasperated breath. He reached for her hand, but she snatched it away from him. "I have nothing to offer you, Savannah. In the end, you'll just get hurt. I don't want to be responsible for hurting you."

"I see," she said quietly. "So you're responsible for me now?" Her chin went up. "Is that it?" He was lucky there wasn't something close enough for her to hit him with, because at the moment, she didn't think she could resist the temptation.

Cody forced himself to meet those angry blue eyes. "No, of course not. That's not what I meant." Frustrated, he ran a hand over his face. He tried again. "I just don't want to be the one who hurts you."

"So you're being noble, then, is that it?" He could hear the temper in her voice. "Let me see if I've got this right. Instead of *possibly* hurting me later, you'll just *definitely* hurt me now and get it over with, is that it?" She wondered how such an intelligent man could be so incredibly stupid.

He dragged a hand through his hair in exasperation. "No—yes..." Frustrated, he drew in a deep breath, wondering why it made perfect sense in his mind, but when she voiced it, he sounded like a blathering idiot.

"Am I supposed to thank you for this...noble gesture?" Her eyes challenged him as she stared at him for a long moment.

How on earth could one man be so dense? So blind? Didn't he know how she felt? What was in her heart? She'd never thought she'd ever be able to trust again. Never thought she'd be able to feel or care or love.

And then he'd walked into her life and turned it upside down.

She looked at him now, studied the planes and angles of his face shadowed by the muted light. In spite of her fury at him, a ribbon of warmth slowly unfurled and wrapped around her guarded heart.

She had no idea why, but she trusted Cody, had trusted him from the moment she'd laid eyes on him. She had no explicable or logical reason. In fact, it made no sense to her. But sometimes logic and reason were surpassed by something far more powerful: emotion and instinct. And her instincts about Cody were strong. No matter what, she had a feeling she could trust him; that he wouldn't hurt or betray her.

As for her emotions, she'd been trying to ignore and deny them, but it would have been easier to ignore a hurricane than the feelings he'd managed to bring out in her, feelings she was certain had died long ago.

She loved him. She'd known it this afternoon when she felt such welcome relief as he'd hauled her into his arms in Judd's office after the accident. Had known it with every breath and fiber of her being.

So how could he be so dense?

Lying here, wrapped in his arms in the dark of night with nothing but the quiet surrounding them, seemed like the most natural thing in the world. She finally felt as if she knew where she was meant to be, where she belonged: in Cody's arms.

Maybe that's why she'd been so scared of him, why she'd been so wary. No man had ever made her feel the way he did. She'd known from the moment they'd met that somehow he was different. And that she'd be different because of him. She hadn't known if she would have the courage to risk her heart, to take a chance. She'd protected herself for so long, afraid of the pain of caring, afraid of the pain of rejection. Now she knew there was no risk, no chance, not with the way she felt about Cody.

She loved him.

There was no question, no doubt. The feelings were pure and strong, so strong she wondered why she'd feared them. There was no fear now, only the depth and breadth of her emotions, the knowledge that this was right, so right.

She knew now the pain, the hurt, would come only from *not taking the chance,* from *not taking a risk.* She'd spent too many years alone and lonely, playing it safe, not wanting to get hurt, that now, *not* to seize the moment and this chance at happiness—even if it meant abandoning her wounded pride—seemed incredibly, unbearably foolish.

Now all she had to do was convince one stubborn, hard-headed man that he was...wrong. Among other things.

"Cody?"

He turned to look at her. Her voice was incredibly calm. Too calm. She'd folded her hands in her lap and was sitting there looking cool and demure. He knew that look; he'd seen it enough over the past few days. It made him instantly nervous.

Looking at her, all tousled, her lips swollen from his, her hair falling sensuously over her shoulders, he felt his resolve weaken and his body harden. Again. Damn! He was tempted to cover her with the sheet so he wouldn't have to see what he knew he couldn't have.

"What?" he asked with a weary sigh.

"You know what I think?" Her voice was so sweet it could have raised his blood-sugar level to a dangerous high.

"What do you think, Savannah?" he asked suspiciously.

She unflinchingly met his gaze with a smile. "I don't think you're worried about hurting *me* at all."

He sighed. "Savannah, I just told you—"

"I know what you just told me. But Cody, you're not worried about hurting *me*. I think you're worried about *you*." Her smile was pure femininity, the kind that confused the hell out of men. "You're worried *you're* going to get hurt."

He looked as if she'd just smacked him upside the head. If she thought it would have done some good, she would have. Savannah's chin went up a notch. Her eyes were blazing when they met his. "If I'm willing to take a chance, to take a risk after what I've been through, why can't you?" she demanded, tossing pride to the wind. If he wanted to walk away from her, fine, but at least he was going to hear what she had to say whether he liked it or not. And judging from the look on his face, he didn't like it. At all. She didn't care. She wanted him to know exactly what he was walking away from.

"You know why you won't take the chance, Cody?" She didn't give him an opportunity to answer. "You won't take a chance because you're afraid, Kincaid. *Afraid!* You're nothing but a big, lousy coward. *In and out of bed.*" She threw the words at him and he took the verbal jab right on his fragile male ego.

He moved so fast he almost dried the spit in her mouth. One moment she was indignantly sliding off the bed, head held high; the next she was flat on her back, arms gently pinned over her head, with him looming over her, larger than life, breathing fire. Blinking in surprise, Savannah swallowed hard. Nerves sang through her, but there was no fear, not of him. No matter how angry she made him, she knew he'd never hurt her no matter what he thought or said.

"Damn you," he growled, staring down at her, his mouth only inches from hers. His eyes were as dark as midnight as his common sense warred with his desire. "I told you I don't have anything to offer you."

"You have yourself," she whispered, freeing her arms and looping them around him to draw him down the last few inches until their breaths mingled.

Didn't she know what she was doing to him? He was drowning and he didn't think he had enough sense to save himself, not this time. Not with her.

"It's enough," she whispered, brushing her lips against his in a teasing motion, breaking the last threads of his control. "More than enough." And if that was all she could have of him, it would be enough. *For now.* "I won't hurt you, Cody," she whispered, enticing him with her words, her scent, her eyes. "I'd never hurt you."

And she wouldn't—couldn't. She'd die before she'd ever do anything to hurt him, because she knew now that someone had hurt him—terribly. Someone had done something that had frozen his heart and left him wary and suspicious, not to mention afraid. Afraid to love, to take a chance, to risk his heart or his hopes. If he offered nothing, nothing could be taken from him. If he offered nothing, he risked nothing. He wouldn't be vulnerable; he couldn't be hurt.

But she wanted him to know she wouldn't hurt him and wanted nothing from him but *him.* It was more than enough, more than she'd ever had, more than she'd ever hoped for all the long, lonely years she'd spent alone.

And she wouldn't let *his* fear or *her* pride deprive them of something so right, so wonderful, and she knew it was right, knew it with the certainty she knew her name.

"Cody?" She licked her lips, and he watched the slow movement of her tongue, mesmerized.

He swore softly. He didn't think; he only allowed himself to feel, to take what he wanted, needed, what she offered. His mouth took hers, coming down so fast, so hard, her head pressed into the pillow. She tightened her arms around him, drawing him in, drawing him closer, but it wasn't close enough. Desperation drove him. From shoulder to hip, he branded her with his touch, pushing the silk fabric of her gown off to find the silk skin hidden beneath. She was naked now, and his hands cupped her breasts. She was so small, so soft, so...perfect. She fit in his hand as if she'd been made for him. Just him. His thumb rasped against her nipple, and she arched toward him with a strangled moan.

Feeling none of the fear she'd imagined, only a driving, wild desire that left her breathless and made her bold, Savannah tore at his shirt in frustration, wanting to feel his skin against hers. Buttons went flying like a hailstorm, and she ran her hands over his bare chest, feeling his strength, his warmth, the frantic beating of his heart.

A fragmented moan tore from her, and she arched clear off the bed as his mouth slid from hers, raining kisses along the tender skin of her neck until his damp tongue gently circled her nipple before drawing it into his mouth. She slid her hands deeper in his hair, pulling him closer, arching upward, filling his mouth, moaning softly as fire raced through her, making her frantic. She shifted her hips upward in a rhythm as old as time, and he moaned, sliding his mouth to her other breast to give it the same attention.

Her hands raced over him. Everywhere she touched ignited. He couldn't wait much longer; the blood was pounding at his temples, and he was so hard he felt as if he were going to explode.

He heard her soft whimpers as he slid a hand down her hip to her inner thigh, caressing her slowly, gently, higher and higher until she sighed his name on a whisper, her hips lifting upward to meet his stroking fingers.

Clinging to him, Savannah dug her nails into the bare skin of his back as his fingers continued to tease, to caress, to bring her slumbering body awake in a way it had never been before, driving her higher until she couldn't feel anything but pleasure and a frantic, desperate need to quench the fire his touch had ignited. Her breathless cries nearly drove him over the edge. Pleasure exploded through her body, making her cry out his name. His mouth caught her cry, dragging her quickly back into the whirlwind of passion. She clung to him, unable, unwilling, to let him go as he quickly unsnapped his jeans and shoved them down, kicking them off.

Holding him, she pressed wet, frantic kisses against his throat, his neck, tasting him, savoring him. She couldn't catch her breath; she didn't care. She no longer needed air, only him.

"Cody, please?" Half plea, half prayer, he had no choice but to respond, everything male in him responding to the elemental female cry of need.

Remembering how small she was, how delicate, he moved slowly, entering her carefully. He heard her soft moan, felt her hands dig into him and he stopped, not wanting to hurt her. His teeth ground together, his breathing grew harsh and his eyes slid closed. She was so small, so tight . . . so wet. He thought he was going to die with pleasure. He began to move slowly, letting her get adjusted to him, but each slow, sure stroke nearly drove him over the edge and out of his mind.

"Don't stop," she whispered, holding him close, lifting her hips to encourage him, to meet each thrust. He couldn't stay still, not with her hips moving against his, pulling him deeper and deeper into her slick, hot wetness. He buried his mouth in her neck, savoring her scent.

He couldn't deny it any longer.

She'd been right; he *had* been scared. Of her. And what she could do to him because of what was between them.

More than he'd ever had with anyone.

More than he'd allowed himself to have, to feel.

More than he'd ever thought was possible with anyone.

It was as if she were a part of him, and he suddenly couldn't remember what life was like without her.

It scared the hell out of him.

She'd offered herself, given herself willingly. And he'd taken what she'd offered, thinking it would be enough. If he assuaged the need and desire she awoke, maybe he could walk away from her.

He knew now it wouldn't be that simple.

Nothing ever was.

Their lovemaking bound him to her more than a steel rope, because he could never go back, would never forget this night, would never forget her.

He would always remember; she'd always be there haunting the recesses of his mind. Her scent. Her touch. Her lips. The way she felt in his arms. Every sigh. Every murmur. Every moment of pleasure. She'd branded him with her own personal signature, and he knew no other woman would ever be able to compete; would never be able to take her place or erase the memories. Because she'd always be there in the one place he'd always guarded like a fortress: his heart.

He was a loner, always had been, always would be. But he wasn't alone now; she was here with him.

For the moment.

It couldn't be more than this…this moment. It couldn't. He'd have to walk away, for both their sakes. He had nothing to offer her or anyone. And he couldn't take what he couldn't give.

She was etched on his mind and buried in his heart. And he knew it was too damn late to do anything about it.

Except run.

Wave after wave of pleasure assaulted him as he continued to stroke faster, slipping his hands under her hips to lift her higher so he could slide deeper. Whimpers of pleasure escaped Savannah as she softly urged him on, her voice a soft caress against his ear. The sound of her pleasure, the feel of her arms holding him, drove him over the edge. With a low growl, he exploded inside of her. The pleasure reverberated through every inch of his body, weakening him.

A breeze blew softly through the room, cooling their heated bodies. Neither moved for long, silent moments. She continued to hold him, her lips pressed against his shoulder. He could still feel her heart beating rapidly, as rapidly as his own. After a long moment, Cody finally rolled to his back, bringing her with him. Content, she curled up atop him, nuzzling her cheek against his bare chest.

Staring vacantly up at the ceiling, Cody absently stroked her back, felt her shiver, then grabbed the sheet to cover them.

"Are you all right?" he finally asked, still stroking her back. He'd never been more aware of their sizes than at this moment, and hoped—prayed—he hadn't hurt her.

Smiling in the dark, she merely murmured, adjusting herself more comfortably atop him.

She was too quiet. It made him nervous. And worried. His hand slowed, then slid up to stroke her hair. "What are you thinking about?"

Lifting her head, she gave him a brilliant smile. It made his mouth go dry. "You."

He found his own lips curling. "What about me?"

She propped her elbow on his chest and her chin in her hand, studying him. "I was just wondering . . . how tall are you?"

He stared at her in confusion for a moment, his frown clearly drawn. He'd had women say a lot of things to him at this point, but this had to be the all-time weirdest question a woman in her position had ever asked him. So why wasn't he surprised she asked it? He almost smiled. Because *nothing* she did surprised him. "You were thinking about how tall I am?"

"No," she corrected, playfully tugging the hair on his chest. "I was *asking* how tall you are."

"Why?" His brows drew together in a frown, wondering what his height had to do with what had just happened between them. Apparently something. "Does it matter how tall I am?"

She was still smiling that beautiful smile, a smile that was making him incredibly nervous. "If it didn't, would I be asking?"

"Six feet four," he said grudgingly. "Are you satisfied?"

Laying her head back down, she laughed softly, rubbing a hand against his bare chest. "Yes. Very. Thank you for asking." She wasn't talking about his answer, and they both knew it. It tickled him to no end that her voice was excruciatingly polite, as if she were standing in the middle of some hoity-toity social situation, instead of sprawled naked across his chest.

He laughed, tightening his arms around her, liking the way she felt against him, the way they fit together. Perfectly. He quickly banished the thought, then waited, wondering what she was up to—something, no doubt—but she didn't say anything. She just lay there contentedly, stroking his chest until curiosity got the best of him. Still holding on to her, he glanced down at her.

"So, are you going to tell me or what?"

"Tell you what or what?" she asked, lifting her head again. There was mischief in her eyes. Even in the dark, he could see it.

He sighed, knowing it was going to be a merry chase trying to keep up with her. "Why you wanted to know how tall I am."

Still smiling, she slowly inched upward until her mouth was hovering just over his. "I wanted to know how tall you were," she whispered, nuzzling his mouth with her own as she straddled him, "because I was trying to figure out *exactly* how long it's going to take me to kiss all six feet and four inches. Probably all night," she admitted with a smile. "Maybe even two," she added hopefully. Her nibbling mouth caught his laughter, which quickly turned into a low moan.

The smell of fresh-brewed coffee woke Savannah up. Smiling, she stretched and reached for Cody, but he was gone; the bed was empty. Yawning, she slid from the bed, clutching the sheet around her naked body as she went to the window, hoping to see him. But he was nowhere in sight.

The door to the barn was open, so she assumed he was probably tending to Miss Sophie. It was so nice to have someone else to help with all the work that had to be done.

It was even nicer to have someone sleeping in the same bed with her, she thought with a smile as she sidestepped an errant button that had gone flying sometime last night. Not that they'd gotten much sleep, she thought, dragging on a pair of shorts and a T-shirt and wondering why Cody hadn't woken her up.

She seemed to remember Cody kissing her before he slid out of bed this morning, mumbling something about letting her have a few more minutes of precious sleep. It wasn't fair that Cody had been doing all her chores; she felt guilty, as if she was taking advantage of him, and that certainly was the case. She figured she could go help him with the morning chores, and maybe they could have breakfast together.

Together.

She couldn't help the brilliant smile that lit her face. All these years that she'd spent alone, she'd never imagined there'd be anyone to share her life, share her sorrows, her troubles, her *love*. It had seemed too much to hope for, too much to want. But that was before Cody had walked into her life.

If she'd thought about it, she would have been surprised how quickly and easily he'd found a place in her heart, maybe because she'd never, ever felt that…connection with any man before. She'd never even realized there could be such a connection, where two people were totally compatible, totally in sync, *until* Cody. He filled all the empty places in her life, in her heart, places she hadn't even known were empty until he'd walked into her life.

Oh, she loved him, all right—there was no doubt about that.

Hugging herself, Savannah glanced at the bed, and a soft smile lit her face.

And Cody loved her.

He didn't have to say the words for her to know it. She knew it with a knowledge born of the wisdom of the ages, a wisdom women had somehow always instinctively known about the men they were destined to be with: They were soul mates.

Now she finally understood what the term meant.

She could see it in Cody's eyes when he looked at her, could feel it in his arms when he held her, could sense it in the way he treated her.

She knew he loved her; unfortunately, she wasn't sure he knew—yet. Somehow, some way she was going to have to break this little tidbit of news to him. Savannah laughed suddenly. And she had a feeling he was *not* going to be a very happy camper when he found out.

Still smiling, she padded barefoot downstairs, stopping long enough to pour herself a mug of coffee, sipping it as she wandered outside toward the barn, thinking.

It was a beautiful day; the sun was bright and high in the sky, but it wasn't quite as hot this early as it would be later on in the day.

"Cody?"

She never even made it to the open door before he came out with a decided frown on his face. Smiling, she stood on tiptoe and kissed the frown. "Good morning. I came to help you with the chores."

The frown remained as he dropped his hands to her shoulders. She glanced up at him in alarm, her eyes searching his. She could tell by his gaze there was something wrong. "Cody, what is it? What's wrong?"

He tightened his hands on her shoulders to halt her progress. She looked so happy this morning, he hated to have to spoil her mood. If he could have done something to protect her from what he had to tell her, he would. The fact that he couldn't only succeeded in frustrating him. "Savannah, don't go in the barn."

"What?" She was trying to look past him through the open barn door, but he was blocking her every which way. "Well, for heaven's sake, why not?"

He hesitated a moment before speaking. Her eyes, wide with confusion, were on his. It tore his insides up. "Savannah, it's Miss Sophie."

Shock and fear slowly stole across her features, wiping away the happiness in her eyes. "Miss Sophie?" she repeated in a whisper, still staring at him. Cody swore under his breath. He knew how much that damn bull meant to her, knew how she'd worked and saved for it, hoping to have some security for the future for her and her son. Not to mention what the bull meant to Joey.

She clutched the front of his shirt for support. "Cody, is she—?"

"He," he automatically corrected. "He's not dead—yet," he added grimly, making her heart pound in double time. "But I think he's been poisoned. There's a telltale scent in his corn. When I went into the barn this morning, he was lying down."

Still holding on to Savannah's shoulders, he felt her tremble, saw the quick flash of tears in her eyes. He knew how she felt; he felt like punching something or someone, too. Knowing someone had deliberately tried to hurt her— again—made his gut tighten and his anger take hold. His determination to get to the bottom of this was growing stronger with every passing moment. As soon as he had the situation with Miss Sophie handled, he was going to see to it. And God help whoever it was when he caught him because that person had chased the happiness from her eyes and replaced it with tears. And he'd pay, Cody vowed. Dearly.

"Oh, God." Immediately all the complications this brought on swam in Savannah's head. Her head dropped to Cody's chest, and she tried to keep the tears at bay. She had saved nearly two years for the bull, had used every single ounce of her savings. If Miss Sophie died, so would all her future security.

Cody drew her into the comforting shelter of his arms, suddenly remembering the night and the memories. She surprised him on so many different levels. She wasn't at all what he'd expected. She was so much more. Maybe if things were different, maybe if he was different— He banished the thought. He wasn't, and there was no changing him. He had to get the hell out of here while he could. He knew it and accepted it. So why was his heart aching and his guts churning?

"Why, Cody?" She raised her tearstained face to his, her gaze searching his. "Why would someone want to poison Miss Sophie?" She shook her head. "I don't understand. It doesn't make any sense."

He sighed heavily, feeling a heavy sense of responsibility. She and her son had been drawn into this through no fault of their own. And he hated the fact that someone was deliberately terrorizing her. "It does, Savannah, if they're trying to drive you off Kincaid land."

She studied him carefully. "But why? Why would anyone want me off Kincaid land?" Savannah shook her head, trying to make some sense of this. "Do you really think that's what this is about?" She needed to know the reasons behind all these terrible things.

He glanced over her head to the land beyond. Someone had been on his land sometime before this morning. *His* land. Even after being gone so many years, he was surprised at how protective and possessive he was. Maybe it was because the land was his legacy. All that was left of his father. And he'd be damned if he'd let anyone chase him or her off of it.

"I'm not sure, Savannah, but I can't figure out any other reason." His face and voice were grim. "I don't know what's going on, but I sure as hell am going to find out." He drew back and looked at her, then raised his gaze to the sprawling horizon. He had that feeling again, as though someone was...watching them. He didn't like it, didn't like having her out in the open, where anyone could see her, target her. The streak of protectiveness that rose up in him was so strong it stunned him. He'd never felt protective of anything or anyone in his life before. Maybe it was because she was so damn determined to be independent and stand on her own two feet. He admired her grit and her courage, but he also realized how vulnerable she was. And he didn't like anyone taking advantage of someone who was vulnerable. A fair fight was one thing; this was something else.

He brought his gaze back to Savannah's, but that feeling just wouldn't go away. "There's not much we can do until the vet gets here, so why don't you go wait inside the house? I'll finish up the chores and handle things out here." Until he got a better handle on things, he wanted her within the safe confines of four walls where no one could get to her.

"Why don't you let me help?"

He shook his head, tenderly brushing the hair off her face. Some of the puffiness of her bruised forehead had gone down. Remembering that someone had done it deliberately only increased his determination to get to the bottom of this and keep her safe. "No, Savannah. I'd feel better knowing you were in the house instead of out here in the open."

In spite of the heat, she shivered, rubbing her hands up and down her arms. "Do you think they'll come back?"

"Not if they've got any brains, at least not while I'm around."

Savannah wanted to weep at his words. He was planning on leaving, and she wasn't entirely certain she could handle that thought this morning, not on top of everything else, especially not knowing how she felt. *How he felt.* The urgency to do something soon to make him realize what they had—what they could have together—was far too immediate to ignore.

She glanced up at him and felt an ache in her heart. Somehow, some way she was going to have to do... something. What, she wasn't entirely certain.

"All right," she said with a resigned sigh, stepping out of his arms, determined to figure something out. "I'll go in, but Cody...?"

"What?"

"Be careful, please?" She laid a hand on his chest, and he instinctively covered it with his own. He couldn't remember the last time anyone had worried about him or cared about him or looked at him the way she was looking at him now. Everything was in her eyes. It was the same way she had looked at him last night—or was it this morning? He really couldn't remember; night had slid into morning, and the only thing he remembered was her and the way she'd felt in his arms. But that look did something to his insides, and he thought again about last night, about how he knew he was drowning, in over his head for the first time in his life, and unable to do a damn thing about it.

Because of her.

Damn!

"Go on in, Savannah," he said, his voice gruffer than he would have liked.

She turned without a word and headed toward the house, but stopped midway to glance back at him.

"Should I call Judd?"

He shook his head. "Already did. When he gets here, give him some coffee, then send him on back." Cody turned and headed toward the barn, pausing to stare across the horizon.

If he was a praying man he'd pray, not just for the ailing Miss Sophie, but for himself, as well.

Chapter Nine

*S*tanding on the bluff with a clear view of Savannah's house, he felt rage rise like bile, almost choking him.

Nothing was going right!

Nothing!

He'd watched them since yesterday, watched as Cody stayed in the house with his woman. His woman! Cody was in there right now with her. In her bed. He could just imagine what they'd been doing. He couldn't stop thinking about the way she'd been pressing herself against him the other day. How could she? The bitch! Thought she was too good for everyone else, but took that damn Kincaid right to her bed. Kincaid had no right to be there! No right at all.

It should've been him!

Nothing was working out right. That damn bull should've been dead from the amount of poison he'd put in his feed, but the vet and Kincaid had worked on him all Saturday and it looked as if he was going to pull through. Because the sheriff had been hanging around all day, he'd had to wait until this morning to sneak down to the barn to check things *out. It infuriated him. He should've just shot the damn animal.*

He'd done everything he could think of to get rid of old man Kincaid and to scare Savannah and her brat kid off the land, but nothing had worked! Nothing! And all because of that damn Cody Kincaid. He should've stayed in Austin where he belonged, and everything would have been fine.

With Cody in Austin and old man Kincaid dead, he'd have been able to get the land he needed. And the woman he wanted and deserved.

But Cody had screwed up everything by coming home.

It wasn't fair that Cody had what should have belonged to him. Not fair at all!

Maybe it was time to take drastic measures. Time to put Cody Kincaid out of his misery. Time for Cody to join his father. With Cody out of the way, there'd be nothing stopping him. He'd have everything he wanted, everything he deserved.

For the first time all weekend, he smiled.

The Sunday-morning sun shone brightly through the open drapes, and the fresh scent of morning wafted through the window. Certain Cody was asleep, Savannah quietly tried to slide out of bed, but Cody hooked an arm around her waist to stop her.

"Where do you think you're going?" he whispered. His voice was deep and husky with sleep, and she smiled as he tumbled her back down, wrapping his arms around her to hold her in place right next to him.

She sighed in contentment. She'd thought she'd grow accustomed to his touch and what it did to her. Her blood seemed to grow thicker, moving slower. Her pulse pounded and her heart beat wildly. Every time he touched her, the riot inside her started all over again, started the fire and need she'd never experienced before. But she hadn't grown accustomed to Cody's touch, because each time he touched her was different. Each time *he* was different. Slow and tender. Gentle and romantic. Or fast and furious. Every sensation was amazing, exciting. She'd never known there were so many feelings, emotions, sensations; had never known one man could bring out so much in her, make her *feel* so much or *want* so much.

"I thought you were sleeping," she whispered, running her fingers against his stubbled chin. His prickly beard rasped against her fingers, and she smiled. She loved the feel of his face when he hadn't shaved, even if it did make him look even more dangerous and disreputable. And desirable.

She'd never actually had a man sleeping in bed with her night after night, and she'd found the past two nights that *everything* about him was fascinating. She couldn't seem to stop touching him. If he got tired of it, he never showed it. Later this morning, Joey was coming home from staying at Louie's for the weekend, and she knew that the private time they would be able to spend would be limited, so she wanted to enjoy every single precious moment they had.

"I am sleeping," he muttered, not bothering to open his weary eyes, enjoying the feel of her small, gentle hands against his face.

Studying him with a quiet smile, she lifted a hand to brush the hair off his forehead. He'd spent most of his time tending to the ailing Miss Sophie, and he'd gotten very little sleep. Last night, she'd curled up in a chair downstairs waiting for him. It had been past two the last time she'd looked. The next time she opened her eyes, she was lying in bed curled in his arms. She hadn't even woken up when he'd carried her upstairs. If she was tired, he had to be exhausted.

"I was just going to make some coffee," she said softly, snuggling closer, laying her head against his chest. His hand went to her head, and he began to lazily stroke her hair. Savannah's eyes slid closed. She'd never realized that just *being* with someone could make her so happy. His presence alone was enough to make her feel . . . complete. He didn't have to say anything; they didn't have to be doing anything. Just knowing he was there, with her, was enough.

"Coffee can wait. There's something else I'd rather have," he mumbled, making her laugh as he turned her on her back and nuzzled his mouth against her neck, nipping the tender, scented skin and making her moan in pleasure. She threaded her arms around him and tilted her head to give him better access.

Her scent still enticed him, and a hint of memory invaded Cody's sleep-clouded mind. He smiled, remembering the first day he'd met her when he wondered if she'd smelled that sweet all over. Eyes closed, Cody moved his mouth up to nuzzle the tender skin behind her ear, smiling as a soft whimper escaped her.

She did.

Every tender inch of her smelled like heaven. And tasted like sin.

He wasn't certain he'd ever be sated.

Too amused to be alarmed, he absently played his fingers along her tender skin and felt the tremors skip over her, immediately igniting a fire in him. He trailed his mouth down the long, slender column of her neck, then lower still to taste the soft, tender skin at the curve of her breast. He felt her hands thread through his hair at the same moment he heard another soft whimper. The sound immediately made him grow hard.

It still surprised and amazed him the way she responded to him. Completely. Totally. Wholeheartedly. She gave of herself as no other woman he'd ever met. She was at times pliant in surrender, and at other times demanding in desire. She was defying everything he'd ever thought about women and she never failed to surprise him.

But so many things about her had surprised him. He'd never actually spent this much time with a woman before, never actually spent more than a few hours in their beds. He'd made a habit of not staying the night, not wanting to have to go through the hassle of hasty explanations and empty promises the next morning. A few hours in a woman's bed was about all he could handle without getting restless to roam, to run.

But with Savannah, it had been different.

Somehow he knew it would be; maybe that's what worried him. From the moment he'd touched her, from that first night they'd made love, he'd never felt that restless need to run. Only to return, again and again, to her, to see the wonder in her eyes when he touched her, to watch her tremble as that wonder turned to breathless desire, then to see her eyes darken and slide closed in bone-melting satisfaction.

He realized he wanted—needed—to feel her go soft and pliant in his arms, to feel her body tighten and dampen in desire as she gave herself to him, knowing with a fierce sense of primordial male pride that he was the only man she'd given herself to in a long, long time. Because in the end, this was all they'd have, and he didn't want her only memories of a man to be painful. He wanted to give her some of the joy and the pleasure that a man and a woman could have together. Maybe that was why it was so important to him not to hurt her.

She'd asked for nothing, not a promise, not an explanation; she only gave, and it had almost overwhelmed him, touching him on a level no other woman had ever touched him before.

But then again, he'd never met a woman like her before.

He wished he could chalk it up to just lust, but lust settled in his loins and was quickly sated and satisfied. This was something different entirely. It wasn't just that they were totally compatible in bed, but more important, they were totally compatible *out* of bed.

It would have made him nervous if he'd stopped to think about it. Just being with her was...easy. No hassles. No headaches. Not that her feisty, independent stubborn streak didn't rear up occasionally, giving him grief, but he found it amusing rather than annoying. Maybe because she tried so hard to prove that she was strong, tough, that she could handle anything. Including him. And she *was* all the things she tried so hard to be: strong, tough, independent. But she was also so much more. Warm. Giving. Loving. And unselfish with her words, her deeds, her love. But more important, she was vulnerable. He could see it in her big blue eyes when she looked at him. She'd shout the rooftops down denying it, yet he knew she was afraid, yet still she forged ahead, head held high, determined to do whatever she set her mind to.

And it tickled the hell out of him.

He thought of the first night in her bed, when she'd accused him of being worried more about himself getting hurt than her. He almost smiled again. No other woman in her right mind would have dared say such a thing to him, at least not while he was still breathing or within earshot. But she'd never even blinked. She'd thrown the taunt at him, challenging him in a way no woman had ever dared, not caring what the consequences might be.

He should have walked away then. But he couldn't.

That first time, he knew she'd been scared. Under the tremors of desire that had racked her body, he had felt the tremors of fear, although she had desperately tried to hide it, and that alone had made him slow, made him gentle. She made him *feel* things, *do* things, he no longer thought himself capable of.

But in spite of everything, he knew he had to leave. He wouldn't and couldn't let a woman—any woman—get to him so that he felt he had to stay. He had to keep on moving in order to protect himself.

It was a fact of life he'd learned at a young age, a fact he couldn't—wouldn't—forget. But he wanted to leave Savannah with some pleasant memories, wanted her to know that not all men were deceitful and dishonest. He'd always been honest with her right from the beginning, but still, he knew she'd probably be hurt, for a little while anyway.

He knew she'd probably curse him left and right, as well, and he damned himself for it, knowing he *was* going to hurt her. But eventually, hopefully, she'd get over it and forget about him.

But how, he wondered, was he ever going to forget her?

"Cody." Gently Savannah reversed their positions, turning him to his back and staring down at him, her eyes both amused and aroused. "You and Judd have been working all weekend."

If they weren't tending Miss Sophie, they'd been sifting through the ashes of the Kincaid ranch house, or Judd was making trips back and forth into town to send or receive faxes. She had a feeling Cody and Judd were on to something, not that they'd confided in her.

"Do you have a point here?" he asked with a lazy smile.

"You've got to be dead tired."

Grinning, he lifted his head and looked down his body. "Not all of me," he teased, making her laugh. "There are parts of me that are downright wide awake and begging for attention."

Still laughing, she planted quick, fiery kisses to his face, his cheeks, his neck, his chest, until he caught her face in his hands and slanted her head to capture her mouth with his own. The kiss started out playful, but quickly turned passionate as tongues touched, tasted, savored. His hands slid to her back, pulling her on top of him, molding her to him as if they were made to fit together.

Fire quickly ignited, engulfing them both. Lost in the pleasure of each other, they were unaware someone was outside . . . *watching*.

And waiting.

Four hours later, Joey came bounding into the kitchen, his face a combination of sweat and pleasure. Judd had dropped him off less than an hour ago, and he'd lost no time making himself useful "helping" Cody with the completion of the henhouse.

For some reason, Joey had been more excited than usual when he'd come home, not that he wasn't always excited whenever he spent time with Louie. But today he seemed not just excited but full of questions.

"Cody says we need something to drink." Swiping an arm across his forehead, Joey hopped up on a chair and looked at his mother carefully. Mindful of the list he and Louie had come up with, he was trying to see if there was anything "good" about his mother that he hadn't noticed before.

"Ma?"

"What, Joey?" She was busy frying chicken at the stove for Sunday dinner, but paused to open the refrigerator to get him something to drink.

"Can you put your teeth in a glass?"

His question made her hit her head on the top of the inside of the open refrigerator. Extracting two colas and rubbing the top of her head, she looked at her son, not certain she had heard him correctly.

"Can I put my teeth . . . where?"

"In a glass."

She handed him the soda, looking at him skeptically. "No," she said carefully. "Am I supposed to?"

Disappointed, Joey shrugged. "Louie says his grandma can take her teeth out and put them in a glass. She keeps them on a little dresser next to her bed at night."

"I see," Savannah said slowly. "And you thought maybe I could do that with my teeth?"

He shrugged again, looking at a bunch of bananas in a bowl on the table, wondering if he could have one so close to dinner. He reached out to snatch one just as she turned to him. He quickly snatched his hand back—minus a banana.

"Sorry to disappoint you, sport, but my parlor tricks don't extend to popping my teeth out and dropping them in a glass." She handed him the two cans of cola, watching him carefully. Now, why did she have a feeling he was up to something—no good, probably? And why did she know Louie had something to do with it?

"Anything else?" she asked mildly. Joey was thoughtful for a moment, his brows scrunched in a frown. He brightened suddenly.

"Do you think you'd ever want to get a tattoo?"

"A tattoo?" she repeated slowly, trying not to grin. "Well, Joey, I haven't actually thought about it. It's not real high up on my list of accessories."

"Will you?" he asked hopefully, jumping off the chair. He couldn't wait to get back outside and talk to Cody about his ma. He hadn't realized there were so many good things about her. "Think about it, I mean. They got all kinds of real neat designs like rats and snakes and stuff." He was inching his way toward the door.

"Charming."

"And Louie says if you don't look at the needles, you won't faint."

"I see. And Louie has a great deal of experience with tattoos, does he?" She arched one brow at him. "His grandma again?" She was definitely going to have to meet Louie's grandma.

"Nah. Louie read it in a book." He was bouncing from foot to foot, itching to move. He had to go talk to Cody. He checked his pocket again, just to make sure he had the list. He did, crumpled up in a little ball.

"Someone ought to take away that kid's library card," Savannah muttered, turning back to the stove to tend to the chicken. "Go take Cody his drink," she finally ordered, suddenly and sincerely grateful she wasn't Louie's mother or grandmother.

Joey didn't have to be told twice. Colas tucked in his arm, he bounded out the door and around the back of the house, nearly tripping over his shoelaces in his hurry. "I got us some colas." Grinning, he handed over half of his bounty to Cody, who paused to wipe his forehead before gratefully accepting the soda.

"Thanks, sport." He snapped open the cola and took a long pull, wondering why Joey was still standing there staring at him. "Something on your mind, son?" Cody asked, wiping his brow again and leaning back against the almost completed henhouse.

Judd had gone back into town this morning to see if the analysis on Miss Sophie's feed was completed yet. They had some ideas, but once they knew for sure exactly what kind of poison was used, it shouldn't be hard to trace, and then they'd know who was behind all this.

Restless, though, Cody hadn't wanted to just sit around and do nothing. On the other hand, he wasn't about to leave Savannah alone to become a target again, especially with Joey coming home this morning. His first responsibility was to see to their safety. But that didn't mean he had to sit around the house doing nothing. The least he could do was finish the henhouse for her. He'd managed to construct a makeshift wire cage to hold the squalling fowl, but he'd needed to do something with his hands, something constructive. And the lure of the outdoors was too much for him to resist. Besides, at least if he was outside, he was almost assured no one could get near the house—or Savannah and Joey—without him knowing about it.

"My ma." Joey shifted from foot to foot, still holding his cola, feeling a little nervous just 'cause this was so important. Louie told him he had to do this right or Cody would never stay. Hands damp with nerves, Joey averted his gaze, staring at the toes of Cody's scuffed boots, wondering if his own feet would ever get that big.

Watching him in silence, Cody took the cola from the boy's hand and popped open the top, then handed it back to him. "What about your ma, son?" Cody asked, trying not to frown. Clearly something was troubling the boy, and Cody absently found his gaze traveling toward the house, where he knew Savannah was safe inside. "Is there something wrong with your ma, Joey?" The thought had his heart beating double time in sudden fear.

Joey's head came up quickly. "Wrong?" Furiously he shook his head. "Nah," he hurried to reassure Cody. "Nothing wrong. Only right." Taking a deep breath, he hoped he'd remember everything on the list. "Did you know my ma's teeth don't come out?"

Cody almost choked on his cola. It took everything he could muster not to laugh. "They don't?" he asked, feigning surprise.

"Nope. That's 'cause she never chews gun. She's got real good teeth." Joey grinned. Cody seemed *real* impressed.

"I see." Cody nodded his head thoughtfully. "Well, son, I guess good teeth that don't come out are pretty important."

"Yep." Pleased, Joey rocked back on his heels and took a gulp of his soda, swiping his mouth with the back of his hand. "And did you know that even though she's got skinny legs and runs like a girl, my ma's legs are pretty sturdy. They reach all the way to the ground."

"I see," Cody said again with a little nod, desperately trying not to laugh. "I guess sturdy legs can be real helpful, too." Not quite what he thought of Savannah's legs, but obviously important to her son for some reason. Joey had some clear path he was going with this list of his mother's...attributes, and judging by the look on the boy's face, as well as the crumbled paper in his pocket he kept referring to, it was obviously something important to him, something he'd given some thought to. So Cody didn't want to deter him or make him think what he was saying wasn't important, but for the life of him he couldn't figure out what was going on.

"And she doesn't need new shoes, either," Joey added, trying not to frown. "Her eyes ain't so good and she has to wear glasses to read, but she doesn't have any knots in her hair. And did you know that her skin's not brown or wrinkly, neither." Joey's brows drew together. "That's 'cause she never goes in the sun."

"I noticed." Noticed that every tender, delectable inch of her was as soft and tender and as creamy white as a newborn babe. Somehow he thought it best to keep that information to himself.

"And she smells good most of the time." Joey frowned. "'Cept when she's been fooling with Miss Sophie."

Cody nodded thoughtfully, the image of his reaction to Savannah's scent fresh in his mind. He deliberately rechanneled his thoughts. "Well, son, it's hard to smell good when you've been mucking around a bull's stall."

"But she's not scared of thunder," Joey rushed on. "And she doesn't eat a real lot."

"Miss Sophie?" Cody asked with a frown, and Joey rolled his eyes.

"No, not Miss Sophie. My ma," Joey said with a little exasperation, looking at Cody suspiciously. "Have you been talking to Louie?"

Laughing, Cody shook his head. "No, son. Not me." He was lucky he could handle *this* ten-year-old, let alone a second one, especially the infamous Louie.

Shifting his weight, Joey sneaked another peek at the list in his pocket, brightening suddenly. "Did you know my ma's a real good teacher and knows just about everything?"

"Really?" One brow rose mildly.

"Yep." Pleased, Joey grinned. "But that's just 'cause she's so old."

This time Cody did choke on his soda. "Son," he finally said when he stopped laughing and caught his breath. "I think your mother is a wonderful woman—"

"You do?" Eyes bright and hopeful, Joey looked adoringly at Cody. Louie was right! Again! His plan worked! It worked! Cody thought his mother was wonderful. That had to mean he thought she was the "right" woman.

"Yes," Cody said slowly, wondering what he'd just said to make the kid beam like a laser. "But it might not be a good idea to let your mother hear you say that she's . . . real old or that she doesn't have wrinkly skin." Amused beyond belief, Cody couldn't help but smile. "Not that those aren't fine things," he hurried to reassure Joey, since the laser seemed to dim a bit. "But let me tell you a little secret about women." He drew the boy closer, then went down on his knee so they were eyeball-to-eyeball. "You see, women can be a bit . . . touchy sometimes, especially about how we describe them."

"But why?" Joey asked with a frown, clearly confused. "It's all good stuff."

"Yeah, son, I know." Cody sighed, lifting his eyes to scan the horizon. Something was making him . . . restless. And it wasn't Joey or their conversation. Bringing his attention back to the boy, he tried again. He didn't know if the kid was old enough to understand women. Hell, he wasn't certain *he* was old enough to understand women. "But women aren't real partial to us . . . talking about them."

Joey felt a sudden rise of panic, wondering if he'd done something wrong. He didn't know you weren't supposed to talk about women. He wondered why. "But Louie said that—"

Cody suddenly stopped listening. Something had caught his eye in the pasture just beyond, where a thick clump of trees grew. Someone was out there . . . watching them. He'd seen something, a flash of color. He didn't think; he just reacted. He clamped his hands down on Joey's shoulders and swiftly rose to his feet.

"Go in the house, Joey." He had to get the boy indoors and out of danger.

"But—" Bewildered by Cody's abrupt change, Joey merely stared at him in confusion. He'd never seen Cody look so mad before. "I was just trying to tell you all the good stuff about my—"

"Go inside, Joey. *Now.* Just do it." Cody's voice brooked no argument, and he firmly but gently turned Joey around, giving him a nudge toward the house. "Go inside and stay there." He was no longer a friend, but a ranger doing his job. "And keep your mother inside until I come back. Now go!"

Hurt and trying to hide tears, Joey took off, wondering why Cody was so mad at him. He had a real angry face and a real mad voice, and Joey didn't know what he'd done. He'd thought he'd done a pretty good job remembering everything good about his ma, but maybe he'd forgotten something, or maybe he'd said something that wasn't so good. Fighting back tears, Joey barreled into the house, slamming the door shut behind him. The sound had Savannah hurrying from the kitchen.

"Joey?" She took one look at his ashen face and trembling lips and immediately knew that something was terribly wrong. "What happened?" She placed her hands on her son's shoulders, stopping him from bolting to his bedroom. Swiping his nose with the back of his hand, Joey averted his gaze so she wouldn't see his tears.

"Cody's mad at me," he said forlornly.

"What?" Savannah frowned. "Joey, are you sure?" This didn't make any sense. She'd never even seen a hint of temper in Cody. Clearly Joey must be mistaken. "What makes you think Cody's mad at you?"

He raised stricken eyes to hers, his eyes moist with unshed tears. "We was just talking, and suddenly he got a real mad look on his face and told me to go in the house. He wouldn't even let me explain."

"Explain what?" Savannah's frown deepened. "Honey, what were you talking about?"

Uh-oh. Joey dropped his chin to his chest, wondering if Louie had a plan for getting him out of *this* mess. If his ma found out about what he and Cody had been talking about, he knew he'd be in deep, serious doo-doo. It was bad enough Cody was mad at him; he didn't want his ma mad at him, too. He sighed dejectedly, wondering if Louie had another plan.

"Joey?"

Head still lowered, he mumbled something she couldn't hear.

Gently Savannah lifted his chin. "I didn't hear you, honey. What did you say?"

"Cody and I were talking about...stuff." He shuffled his feet, swiping at his nose again. "Just...stuff."

"I see," she said quietly, not seeing at all but trying to make some sense out of this. Clearly something had happened. She wasn't imagining the hurt look on her son's face, but she couldn't envision Cody doing anything to hurt Joey, especially when he'd gone out of his way to be kind and patient with the boy. Something wasn't right. "Did Cody say anything else, honey?"

"Yeah," he admitted reluctantly, and Savannah wondered if she was going to have to start pulling the words out of her son's mouth with pliers.

"What else did he say, honey?" She waited patiently, watching him, her heart aching at the stricken look on his face.

Sniffling and feeling miserable, Joey swiped at his nose again. "He told me to come in the house and stay here. Said to keep you inside, too, until he came back."

"Came back?" Savannah frowned, worry and fear mingling to tighten her stomach. She glanced out the window of the back door. "Where did Cody go?"

Joey turned and stared dejectedly out the window. "I don't know," he said forlornly, hoping that Cody wasn't so mad at him that he was gone for good. Joey swiped his nose again, trying hard not to cry at the thought of Cody maybe never coming back. Sniffling, he looked at his ma, hoping Louie had another plan, because if he didn't, he had a feeling Cody was never, ever going to stay and be his dad.

And he had a feeling when his ma found out, she was going to be real, real mad.

Chapter Ten

Cody kicked the black stallion into a run and rode hard and fast across the open land, heading due north past the pasture where his daddy was buried, knowing time was at a premium.

He knew he'd never be able to maneuver his Jeep across the rough terrain near where he'd seen the movement; the land was too rough, the trees too dense. So he'd hopped in the Jeep and headed toward his father's ranch to saddle the stallion. He'd also retrieved his gun from the glove box of the car. Normally he never took his gun off, but since he'd been staying at Savannah's, he didn't want to scare either her or Joey by wearing it so conspicuously, and leaving a loaded gun in the house with a child wasn't an option. He'd learned to respect the power of weapons early in his life, so he'd simply kept it safely locked in his glove box.

Now he was grateful he had. This was the first real break he'd had, the first time the coward had actually gotten close enough to be seen, and he wanted to catch him before he disappeared.

Cody's hands tightened on the reins as he urged the horse on. He tried to keep his emotions in check and his temper cool. He needed a clear, calm head.

As Cody rode, eating up the land, he thought of the afternoon the henhouse had caught fire, remembered the fear in Joey's eyes and the stark terror in Savannah's. The images ate at his mind. He remembered, too, the way he'd felt when Judd had called to tell him about Savannah's accident. He'd never been a man prone to fear. Just wasn't part of his nature—he couldn't allow it to be, not with his occupation. Fear was an enemy, as was any emotion that destroyed or disrupted your concentration. But when he thought about Savannah's accident, for the first time in his life, he knew fear in a way he'd never experienced. It left a cold, bitter taste in his mouth, and it wasn't a taste he cared much for, nor one he ever wanted to experience again.

And he wouldn't, not if he had his way.

Whoever this bastard was, he itched to get his hands on him for all that he'd done. The fear became cold, hard fury that someone had dared take so much from him. His father. His land.

And almost Joey and Savannah.

Climbing the steep, rough hill toward the clump of trees, Cody drew out his gun, his eyes searching, his movements quick. The air suddenly seemed still and quiet, too quiet. Every nerve in his body was screaming. Even to his own ears, his breathing was fast and harsh. He concentrated on the quiet sense of anticipation and wild rush of adrenaline.

He felt a profound sense of danger and his eyes suddenly narrowed. He pulled in the reins, slowing the horse down. The world seemed to grow even quieter. He could feel the hot sun beating down on him. Hear the squawk of a hawk high in the air, the sound suddenly electrifying in the sudden, eerie quiet of the day. His senses kicked into high gear as his gaze took everything in.

Someone was watching him.

He couldn't see anyone, but he could feel it, sense it, and anticipation quickened his pulse as his gaze continually scanned the horizon, wishing the bastard would come out in the open and show his face.

Like a man.

Something bright red caught Cody's attention, and he urged the horse forward. Stuck on a clump of trees was a piece of material. Bringing the stallion to a halt, he leaned over and plucked the bright red fabric loose. From the jagged way the material was torn, it looked as if he'd gotten caught up in the trees, and in his rush, had torn a piece of his shirt. He was either careless. Or foolish. From the looks of things, probably both.

Still fingering the shirt, Cody glanced around, trying to absorb something of the man from the material. He was damn close, so close he could almost smell the other man. Smell his fear and his confidence, but it was a misplaced confidence because he'd made a mistake—a fatal one.

Knowing that, Cody allowed his emotions to slip. He wanted this guy in a way that made him ache, not just for himself and what he'd done to Savannah and Joey, but for what he'd done to his father. Knowing someone had deliberately and intentionally harmed something that was his only fueled the fury growing low and slow in his belly. He ached to even the score and make things right, for himself and his father. He didn't much like cowards, never had, never would. And killing an unarmed man and terrorizing a woman and a helpless child qualified as the actions of a coward in his book.

The material of the shirt seemed to burn his hands. Not many men in the county had a fondness for bright red shirts. Shouldn't be too hard to trace.

A sound caught his attention, and Cody whirled, his gun drawn and cocked, his eyes narrowed. He saw the flash of light a moment before he felt the pain of the bullet slam into him, knocking the breath from him. The shirt slipped from his hands as he tumbled forward off his horse, but not before the face in the distance registered.

* * *

"Louie, I'm telling you somethin' happened. Somethin' bad. Your plan didn't work." Switching the phone to his other ear, Joey curled his legs under him on his bed as he tried to stretch the phone cord further. "He got mad. Real mad. Honest, I wouldn't lie.... Yeah, I told him all that." Sighing, Joey rolled his eyes, feeling miserable. "Louie! Would ya listen? I told him *everything*. I even told him about her being real smart and...Louie? Louie?"

Frowning, Joey looked at the receiver, but there was no sound. He couldn't even hear Louie breathing anymore. Wondering if Louie had hung up on him, Joey dialed Louie's house again, but nothing happened. Slamming the phone down, Joey hopped off the bed.

"Ma?" He headed into the kitchen where his ma was just sitting at the kitchen table. He frowned. "What ya doing?"

She glanced up at him. Ever since Joey had come barreling into the house, almost in tears, telling her Cody was mad at him, she'd had a terrible feeling something was wrong. She glanced out the window, wondering where Cody had gone and wishing he'd come back.

"Nothing, son, why?"

"How come you're just sitting here doing nothing?" His ma never did just nothing. She was always doing something. Dishes. Sewing. Cooking. Laundry. He couldn't remember ever seeing her just sitting before. It seemed real strange. There was a pile of potatoes in front of her and a small knife next to the potatoes, but she didn't seem to be doing anything with them. "Are you mad at me, too?"

She forced a tenuous smile, absently fingering the knife. "No, honey. I'm not mad at you."

He breathed a sigh of relief. "Good, 'cause Cody's mad at me, and now I think Louie's mad at me, too." He looked so dejected, she reached out an arm to draw him close.

"What makes you think Louie's mad at you?" As long as they'd lived in Silver Creek, Louie and Joey had been inseparable; she couldn't even imagine Louie being mad at her son. At least not for more than two minutes max.

"He hung up on me." She felt him relax against her, realizing this was one of those times, in spite of the fact that he was an almost-grown-up ten-year-old, that he needed a mother's hug.

She frowned. "How come?"

Joey shrugged. "Don't know. I don't like people being mad at me." She hugged him close for a minute until he started squirming.

"Well, I'm sure if you call Louie back and you two talk, you'll be able to settle things."

"Nope. Tried it. Something's wrong with the phone."

Suddenly feeling fearful and not knowing why, Savannah was on her feet in an instant, heading toward the wall phone. "What do you mean something's wrong with the phone?"

A movement caught her eye, and she came to a dead standstill, frowning, not recognizing the strange vehicle that had just come to a screeching halt in front of the house. A frisson of fear washed over her when she saw James Hooper get out. Her fear was so palpable she could feel it in the air, and she shivered.

Instinctively she went to the back door and pulled it open, stepping out onto the porch. "James?"

"Afternoon." Smiling, he tipped his hat at her. "Miss Savannah, I'm afraid I've got some bad news for you." Fingering his Stetson, he took a step closer to the porch and her. She rubbed her suddenly chilled arms, trying to bank down her sudden apprehension. But fear leapt to her throat, almost clogging her voice.

"What kind of bad news?" She watched him carefully. Savannah tried to suppress the sudden urge to run into the house and slam the door in his face.

James came up on the porch, his eyes never leaving hers. "Miss Savannah, I'm afraid Cody Kincaid's had an accident. We tried phoning you, but seems to be something

wrong with your phone." Concern etched his features as he
fingered his hat, trying not to look directly at her.

"Cody's had an accident?" Horror washed over her, and
she clutched at James's arm, feeling the color drain from her
face. "What's happened? What kind of accident?" Fran-
tically she glanced around, hoping Cody would suddenly
materialize and this would all be a bad dream. "Where is
he?" Her fingers absently dug into the flesh of James's arm,
and he gently pried her loose with a sympathetic smile.

"Now, don't go fretting, Miss Savannah. Cody's at my
daddy's house. Seems he took a bullet in the shoulder, but
it's not too serious. Like I said, we tried phoning...." His
voice trailed off, and he shrugged.

"A bullet in his shoulder?" Stunned and horrified, Savannah merely stared at him. "Cody's been shot?"

She felt as if her knees were going to buckle, and tried not
to recoil when he reached out a hand to steady her. His
touch sent another shiver of fear and apprehension rolling
over her, but she forced her own personal feelings back and
tried to clear her mind to think rationally.

Who on earth would want to shoot Cody? And more important, why? Somehow she knew this was all related to
what had been happening the past few weeks. John Kincaid's death. The henhouse fire. Her accident. The poison-
ing of Miss Sophie. And now Cody had been shot. But why?
Why was someone doing all this? She wanted to scream in
frustration and rage. There didn't seem to be any solid answer. Thinking clearly now was impossible when her mind
was filled with worry about Cody.

"James?" Her voice held an unspoken question. She
couldn't seem to put into words her very real fear. She held
her breath, clutching her trembling hands together in worry
until James smiled softly.

"I do believe Cody's gonna be fine, ma'am." She let out
a relieved sigh. "Daddy thinks it's just a flesh wound, but
Cody's lost some blood, so Daddy thought it best not to
move him until the doc can have a look at him. He put a call

into him, as well as one to the sheriff, but Cody asked that someone come tell you so you wouldn't worry."

"Take me to him." Realizing her words sounded like a command, Savannah struggled to get a hold of herself, swallowing the fear and the bile that rose in her throat. All she could think of was Cody. He had always been so strong, so safe, she couldn't imagine him being hurt, shot, *needing her.*

Maybe it was time she realized—they both realized—that they needed each other.

"Yes, ma'am," James said agreeably. "That's exactly what I intend to do." Feeling a profound sense of relief, as well as a sense of foolishness for her rather rude behavior, especially when the man was merely trying to be a good neighbor, she forced a smile for James, embarrassed.

"James, I'm sorry. Please forgive my manners. I appreciate your kindness." She touched a hand to her forehead, trying to stay calm. Her behavior in light of the circumstances had been unbelievably rude, but she couldn't help it. The thought that Cody was hurt and needed her colored everything.

Until this moment, she hadn't realized how much she'd come to depend on Cody, to need him, to lean on him. Now, knowing he was hurt, knowing he *needed* her, she realized she had to draw from that reservoir of strength she'd used all these years in order to be strong.

But, dear God, it was hard.

At the moment, she didn't feel very strong, and she didn't feel very brave. She felt scared and helpless, and all she wanted was to see Cody and hold him in her arms so that she'd know he was safe—so she'd feel safe.

Blinking back tears, she tried to take a deep breath to calm herself. It wouldn't do for either Cody or Joey to see her trembling like a rabbit caught in the cross hairs of a rifle. She had to be strong right now—for everyone's sake.

"If you're ready, I'll be happy to take you to Cody, ma'am." Completely solicitous, James took her arm to lead her to the car, but Savannah came to a sudden halt.

"Wait. I have to tell my son where I'm going." Her mind was whirling a hundred miles a minute as she hurried back into the kitchen. Joey was standing at the sink, watching them through the window.

"Joey, listen. Cody's . . . had a little accident." She chose her words carefully, not wanting to scare her son. "James is going to take me to him."

"What kind of an accident?" Suddenly frightened, Joey was frowning, craning his neck to look out the window. "Where is Cody?"

"At the Hooper ranch, son. Now, please don't ask me any questions, I'm going over there and I promise I'll bring Cody home soon. Stay here and don't go anywhere."

"Can't I come? Please? I want to see Cody."

"No, honey. Not now." She paused and kissed the frown on his forehead. "Don't worry. Cody's going to be fine, I promise." She ruffled his hair and tried to smile. "Mr. Hooper's already called the sheriff and a doctor, so Cody will be in good hands. I'll be home as soon as I can. And keep trying the phone. James said they tried calling me but couldn't get through. I'm sure if you patch things up with Louie, you'll feel better," she added, hoping it would distract him from worrying about Cody.

"I told you, ma. It went dead when I was trying to get through to Louie. I'll keep trying, though." He had to get through to Louie, had to tell him all about what was going on. Louie had better be able to come up with another plan, one that wouldn't make Cody mad 'cause once Cody was better, he was going to try again.

"Good." She yanked open the back door again, anxious to get to Cody. "Now, stay here until I get back. Don't leave the house." With a wave, she ran out the door toward James's car.

Judd Powers had just walked in the back door of his house when the phone rang. He snatched it up as he passed. He'd just gotten the definitive analysis on Miss Sophie's corn feed and was headed over to see Cody, but he'd decided to stop home first.

"Sheriff Powers." He listened for a moment, his hand tightening on the receiver. "What do you mean, 'How's Cody?'" Judd frowned. "Joey, what are you talking about? Isn't Cody there with you and your ma?" Swearing softly under his breath, Judd began to pace, listening carefully. "How long ago did they leave? And you're sure she left with James Hooper?" An unnatural feeling began to spread through his gut. The pieces of *who* were suddenly falling into place, but what he couldn't figure out was why. "All right, Joey, now listen to me and listen very carefully. I want you to stay in the house and lock the doors. Do you hear me? One of my deputies will be there in ten minutes to pick you up. He'll bring you to my house until your mother gets back. You can keep Louie company. All right? Now, stay put and don't let anyone else in but my deputy. Got it?"

Still swearing, Judd slammed out the door, adjusting his hat along the way. He knew time was of the essence if James had Savannah, but he couldn't take a chance on leaving Joey home alone and unprotected. He radioed his office as he tore out of the driveway, trying to make some sense of this. But only one question kept reverberating through his mind: what the hell had happened to Cody?

"James?" Savannah glanced around. "Where are you taking me?" So absorbed in her own thoughts, she'd just realized that the landscape suddenly looked strange. "This isn't the way to your father's house."

They were driving along one of the barren, lonely roads that wound its way toward the many desolate bluffs overlooking Kincaid land. She remembered Cody telling her about playing along these bluffs when he was a boy, camping out under the stars. It had sounded so blissful, so peaceful, but it didn't seem peaceful now. Only frighteningly desolate and eerie.

The feeling of apprehension returned, and her hand instinctively went to the handle of the car door.

"I wouldn't try it if I were you," James said calmly, turning to her. It was then she saw the small pistol in his hand. It was pointed directly at her. One of his hands was on the wheel, the other on the gun. "You might hurt yourself jumping from a moving vehicle, and I sure wouldn't want anything to hurt that delicate skin." His smile froze the blood in her veins, and the breath seemed to back up in her throat.

She couldn't take her eyes from the gun. Terror gripped her. This had to be a joke, a sick, crazy joke. Slowly she raised her horrified gaze to his, and then she saw it: the madness. It was as clear as the air that surrounded them, as clear as the fear that pounded through her veins, nearly knocking the breath from her. This was no joke; this was very, very real.

"You," she breathed, her hand tightening on the door handle of the car as everything seemed to fall into place. "It was you all this time." The car was moving too fast for her to jump, and she realized she was trapped. Trapped with a madman.

"Yes, dear."

"Cody." Her heart pounded into triple time, and without thinking, she grabbed James's arm. The gun wavered in his hand, and the car swerved as he tried to make adjustments. "What have you done to Cody?"

"I'd be careful about grabbing me," he said calmly, steering the car back on course. He glanced down at the gun and chuckled softly. "We wouldn't want this to go off accidentally, not after I've gone through so much trouble to have you to myself."

His eyes, clouded by madness, slid over her, intimately caressing her. Revulsion at his words almost made her sick. "I'd at least like an opportunity to enjoy you."

The way his eyes slid over her made her cringe, and she shrank away from him, wishing the door would melt so she could just slip through it and away from this madness. And him. She'd die before she ever let the likes of James Hooper lay a hand on her. She'd almost beaned him once with a cast-iron skillet, and skillet or not, she'd do it again if he even dared try to touch her.

"Cody will kill you if you even think about laying a hand on me." She knew the words to be true, as true as any she'd ever uttered. She remembered the fiercely possessive, protective look on Cody's face the day he'd come charging into Judd's office to get her after her accident. The memory brought a feeling inside so strong she wanted to weep again. Maybe Cody hadn't said the words, yet she knew he wasn't a man of many words, but a man of action. And every action and every touch had told her, shown her, that he loved her, loved her in the same way she loved him.

"You think I'm afraid of Cody Kincaid?" James laughed outright, clearly amused and mad.

Her eyes slid closed against the hot rush of tears that came without warning. Only a fool wouldn't be afraid of Cody, especially in light of what had happened. If she were so inclined, she'd pity James, for clearly he had no idea the wrath Cody would bring down on him when he found out what he'd done.

She'd give anything right now to have Cody here with her, holding her, making her feel safe, telling her—even ordering her—to do something, anything. She feared she might never see Cody again, and suddenly she simply couldn't bear the thought.

"Now, don't go wasting your tears, at least not on Kincaid." James's eyes went over her again in a way that made her self-conscious about the shorts and T-shirt she wore. She crossed her legs, huddling closer to the door, her eyes never leaving him.

Chuckling softly, he pulled the car over to the side of the barren, desolate road and shut off the engine. With a hand free now, he leaned over and ran a finger down her face. She recoiled in horror at his touch. It only made him chuckle more.

"You know, he never deserved you. No, sirree. Kincaid just never deserved a fine lady like you." He leaned close, forcing her to inch nearer to the door. It was locked, or she would have hit the handle and bolted. "You know," he whispered, his face so close to hers she felt the warmth of his breath fanning over her. She wanted to gag. "It was me you should have taken to your bed. Not that...interloper." Sadly he shook his head as if she'd made a grave error in judgment. "But you weren't interested, were you? Thought you were better than me. Thought you were better than everyone in town. Always walking around with your nose in the air, so high and mighty."

A slow, disquieting grin slid across his features, chilling her. The madness was growing, gathering steam, mixing with anger, and she realized with sudden clarity just how dangerous he really was.

"I watched you," he whispered, trailing a hand down her arm, then clamping a hand down hard on her wrist until she nearly winced in pain. She tried to pull free, but he held on tight. "I watched the two of you, watched you pressing yourself up against him, kissing him. Watched his hands paw all over you, touching you. Shameful was what it was." His voice had dropped to a husky whisper even as his hand tightened painfully on her wrist. "You should have been mine."

Her eyes, frantic with fear and fury, searched his. Although he was only about six or seven inches taller than her, he outweighed her by at least a hundred pounds. But she wasn't about to just sit here and become a pawn for some deranged madman. She had to think! She had to do something.

"You mean you watched us?"

Horror mingled with fear, and she merely stared at him, her eyes wild, her mind racing, hoping she could keep him talking while she thought of something to help her escape. The mere idea that he had watched her and Cody had her fists clenching.

"I watched," he whispered. "And I saw you."

Furious, she lashed out at him with her free hand, wanting to hit him, to scratch him, to do anything to him, anything that would help her get away. He captured her free hand, laughing and yanking hard until she cried out in pain. It seemed to amuse him. Holding on to her wrists with one hand, he picked up the small revolver and tucked it into his pocket, then threw open the car door and half pulled, half dragged her out.

"You know none of this would have happened had that boy just stayed in Austin where he belonged." His anger was growing as he dragged her by her wrists behind him. She stumbled, trying to get her balance on the rocky, uneven ground. James kept talking, his voice eerily calm, as if he was talking to himself. "Why, with his daddy dead and no one to claim the land, it would have been real simple and real cheap for my daddy to buy it. And I would have made it possible. Me!"

Turning toward her, he dragged her close and upright until his face was close to hers. She tried not to cringe at the craziness she saw so clearly. He grinned then, clearly pleased with himself. "All these years my daddy thought I was useless, didn't think I could handle things, but I showed him. I showed them all! We would have had that Kincaid land, and for a song, too, and it would have been all my doing." He patted his chest proudly. "It would have been my finest accomplishment. I brought you up here so you could see what I accomplished, all that I've achieved."

He spread his arms wide. "This was all going to be mine. *Mine.*" His gaze swung back to hers. "And so were you." He frowned, suddenly desolate, and he shook his head as if remembering. "But then Cody had to come back and ruin everything."

"You . . . killed John Kincaid?" Horror had her merely staring at him in disbelief.

"Why, of course, my dear." Clearly proud, he smiled at her as he drew a small piece of rope out of his pocket. Carefully he began to bind her wrists together in front of her. She decided against fighting him—for the moment. She wanted to keep him talking, hoping to catch him off balance and distract him. But she knew she couldn't act impulsively; to do so could be deadly. She had to keep her wits about her and outthink him.

"It was quite simple really. He was old anyway, and he didn't need that land nearly as much as my daddy did. His time had passed." Examining the binding holding her wrists, he smiled at her. "Fire can be such a nasty thing. But Kincaid was dead before he ever hit the ground. Put up a struggle, though."

He shook his head, nudging her toward a boulder. Savannah sat, gauging the distance to the edge of the bluff from where he was standing. Facing her, his back was to the bluff, and for a moment, her own thoughts horrified her. She'd never thought about killing before, but then again, she'd never been trapped by a madman before. A madman who had clearly killed once and appeared quite prepared to do it again.

"Old man Kincaid was just as stubborn as that son of his." His glazed eyes met hers. "But now we don't have to worry about either of them, do we, dear?"

Savannah swallowed hard. "What...what have you done to Cody?"

James looked at her for a long, hard minute, and then a slow, satisfied smile lit his face. "Why, it's simple, my dear. I killed him."

His shoulder was bleeding like a son of a bitch, and it hurt like hell, but it was nothing compared to the white-hot rage bubbling inside his veins.

James Hooper was a dead man.

Dragging himself to his feet, Cody scooped his gun off the ground with his good arm and whistled softly, bringing his stallion running. He ripped off what remained of his shirt and managed to tie a makeshift tourniquet to stem the bleeding. It wasn't the first time he'd been shot, and luckily, it was little more than a flesh wound. But in order to manage what he had to do, he had to get the bleeding under control. Now. It took several attempts and a few long, strong, strings of curses before he had the tourniquet on properly. The pain he would deal with later.

Annoyed and frustrated with himself, he mounted his horse, wincing as he gathered the reins. As if sensing his urgency, the stallion's hooves seemed to fly over the land. Pain or not, there was only one thing on his mind: James Hooper.

The bastard.

He'd seen him clearly a moment before the bullet had slammed into him. There was no doubt about it. No doubt, either, that he'd probably used the same rifle he'd used to shoot out Savannah's tire. Knowing how close James had come to killing Savannah and Joey made Cody's blood run cold.

He'd already tried once; Cody had no doubt he'd try again.

What he couldn't figure out was why. What the hell did James hope to accomplish by hurting Savannah and Joey?

Cody shook his head. This didn't make any sense. And why had James killed his father?

Paul Hooper couldn't afford the Kincaid ranch—that was clear. He was in debt up to his eyeballs, so what was the point of all of this?

Just the thought brought another fire to his gut. He didn't know, but one thing was certain. He was going to find out, and *then* he was going to make him pay.

Now all he had to do was find him.

Another thought crowded Cody's mind, causing his blood to run cold.

Before James got to Savannah.

Chapter Eleven

Savannah wanted to scream and scream and never stop. The urge came so quickly, so strongly, she had to clamp her teeth over her lip to stop herself. More horrified than she believed possible, she simply stared at James, unable and unwilling to comprehend his words. She swallowed the huge lump in her throat, fighting back tears of grief, tears of anger, tears of rage.

"You . . . you killed Cody?" she whispered, forcing the words out. She wanted to weep, to strike out at him, to hurt him the way she hurt right now, with a pain that was as sharp as a pick and went straight to her soul.

She shook her head, blinking away the quick, hot rush of salty tears that filled her eyes. Cody. Dear God. *He'd killed Cody.* An anguished sob escaped her, and she saw his smile. It only infuriated her, mingling with her grief and giving her a sense of purpose, of determination. Lifting her bound hands, she dashed at her eyes, not wanting to give James the satisfaction of seeing her tears.

She couldn't believe it, wouldn't believe it. It wasn't possible, it just wasn't possible.

Cody was dead.

No!

God wouldn't have given her something so bright, so wonderful, only to take it away. Not now, when she'd never even had a chance to tell Cody how much he'd meant to her, how she felt about him, how much she needed—wanted him. The unfairness of it all made her want to weep again.

"Yep." James's smile broadened, and he casually examined his nails as he paced a path in front of her. "Shot him dead right off his horse." He looked at her, his eyes gleaming. "And I enjoyed every blessed minute of it, missy." He shrugged as if taking a man's life were of no more importance than the debris blowing at his feet. "Every single blessed minute." He shrugged. "Had no choice. He was all that stood between me and pleasing my daddy, giving him the one thing he wanted and needed to keep our little ranch going."

"But surely you can't believe you'll get away with this?" She shook her head. No one could be that mad.

"Now, Miss Savannah, of course I'm going to get away with this." He nodded his head confidently, as if trying to make her understand. "Why, who's going to stop me?"

She struggled to understand, to put the jagged pieces of this puzzle together. "But why...why did you start the fire in the henhouse? Why...why shoot out my tire? Why kill Cody?"

Grief and rage mingled, clogging her throat, clouding her mind, but she struggled to keep a clear head. She needed to understand, to try to figure out what James's motives were and how desperate he really was so she could try to devise a way to help herself. Because she knew now, with an aching heart, that she was alone in a way she'd never felt alone before.

Because now Cody was gone.

No! She'd never believe it, never accept it. She couldn't, because if she did accept it, she knew she would die, too.

Everything inside of her would slowly fold up and simply wither and die.

Life had no meaning without him.

She was almost certain she could feel her heart slowly cracking, breaking into little pieces, but she knew she had to try to stay strong, not just for her sake, but for her son. He would be devastated when he found out about Cody. She knew her son well enough to know that she wasn't the only one who had fallen in love with Cody. Her heart broke a little more when she thought of Joey. She'd tried so hard to protect him, to do everything right. Now she understood that a parent could never hope to do everything right, only try the best he or she could. Sniffling, she blinked away her tears. For Joey's sake, she had to find some way out of this mess. She'd brought him into this world, and she was determined to see him through it. But she knew her life would never be the same, not without Cody.

She glanced up at James. For the first time in her life, she knew hatred, knew how it burned and ate at you, fueling something frightening inside. The rush of hatred she felt for James for what he'd taken from her was so strong it stunned her. But she had to control her emotions, had to try to reason with him, keep him calm until she figured out what to do, how to free herself. She hadn't spent most of her life being strong and taking care of herself merely to be defeated by a madman. The sheer audacity of what James had done, and was about to do, was enough to fuel her fury. How dare he! The fury grew low and quickly, pushing aside all the other emotions, and she allowed it, grateful that now something else occupied her mind but grief.

She was going to outsmart this bastard. Even if it was the very last thing she did. Not just for her sake and Joey's, but for Cody's, as well.

"James, please?" She hated the pleading tone of her voice, but she was desperate for answers and pleading for time, time to come up with a plan to save her life. "Explain this to me. I . . . I don't understand." She spoke carefully, keeping her eyes on his, all the while slowly twisting her wrists, trying to loosen the bindings.

With a benevolent smile, he stroked her cheek with a finger again, clucking his tongue as she tried not to recoil from him. "I'm sorry, Miss Savannah. I forgot you're just a woman and all this ranching business is probably a bit over your head." Smiling, he continued, his tone so blatantly patronizing, it infuriated her. The man was truly an idiot! But she welcomed the anger, for it helped stem her raging grief—for the moment. And perhaps all she would need was a moment. She had to stay calm and keep her wits about her in order to try to escape.

"You see, darlin', with Cody's daddy dead and him in Austin, the Kincaid ranch could have been sold at auction, and for a song, too. And me and my daddy could have bought it up lickety-split, and no one would have been the wiser. My daddy would have had the water he needed from Silver Creek in order to maintain our livestock, and I would have proved to my daddy that I was worth something." He grinned, and his eyes glinted with an unholy light. "I figured with Cody's daddy dead, it would take nothing to run you off the land."

"The fire in the henhouse," she whispered with sudden understanding.

He nodded, pleased she understood. "That's right, darling." A momentary frown of concern crossed his beefy features. "I was certain after what happened to Cody's daddy, that another fire would be more than enough to send you packing. A woman alone, with a child to tend to and no man around to protect her..." He chuckled softly. "Well, I figured it would be more than enough to send you on your way."

Obviously this man needed a new way of figuring if he thought that he could scare her into leaving her home.

He chuckled, then sobered so quickly it stunned her. She watched him, mesmerized. His emotions and actions were hair-trigger, changing and swaying with the wind, which only frightened her more. "Although I do confess I didn't know your little boy would be in there. I hope you believe me that I never truly intended to hurt the child.''

She believed no such thing. James would have killed anything and anyone who stood in his way.

He sighed heavily, still pacing in front of her. "I must admit, though, at the time, I didn't realize Kincaid had come back. That changed everything.''

Something moved into his eyes, something other than madness, something far more frightening and dangerous. Rage. Pure, unadulterated rage. He took a step closer, and she braced herself, poised for anything, aware only of the terrible pounding of her heart. When his hand snaked out and caught her by the throat, she felt her breath leave her in a rush.

"Nor did I know you'd take him to your bed.'' His fingers were tightening, and she could barely breathe. Hot tears filled her widened eyes, but she never took her gaze from his. "Why?'' He looked truly perplexed. "Why did you do that, Miss Savannah?''

She tried to swallow, tried to breathe, but it was growing impossible. She tried to stay still and calm, but it was more and more difficult. The violence and rage in him were so strong they were emanating from him in waves and terrifying her.

Lifting her bound hands, she plucked at his. "James, please?'' she gasped. "Y-you're . . . hurting me.''

His fingers immediately loosened and he stepped back, looking truly contrite and surprised. "I'm sorry. I truly am.'' Gently, reverently he ran a hand down the length of her hair, brushing it off her face.

She remembered Cody's gentle hands doing the same thing. And she wanted to weep again.

"But you should never have done that.'' He shook his head and his face grew grim. "No, siree. You should never have taken that man to your bed.'' He lifted his glazed eyes to hers. "You were mine, Miss Savannah. Mine!'' The vehemence in his voice caught her off guard, and she cringed, shrinking back from him. "I've watched and waited, biding my time all these years, being patient, just waiting for the day you realized we were meant to be together. I thought for sure once I had the Kincaid land you'd see that.''

Oh, God. He'd been watching her all this time. Her skin began to crawl, and she wondered just how long his madness had been going on and why no one had ever seen it before.

Now she understood why the man had always given her the creeps. Why he seemed so odd. He wasn't odd; he was deranged.

He smiled suddenly, but sweat was pouring off his face. ''But now that Cody's dead, I'll have his land and his woman.'' Pleased, he chuckled, absently mopping his brow with the back of his hand. ''Now there's nothing standing between us.'' His eyes caressed her face, and he looked at her in fascination, the way a child might look at a favorite doll. Slowly, carefully he laid a hand against her cheek, and she struggled not to scream. ''We can finally be together,'' he said softly. ''You'd like that, Miss Savannah, wouldn't you?''

She couldn't answer, couldn't find the words to tell him she'd rather die a thousand deaths than let him touch her.

Suddenly he was looming over her menacingly. The hand at her cheek slid to her throat. And tightened. Slowly, carefully he pulled her upward until she was on her feet, facing him. Her legs were shaking so badly she would have collapsed in a heap if he hadn't had a hold of her throat.

He pressed his sweating face close to hers, his hideous mouth dangerously close. ''You'd like that now, wouldn't you, Miss Savannah?'' His fingers tightened until she was standing on tiptoe, the toes of her sandals barely scraping the dusty ground. ''Answer me,'' he demanded, shaking her like a rag doll. ''You'd like that, wouldn't you?''

She couldn't answer, couldn't speak—at the moment, all Savannah could do was close her eyes and pray.

Judd was just coming out of the Hoopers' front door when he spotted Cody, riding hard and hell-bent for leather.

Too grateful he was still alive, Judd didn't bother with pre-liminaries as he took the stairs three at a time and headed toward him. "He's got Savannah."

With his limp, bloody arm hanging at his side, Cody brought the stallion to an abrupt halt and swore long and hard as fear unlike anything he'd ever known before clenched at his guts.

Savannah.

His eyes slid closed on another oath. The bastard had Savannah.

"His old man have any idea where he might be?" Cody's eyes were cold and empty, so empty Judd almost shivered.

"Thinks he might have taken her to one of the bluffs overlooking Kincaid land." Judd's eyes strayed toward the distance, where the vague outline of the bluffs could be seen glinting against the sunlight. "Said James used to go up there and hide when he was a boy." Judd had a feeling there was no place on earth James could hide now, not where Cody wouldn't find him.

"He thinks I'm dead." Cody's eyes were dark, his face grim. "He won't be expecting me."

Judd let out a heavy sigh, glancing at Cody's arm. At the moment, he wasn't certain who was more dangerous—James or Cody. The look on Cody's face was enough to frighten the dead. If the circumstances were different, he might pity James Hooper.

Judd nodded. "I figure I'll go up the paved road with the Jeep, but I'll let him know I'm coming." He paused, won-dering if what he was about to say would be James Hooper's death sentence. He thought about it, then dismissed it, re-alizing he had a helpless citizen to protect. He had to put Savannah's safety and well-being before the welfare of a murderer. "Why don't you head up the other side of the bluff? If he's not expecting you, we might have a chance to take him by surprise." *Before anyone else gets hurt,* Judd thought, but reconsidered before saying it.

With a nod, Cody nudged his stallion around, prepared to ride. Judd's voice stopped him.

"Cody?"

Itching to move, Cody tightened his hands on the reins. Glancing back over his shoulder, he waited, saying nothing.

Judd shifted nervously. "James is a very sick man." The lawman in him warred with his very real human emotions, and he had to dig deep to find some sympathy.

Without a word, Cody spurred his horse, leaving a cloud of dusty earth in his wake.

His mind was blank as he rode; nothing filled it but determination. But it was his heart that was heavy and hurting in a way he'd never believed possible.

A vision of Savannah floated across his eyes, and he blinked, trying to keep his mind focused on what he had to do. The thought of James touching her... No, he couldn't even bear the thought. Couldn't bear the thought of another man ever touching her. *No one* would ever touch her again. Not while there was still a breath left in his battered body.

She was his.

He finally accepted it, acknowledged it with a fierce sense of male pride and possessiveness that made him ride harder, faster.

He laughed softly, but the sound was bitter and ragged as he tore across the land, man and horse moving as one. He remembered the other night when he'd thought about leaving—running—realizing now how foolish he'd been. There'd never been anywhere for him to run, not since the day he'd set eyes on her in the north pasture, standing bold as brass, no bigger than spit in a well, hands on her hips, chin thrust to the sun, giving him sass, trying so hard to be strong, to be brave, to be independent.

He couldn't help but smile at the image, but it made the ache in his heart deepen. He could run, or at least he could *try* to run, but she'd always be with him, as much a part of him as the blood that slid through his veins.

He loved her.

The depth and breadth of what he felt for her stunned him, humbled him. Maybe now he understood a bit about the love his father and mother had shared. It wasn't something he ever thought possible for himself. He didn't think himself capable of that kind of emotion, that kind of caring, that kind of devotion.

But then again, that was before he'd met Savannah.

He almost smiled again as her image floated through his mind. He thought about all the years before her, long, lonely years when he'd drifted from woman to woman, feeling nothing but an urgent need to run, to roam, to keep himself emotionally distant, never letting anyone close, never really wanting anyone close. He realized now it had been an empty life. Lost memories and wasted years, he thought now with some regret.

Savannah had been right when she'd called him a coward.

A coward, yes.

A fool, no.

He couldn't have run, couldn't have stayed away from her, even if he tried. His intentions had been strong, honorable; he *had* tried to walk away but had found he couldn't because for the first time in his life, he'd found something he wanted, something he needed more than he wanted or needed to run. He'd found someone who'd given him a reason to stay and never look back. He had no regrets.

He'd never thought he'd ever need anything or anyone in his life. He'd thought he was enjoying his solitary, lonely life.

A grim smile tugged at his lips.

The Lone Ranger.

Now he knew differently. Now he knew how rich and full life could be, knew, too, how much fun and joy life could be. But it would be nothing without her.

His hands tightened on the reins as he spurred the horse on. He needed her, knew it as surely as he knew his name. He needed her, and Lord knew she needed him. This time he did smile. Not that she'd ever actually admit it, but she didn't have to. He could see the need in her eyes every time he came near her, touched her, loved her. He saw the need and so much more, finally saw what he couldn't or wouldn't see before. He could see the love. Uncompromising. Unflinching. Unconditional. It was there for him and the entire world to see, without shame, without apology, without conditions.

And damn if that didn't beat all.

His only regret was that he hadn't told her how he felt, but perhaps he couldn't admit it or accept it until now. Now, knowing he might lose her, really lose her, made him realize just how much he loved and needed her.

He'd never felt fear, never felt pain, never felt anything similar to what was seeping through him now like a slow-moving poison. He *couldn't* lose her. He *wouldn't* lose her.

Riding hard, his jaw set, his stance steady, Cody narrowed his eyes in determination as he pulled in the reins to start the slow, treacherous climb up the bluffs.

To Savannah.

"I didn't mean to scare you, Miss Savannah."

All solicitous, James released her so abruptly, she stumbled backward, almost falling over the boulder. She thought she heard the sound of a car engine, then shook her head, certain she was just imagining it. James caught her by the shoulders, his fingers digging painfully into her tender skin as he dragged her closer to him once again.

"But you didn't answer me." His eyes went over her face, slowly, carefully, as if memorizing her every feature. The sun beat down on them unmercifully, and she could feel her body grow damp with fear and perspiration.

Her lips were parched, and she was so thirsty she almost felt dizzy. Absently she licked her lips, and watched in horror as his thumb snaked out to touch her dampened mouth.

"Such a pretty mouth. So delicate. And sweet, I'll bet." His eyes were unfocused, wild, and she was certain he didn't realize how hard he was dragging his thumb against her lip. The urge to bite him, and bite him hard, was so strong, she

fought it back. She knew she would probably only have one
chance and she had to make sure she was smart and used it
wisely.

Her life depended on it.

"Did Cody Kincaid find your mouth sweet?" His voice
had taken on a singsong quality that would have been com-
ical coming from a man his size if it wasn't so terrifying.

"James Hooper, this is Sheriff Judd Powers."

The sudden sound of a man's voice echoing up the gravel
path panicked him. He was still sweating profusely, and his
hands began to shake. As Savannah nearly sagged in relief,
James grabbed her, winding his arm around her throat and
pulling her back against him.

"Keep your mouth shut," James hissed in her ear, reaching in his pocket for the small, pearl-handled pistol. His
hand trembled violently as he held it to her head. "If he
comes up here, I swear I'll shoot you."

Eyes wide, she swallowed hard, trying to keep her wits
about her. She had no doubt he'd do just that. But she
couldn't simply stand by and let him kill Judd.

"We know you've got Savannah Duncan up there with
you," Judd continued through the bullhorn. He had parked
his vehicle less than a quarter of a mile away and climbed
until he'd spotted James's car. He knelt behind it now for
protection. "Let her go, James. It's over. Let her go before
someone else gets hurt."

"No. Never." His arm tightened around Savannah's neck,
and she gasped for air. He had to think. He had to figure a
way out of this. He'd gone to all this trouble to get the Kincaid land. He couldn't fail again. He just couldn't. What
would his daddy think?

No. He couldn't let his daddy down, not again. Not ever
again. He had to do one thing right in his life. Just one
thing. He had to get that land for his daddy. Even if he went
to prison, at least his daddy would be proud of him. He
would have saved the ranch, and no one could take that
away from him. He'd be a good son, then, the kind of son
his daddy had always wanted, hoped for.

"Sheriff?" he called, trying to concentrate. He was trying to remember everything, trying to remember why he was up here. But his thoughts kept scattering like leaves in a fall breeze. He frowned, concentrating hard. "I'll make a deal with you."

His words caused Judd to pause. The man clearly had to be deranged if he didn't understand that he had no position to deal from. There was nowhere for him to go, but until Judd knew Savannah was safe, he had to play the game. "What kind of a deal, James?"

James licked his lips, thinking. He brightened suddenly. "I'll trade you the deed to Kincaid land for the woman."

"You want my land, you come and take it from me." Cody's gun was already cocked and aimed, his finger itching to pull the trigger. Cody saw the gun pointed at Savannah's temple, and his blood ran to ice, almost freezing him in place. He knew he couldn't look at Savannah; he couldn't afford to take his eyes off of James or let anything disrupt his concentration. He'd have one quick, clean shot if he was lucky, and if he flinched or hedged even for a second, it would mean Savannah's life.

James never heard Cody creep up behind him. The sound of his voice caused him to panic. He whirled, taking Savannah with him.

Relief and joy flooded through Savannah as she laid eyes on Cody. Dear God, he wasn't dead. He was alive. Alive! Her aching heart nearly burst with joy, overflowing with love, but she didn't have time to think, only to react as James gave a roar of disbelief and lifted the gun from her temple and pointed it at Cody.

"Noooooo!" she screamed, and lunged at James with her entire body, knocking him off balance and the gun from his hand. They fell to the ground in a tumbled, tangled heap. Sobbing, Savannah beat at him with her bound fists, tears of rage, relief and frustration slipping unheeded down her face. Her banked temper escaped. With a rush of flying fists and feet, she pummeled James as words that would have made a longshoreman blush spewed from her mouth.

"Whoa, whoa, whoa." Holstering his gun, Cody grabbed her around the waist with one arm and hauled her off James just as Judd slipped the cuffs on the dazed and dirty man, pulling him to his feet.

Looking quite confused, James glanced around as if he wasn't quite certain where he was. His eyes focused on Savannah for a moment, and a slow, almost innocent smile flitted across his face.

"I'm sorry, Miss Savannah," he said quietly. "I meant no harm. But you see, my daddy needed that land."

If Cody hadn't been holding on to her, she would have been on him again. Savannah muttered something under her breath as Judd led the man away, something that made Cody almost blush as he shook his head with a smile.

Although reluctant to release her, he set her on her feet but kept an arm around her to keep her close as his eyes went over her quickly, wanting to assure himself she was all right. Except for being a little tousled and dirty from fighting on the ground with James, she appeared to be fine, at least on the outside.

Awed that Cody was really alive and here with her, Savannah could do nothing, say nothing but stare at him, drinking in the sight of him. Without a word, he slid a knife out of his pocket and unbound her wrists, rubbing the raw, tender skin.

"Cody." She finally found her voice, and relief rushed through her, making her weak. She turned in his arms and collapsed against him, burying her face against his chest, clutching at him, so grateful and relieved he was here and alive she simply couldn't speak. She just wanted him to hold her as sobs racked her body.

"Easy. You're all right." He said it as much to reassure himself as he did to reassure her. He ran a hand down her hair, felt her trembling, then hauled her closer, surprised to find his own hands were shaking and his knees were a bit wobbly. "Did he hurt you?" he whispered, stroking her hair, needing her close. She shook her head defiantly, and he couldn't help laughing, releasing the tension that had been wound up inside of him. "And to think I was worried," he teased.

Her head came up, and she saw his smile, that beautiful wonderful smile that made her heart tumble over.

"I . . . I thought you were dead." Sniveling, she snuggled closer. "God, Cody, I don't ever, ever want to go through that again." Her eyes went to his, and she saw something that touched her heart, something she recognized because she saw it every time she looked at him: love. She wondered if he knew it. Absently her eyes drifted over him, and she touched his arm, trying not to shiver at the ugly, bloody wound. "What happened?"

"James took a shot at me." He glanced at his arm. The bleeding had stopped, and now a dull ache remained, but it was nothing compared to the ache he'd felt a few minutes ago when he thought he'd lost her. "Lucky for me he's a bad shot." He held her away from him for a moment, the fear having thankfully passed. Now all that was left was a huge sense of relief and a little bit of fury. "Savannah, you scared the living hell out of me. What were you thinking lunging at him when he had a loaded gun? You could have been killed. When I heard you scream and saw you move . . ." His voice trailed off, and he tried to rein his emotions in, without much luck. His eyes grew dark, his face grim, when he realized how close he'd come to losing her. "If you ever, ever do anything stupid like that again—"

"Stupid?" Her eyes widened. Mindful of his arm, she thumped him on the chest. "Stupid!" She inhaled a great gust of air through her nose. "Did you expect me to just stand there and watch him shoot you?" Eyes blazing, she raised her chin a notch. It amused him and assured him more than words ever could that she was fine. "How dare you—"

"Savannah." He said it so softly it stopped her words.

She glanced up at him, then blinked. "What?" she asked suspiciously.

"Shut up." With a sigh, he hauled her off her feet and covered her still moving mouth with his own. He was trying to kiss her—*trying* being the operative word—but it was hard when he was also trying not to laugh because her mouth was still moving under his, still spewing words *at* him *about* him, no doubt.

He deepened the kiss, tilting her head and slanting his mouth more fully over hers. He finally heard her sigh, felt her arms slide around him and her body lean into him as her mouth finally opened in welcome. He breathed a sigh of relief, then finally released her.

"Savannah, you've had a hell of a day." Draping an arm around her shoulder, he led her down the path. "Let's go home."

"Home?" She glanced up at him. Her eyes questioned his. Usually he said *back to your house* or something along that line. He'd never, ever said the word *home* before, and she tried not to let the hope in her heart flare up. "Home?" she repeated, and he nodded.

"Yep, home."

Her feet slowed. She was hot, tired and weary with fatigue and fear, but this was far too important to wait. She'd waited too long—hoped too long. This was something she needed to know. Now.

"Cody, home is usually a place where you live."

"Yes, I know," he said with a smile, trying to move her along. She wasn't moving. "But I appreciate you pointing that out to me." He nudged her with his hip. She began walking slowly again.

"Permanently. I mean, usually a home is where you live permanently."

"Know that, too," he admitted, trying not to be amused by the fury he saw gathering in her eyes.

She came to a dead stop, chin up, hands on hips. "Does that mean you intend to stay?" She wished her voice wasn't so hopeful, wished her heart wasn't in her voice. In his hands.

He was thoughtful for a moment. "Yep."

He tried to get her moving again. She wasn't having any of it.

"For how long?" Her eyes sought his, and she tried to hide the fear and rampant disappointment that had started to build. "How long do you intend to stay?"

He moved his jaw in thought, glancing out at the land below, land that had been in his family since before the Civil War, land that men had fought for, died for. Land that his father had been killed for. And he knew as sure as he knew his own name, this *was* home.

Until he'd met her, he hadn't realized it, maybe because until he'd met her, it hadn't been a home. It was now. This land was a part of him. Just as much a part of him as she was. His gaze shifted to her, and he tried not to grin.

Maybe it was time he told her. If only to save himself some grief.

"Well now, Savannah, it's hard to tell how long *permanent* will be." He shrugged. "But I figure until I draw my last breath seems permanent enough." He saw the joy leap in her eyes, felt it in his heart. "I want to marry you, Savannah. Unless, of course, you have an objection."

"The only objection I have is that it took you so long."

Laughing, she launched herself at him, nearly knocking him over. He caught her with his good arm, holding her close as she planted kisses all over his face. Shaking his head, he finally let her slide to her feet, knowing if he didn't, it would be a much longer time before they got home. And after the day she'd had, he'd just as soon have a nice, warm, comfortable bed under her rather than a dusty, rugged road.

Still in his arms, she smiled at him. "What made you change your mind?"

He sighed. "Well, I figure with the trouble you keep getting into, it's not safe to leave you on your own." He kissed her quick and hard. "Someone has to stick around to keep you out of trouble."

"There is that," she agreed, knowing that whatever the reasons, he was staying for all the *right* reasons. Maybe he hadn't said the words, but she didn't need words. She'd had the words once, but they were merely empty promises. She'd rather have the feelings, honest and real, and they were there in Cody's eyes when he looked at her, held her.

"Besides," he added, "it's not often I'm going to find a woman whose teeth don't come out, or who smells like a bull sometimes." He tried to keep the laughter out of his voice when she groaned.

"Joey?" she asked, and he nodded, enjoying her embarrassment. "I'm going to strangle that child. And Louie," she added, knowing somehow, some way, when she got to the bottom of this, Louie would have been part of it.

"Hey, don't be mad. It's not often a boy extols the virtues of his mother in the hopes of snaring a husband for her."

She groaned again and he laughed.

"Then, of course," he continued, "there's the fact that you're not scared of thunder, and your skin's not brown and wrinkly, add to it the fact you don't have knots in your hair, and I'd say I'm getting a pretty good deal." The best deal of his life.

"I love you," she whispered, brushing her lips against his. His eyes met hers, calm, steady.

"I love you, too."

"I know that," she said with a grin, letting loose a relieved sigh she seemed to have been holding forever. Well, at least since she'd met him. "I guess I've always known it," she admitted softly, trying not to grin at the look on his face.

"Did it ever occur to you to tell me?" he asked in amusement as they started walking down the path. "Seeing's how you seem to tell me everything else?"

"What? And spoil the surprise?" She laughed, taking his hand. "Not a chance. I figured a smart man would eventually figure it out on his own."

"And if I didn't?"

She shrugged, hiding her fear in her heart. "Then you obviously didn't deserve me." She frowned. "Although, you did give me a few moments of worry," she admitted reluctantly as he unhooked the stallion's reins from a tree.

"Just a few?" he asked with one brow raised.

"More than enough."

His eyes were steady on her. "And if I would have left?"

She waited a heartbeat. "I would have followed you to the ends of the earth and hunted you down like a dog, and I would never—*never*—have given you another moment of peace."

Laughing, he grabbed her in a hug, believing her.

"Cody," she began slowly, laying her hands on his chest. "Joey... Joey and I are a package deal." They'd never talked about this, never even discussed it. She had no idea what he thought or how he felt. She'd just assumed...

"You think I didn't know that?" he asked, seeing relief flood her face. "Hey, I figure taking care of you is more than enough for two men to handle." He winked at her. "What do you think?"

Her eyes softened, and she reached out and touched his face. "I think if I didn't already love you, I'd love you for that alone."

"Care to show me?" he asked, wiggling his brows at her and making her laugh.

"Just as soon as we get home."

"Home." He said the word as he helped her on the horse, then climbed on behind her, nudging the horse with his heels. "That has a nice ring to it, but it will only be temporary."

Everything inside of her stilled for a moment. "Temporary?" She turned back to face him, fear in her eyes, in her heart.

He smiled and kissed her nose. The wariness had leapt into her eyes again, as well as the vulnerability. He had to remember this was new for her, had to remember not to be careless with his words, to be clear so she always knew, always understood, she could depend on him.

She wasn't used to men honoring their words, their commitments. But she'd get used to it in time; he was certain of it. And they had plenty of time. A lifetime really, not certain at the moment if even a lifetime with her would be long enough.

"Yeah, temporary. Until we rebuild the big house."

She let out another relieved sigh.

"I'm going to take a leave from the rangers. I'm sure Judd can use an extra man, and if not, I've got more than enough to keep me busy. We're going to need more room, because I don't intend to continue sharing a room with Joey. Let his brother or sister do that."

"You want children?" she asked in surprise.

"God willing," he admitted. "If it happens, great." He shrugged. "If not, it's not a problem, I figure we already have a son." He thought of Joey, the fatherless little boy who needed him so much. Until now he hadn't known how important it was to be needed. He'd have his son, a namesake to carry on, to inherit the land. "A Kincaid," he said softly, realizing until this moment he hadn't realized how important it was to him.

"And don't worry," he hastened to add, wanting to head off her worry at the pass. "Joey and I already had *this* conversation."

She was going to have to have a serious conversation with her son. *Their* son. She liked the sound of that.

"There's just one thing, Savannah, one thing I am going to insist upon."

He sounded so serious she turned to look at him, apprehension gripping her. "What?"

"Miss Sophie."

She frowned—this was not at all what she expected. "What about Miss Sophie."

"We're changing her damn name."

Savannah grinned and her chin went up. "No, we're not."

His eyes, amused, adoring, met hers. "*Yes,* we are."

"Nope." She shook her head.

"It's not open for discussion."

"Everything's open for discussion." Still facing him, she kissed his chin. He hadn't shaved, and his beard scratched her delicate skin. She loved it. "How do you feel about 'Miss Amelia'?"

He gave her a look that told her, without words, exactly what he thought of it. "Out of the question."

She kissed his nose. "How about 'Penelope'?"

"Don't be ridiculous."

She moved her lips to his eyelids, not caring he was trying to steer them home. "How about 'Endurance'?"

He drew back, stunned. "Endurance?" Shaking his head, he laughed. "That's not a name, that's something I need— to deal with you."

"It's a name," she insisted, moving her lips to his. She knew he was helpless. One arm was bandaged, and the other was holding the reins. She didn't feel the least bit guilty about taking advantage of him. "How about 'Regan'?"

"That's not a name, that's a damn president."

"No it's not," she murmured. "That's my mother."

"Your mother was the president?"

"No." She laughed. "My mother was a Regan. Susan Regan. That was her maiden name."

Her mouth moved against his. She was pressed against him, and he could feel every soft, feminine inch of her, weakening his resolve.

"How about . . . 'Cynthia'?" she whispered, teasing the corners of her mouth with his tongue. " 'Miss Cynthia' has a nice ring to it." He frowned and she tried not to smile. "Or 'Patience.' How about 'Miss Patience'?"

"Patience is also something I'm going to need." Abruptly he thrust the reins into her hands. "Here. Hold these for a minute."

"What?" She took the reins with a frown. "Why?"

She found out why when he used his good hand to pull her close and kiss her senseless. Dazed, she blinked up at him when he finally let her go.

" 'Jack,' " he said firmly, taking the reins from her. "We're going to name that damn bull Jack."

She started to protest, but his mouth swooped down again, capturing hers. She wound her arms around him. "Well, maybe 'Jack' has a nice ring after all," she murmured against his lips, conceding defeat. "Cody?" she said after a moment.

"What?"

She sighed dreamily, laying her head against his broad chest. "How do you feel about 'Carrie'? Or 'Barry'?"

He scowled. She was back to that again. "No. Not even a consideration. And don't even ask about Megan or Lauren," he added, with another scowl, his patience straining. "'Jack,' Savannah," he said firmly. "We are renaming that damn bull 'Jack.'"

She thumped his chest. "Not for the bull, for a baby."

He simply stared at her as his face went pale. "For a baby?" He almost choked out the words as she nodded. "I...I..." He blinked at her, stunned, making her grin. "I...suppose I like it fine." He suddenly grew suspicious. "Savannah?" he said cautiously, his gaze searching hers. "Are you...I mean are we...?" He let the question hang in the air as emotions ran over him. "Well, are we?"

"Well," she said slowly, trying to contain her grin, "if we're not yet, I'm sure with practice we sure will be."

"Practice," he repeated dully, still not certain.

"Yes, Cody, practice." She kissed his chin again. "You have heard the old saying 'Practice makes perfect'?"

He nodded, still a little stunned. She kept kissing him.

"Well, it also makes babies." She laughed at the expression on his face. "So I figure we'll either get perfect or get pregnant—either way we can't lose."

"Perfect or pregnant," he repeated dully. Somehow he had a feeling this logic made sense to her. And damned if he wasn't beginning to understand it. And her.

He glanced at Savannah and couldn't help but smile, knowing she was deliberately trying to drive him crazy. Eventually, it was probably going to work, but it was his own fault. He'd known all along she was going to lead him on a merry chase, had known it from the day he laid eyes on her, so he figured he'd better get used to it.

But he wouldn't want it—or have it—any other way.

"Let's go home, Savannah," he said, nudging the horse with his heel. "I think you've *finally* done me in."

"And I haven't even done anything. Yet," she added mischievously, her voice and words a loving promise.

His easy laughter warmed the air as the Lone Ranger, no longer alone, took them the last few miles toward home.

Epilogue

Savannah was nervous. Standing before the full-length mirror in Miss Tulip's elegantly decorated bedroom, she checked the set of her bridal veil for the tenth time.

"Stop fussing," Miss Tulip scolded, trying to hide a smile as she did a little fussing of her own. Today, as Savannah's attendant, she was dressed in flaming floral with her ever-present matching bonnet set atop her head. She had to admit, she did look spiffy. Cocking her bonnet to the other side, she set it at a jaunty angle before letting her gaze drift toward Savannah's reflection in the mirror. "You look pretty as a picture, dear," she said softly, placing a gentle, loving hand on Savannah's arm.

In the past two weeks, since she'd offered—insisted—on hosting Savannah and Cody's wedding, she'd come to feel like part of the family—their family. And little Joey. Oh, just the thought of the little tyke set her heart to racing. She'd managed to convince Savannah and Cody to leave Joey with her while they went on their honeymoon. And, oh, the mischief she and Joey had planned!

"Where's Joey?" Savannah asked, placing a nervous hand on her fluttering tummy. She hadn't realized how nervous she'd be now that the day of her actual wedding had arrived.

"He's with Cody, dear." Miss Tulip adjusted Savannah's veil, tsking a bit. "They should be going down momentarily. Cody and Joey are having a final man-to-man talk, I believe."

Unconsciously Savannah chewed her lower lip, worrying about the time. Everyone in town had gathered for the wedding, and now they were all seated downstairs... waiting. She could hear the faint strains of the organist as he warmed up. It just made her more nervous. "I hope Joey remembers he has to walk me down the aisle."

"That boy's been doing nothing but practicing for the past two weeks, dear. How could he forget?" Smiling, Miss Tulip patted Savannah's arm. "Just relax, dear, I'm sure he'll be here momentarily."

Still worrying her lower lip, Savannah couldn't help but wonder what Joey and Cody were talking about.

"Son, before we go down, there's a couple things I think we should talk about." Dressed in identical black tuxedos, Cody went down on his knee so he was eye level with his son. He slid an arm around Joey's waist, drawing him close. He'd rehearsed this speech for almost a week, wanting it to be right. He hated to admit it, but he was nervous. Not about the wedding. No, he'd never been more sure about anything in his life. But this parenting stuff was new to him, and he wanted to do it right.

"You know, Joey, sometimes parents do things that their children don't understand. They think that their parents don't understand or approve or sometimes that they don't even like them." Cody smiled, aware that Joey was hanging on his every word. "That's not true. It's just that being a parent is almost as hard as being a kid. You know how you have to do your homework even though you don't like it?"

"Yeah." Joey nodded his head, brushing the hair out of his eyes.

"Well, even though you don't like math, you know you have to do it for school, right?"

"Yeah."

"Well, sometimes it's like that being a parent. You have to do things you don't like, and sometimes you have to do things that your kids don't understand. Like that day a couple of weeks ago with James Hooper. Remember we talked about this and I explained that I wasn't angry with you that day. I just needed for you to go in the house."

Joey rubbed his nose. It was real itchy 'cause of the flowers all over the place. "'Cause you were worried?"

Cody smiled. "Yes, son. I was worried."

Joey sighed. "Ma told me. She already explained about old man Hooper's son." He was quiet for a moment, plucking at the cummerbund at his waist. It was making him sweaty. "You just didn't want him to hurt me, right?" he asked hopefully, wanting to be sure.

Cody smiled.

"That's right." Cody paused for a second. "You know, Joey, today I'm not just marrying your mother."

Joey's eyed him suspiciously. "You're not?"

"No, son. In a way, I'm marrying you, too. Once your Mom and I are married, then you'll be my son, too." Cody paused for a moment, realizing Joey's eyes, so wide, so hopeful, were on his.

"Then that means you'll be my dad, a real dad just like Louie's dad, right?"

Both child and man held their breaths for a moment suspended in time. Finally Cody smiled. "Yes, Joey. Then I'll be your real dad. Just like Louie's."

Joey's eyes rounded into saucers, and he couldn't contain his smile. "Forever?" He could feel the excitement bubbling inside of him like when he shook a can of soda too much.

"Yep." Cody smiled in relief. "Forever and ever, no matter what."

"Wow," Joey breathed, ready to bound off to tell Louie. But Cody held him in place.

"Where you going, son?"

"To tell Louie." Eyes shining, Joey shook his head. "Wait until he hears this. His plan worked. It really worked! You're going to be my dad!" Excited, Joey whirled in a circle, almost making himself dizzy.

Cody wasn't entirely certain he wanted to know just *what* plan. He had a feeling he would be getting very well acquainted with Louie and his "plans" in the future.

"It can wait a minute." Cody glanced nervously at his son. "Joey, I'm kinda new at this fathering stuff, so you're going to have to be patient."

Joey stopped whirling and frowned. "I never had a dad before, so I guess we're even." He brightened suddenly. "Maybe Louie could help us."

Shaking his head, Cody groaned at the thought.

"Maybe not," Joey said when he saw Cody's expression.

Cody hesitated for a moment. "Joey, I want you to know even though I've never been a dad before, and even though I'm kinda new at this, I'm going to be the best father I know how." Cody slid his arms tighter around his son. "I love you, Joey. And I love your mother, too. And I want you to know I'm going to take very good care of both of you."

Joey's grin went from ear to ear. "I'll take good care of you, too."

Cody fished in his pocket for something, pulling out a gold medallion on a chain, a chain that he'd had repaired just a few days ago. "Joey, I want you to have this."

Frowning Joey, looked at it curiously. "You got one just like it."

"I know." Cody slid the chain over Joey's head. "This one belonged to my father. He gave me mine, and now I'm giving you his. This makes you a Kincaid." He touched the medallion gently, thinking about the years and the tears and all the love it represented. Now he understood a little bit about his father, a little bit about the way he'd acted and treated him. When you were a parent, you wanted so much for your child; you wanted life to be perfect; you wanted there to be no pain, no mistakes. You only wanted life's best for them, and so you protected them with everything you had inside, protected them and loved them, no matter what.

He knew now, and finally understood his father and why he did all the things he'd done. It was love, pure and simple. And his father had loved the best way, the only way he knew how.

He knew now because that's the way he felt about Joey. Maybe Joey wasn't his son by blood, but he'd learned a long time ago that sperm didn't make a man a father—loving and caring for a child did.

Cody fingered the medallion. "When you have a son," he said quietly, "you can pass it on to him."

"Does this mean I gotta get married?" Worried a bit, Joey touched the medallion. "'Cause I don't wanna hafta kiss a girl." And he suspected you had to do a lot of kissing if you got married, and he wanted no part of that.

Laughing, Cody squeezed Joey's hand. "Come back and tell me that in about six years, Joey. You'll change your mind about kissing girls by then, I guarantee it."

"Nope. Never."

Standing, Cody held out his hand. "We'd better not keep your mom waiting." Cody paused before opening the bedroom door. "Joey, I want you to always remember something. We may not always agree about everything. We may fight and argue—"

"Nope. Never." Shaking his head furiously, Joey held Cody's hand tighter. "I'm never gonna argue with you 'bout nothing."

Cody laughed, wishing Joey's words were true. "Yes, you will, but I want you to always remember something." He knelt down until he was eye level with him again. "I love you, Joey. No matter how angry we get at each other, no matter what happens between us, as long as you remember that whatever I do, I do because I love you."

Shy suddenly, Joey scraped his toe against the carpet. "I...I love you, too...Dad." Hopeful and holding his breath, he raised his eyes and saw Cody's smile.

"And I always want you to remember, Joey. You can come talk to me about anything, any problem. No matter what. Just talk to me about it, and I promise I'll try to help." Still holding his son's hand, Cody pulled open the door.

"Dad?" Joey was frowning a bit and dragging his feet.

Cody paused before going through the doorway. The guests could wait. Joey was more important. "Something wrong, son?"

Joey was thoughtful for a moment, wondering if he should tell him. Nah, he and Louie would figure it out. Louie would come up with another plan. After all, he was the Plan Man. Besides, he wasn't certain a new dad would be able to handle the news that their new fourth-grade teacher was a...vampire. And this time it wasn't just Louie's imagination. He saw it with his very own eyes. Miss Logan, their new fourth-grade teacher, had a...black tongue. And *everyone* knew vampires got a black tongue from sucking all that blood. Joey fairly shuddered at the thought, deciding it was probably best not to talk to his dad about this—yet.

"Son?"

"Nah, it's nothin'," Joey said with a smile, bounding into the hallway and dragging Cody with him. "Let's go get married."

Laughing, Cody let his son drag him along. He stopped in front of the closed bedroom door. "I think you'd better get your mother now." He ruffled Joey's hair. "I'll meet you downstairs, son."

Joey smiled. "Okay, Dad." Joey waited a moment before knocking on the bedroom door.

He had a dad.

A *real* dad of his very own.

Forever and ever. Just like Louie. Life was perfect.

Except for one teeny-weeny little problem—Miss Logan. The evil vampire teacher. Somehow, some way they were going to have to find a way to get rid of her. Soon. Real soon.

Still grinning, Joey knocked on Miss Tulip's bedroom door.

Louie would come up with a plan; he was sure of it. After all, if Louie could come up with a plan to get him a dad, surely he could come up with a plan to get rid of an evil old vampire teacher. Piece of cake!

And if that didn't work, he knew he could always talk to his dad about it. His dad could probably do *anything*. Even get rid of evil vampire teachers. The thought made Joey so happy he felt as if he was going to burst again.

The door opened, and Joey's eyes widened as he saw his mother. She was dressed all in white. She reminded him of an angel. He had to swallow a couple of times before he could say anything.

"Come on, Ma. Dad's waiting." He grinned as Savannah took one hand and Miss Tulip took the other. The three of them headed downstairs together. Joey couldn't stop grinning.

He had a dad. A *real* dad.

And once they got rid of the evil vampire teacher, life would be just perfect!

* * * * *

Pick up the next Silver Creek County *book—*
THE LONESOME LITTLE COWBOY—
coming in May 1997, only from Silhouette Special
Edition.

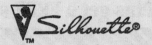

Take 4 bestselling love stories FREE

Plus get a FREE surprise gift!

WELCOME TO SILVER CREEK COUNTY

A place full of small-town Texas charm, where everybody knows your name and falling in love is all in a day's work!

Award-winning author **SHARON DE VITA** has spun several delightful stories full of matchmaking kids, lonely lawmen, single parents and humorous townsfolk! Watch for the first two books,
THE LONE RANGER
(Special Edition #1078, 1/97)
and
THE LADY AND THE SHERIFF
(Special Edition #1103, 5/97).
And there are many more heartwarming tales to come!

So come on down to Silver Creek and make a few friends—you'll be glad you did!

*If you're looking for irresistible
heroes, the search is over....*

Joan Elliott Pickart's

Tux, Bram and Blue Bishop and their pal,
Gibson McKinley, are four unforgettable men...on a
wife hunt. Discover the women who steal their
Texas-size hearts in this enchanting four-book series,
which alternates between Silhouette Desire
and Special Edition:

In February 1997, fall in love with Tux, Desire's
Man of the Month, in **TEXAS MOON,** #1051.

In May 1997, Blue meets his match in **TEXAS DAWN,**
Special Edition #1100.

In August 1997, don't miss Bram's romance in
TEXAS GLORY—coming to you from Desire.

And in December 1997, Gib takes more than marriage
vows in **TEXAS BABY,** Special Edition's
That's My Baby! title.
You won't be able to resist
Joan Elliott Pickart's **TEXAS BABY.**

You're About to Become a
Privileged Woman

Reap the rewards of fabulous free gifts and benefits with proofs-of-purchase from Silhouette and Harlequin books

Pages & Privileges™

It's our way of thanking you for buying our books at your favorite retail stores.

✂ **PROOF OF PURCHASE** SSE-PP21

Offer expires March 31, 1997

Pages & Privileges ™

Harlequin and Silhouette— the most privileged readers in the world!

For more information about Harlequin and Silhouette's PAGES & PRIVILEGES program call the Pages & Privileges Benefits Desk: 1-503-794-2499

Silhouette®

SSE-PP21

COMING NEXT MONTH

#1081 NOBODY'S BABY—Jane Toombs
That's My Baby!
When Karen Henderson claimed Zed Adams fathered the infant nestled in her arms, the disbelieving rancher was caught off guard! Could these two come together for the sake of a child?

#1082 THE FATHER NEXT DOOR—Gina Wilkins
Margaret McAlister's perfectly predictable world was turned upside down the minute Tucker Hollis and his two rambunctious children moved in. She and Tucker were exact opposites, but you know what they say about opposites attracting....

#1083 A RANCH FOR SARA—Sherryl Woods
The Bridal Path
To save her father's ranch, spirited Sara Wilde challenged ex-rodeo champ Jake Dawson to a bull ride. But when the smitten cowboy upped the stakes to marriage, Sara faced the gamble of a lifetime!

#1084 RUGRATS AND RAWHIDE—Peggy Moreland
Retired bronc rider JD Cawthon dreamed of building a successful horse farm, but everything changed after he succumbed to an old desire...and Janie Summers became pregnant. So what was a respectable cowboy to do?

#1085 A FAMILY WEDDING—Angela Benson
To give his young daughter a mother, widower Kenny Sanders wed longtime friend Patsy Morgan. It was a marriage in name only—but how long could they deny their feelings had blossomed into love?

#1086 VALENTINE'S CHILD—Natalie Bishop
Sherry Sterling returned to her hometown to confront J. J. Beckett with the secret that had driven her from his arms years ago—their child. But could she walk away from the only man she'd ever loved?